EVIL CHASING WAY

**Books
by
Gerald Hausman**

GUNS
Turtle Dream
Ghost Walk
Tunkashila

STAR SONG *series*
Evil Chasing Way

Coming Spring 2018

Book 2
Hand Trembler

EVIL CHASING WAY

GERALD HAUSMAN

SPEAKING VOLUMES, LLC
NAPLES, FLORIDA
2017

Evil Chasing Way

New Mexico map illustration by Mina Yamashita

ISBN 978-1-62815-519-8

Foreword

"All stars are more or less evil, but Black Stars are feared most of all as they cannot be seen as they move through the sky. To them is attributed all the sickness, accidents and frights that occur to people who are abroad at night. Those who have no trouble when they travel often at night are suspected of being guarded by evil spirits."

—Hatrali Begay, Navajo Medicine Man

"With his dark staff and the dread evil-chasing power of lightning, Nayenezgani comes down through mountains, mists, mosses and waters, and flings aside Coyote and Owl, and other creatures of ill-omen."

—From the Navajo Evil Chasing Prayer

Northern
New Mexico...

Legend: pueblo sites
ⓜ mutilation
ⓢ saucer sighting

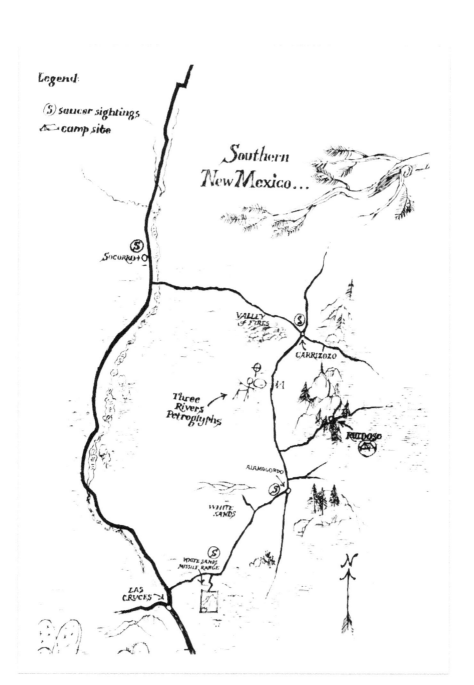

Chapter One

Tesuque, New Mexico, 1978

We arrived at dusk with four pails of garbage in the back of the pickup, my younger daughter, Sarah, who is three, and myself. I don't like the dump at night but we had a houseful of trash and company coming. So I had loaded up the truck. Sarah wanted to come with me. She likes to see the burrowing owls that feed on the rats that eat the garbage.

The sun was down behind the Jemez mountains, a night wind was moving through the arroyos. The dump was in a hollow, the chamisa hills all around with Los Alamos in the distance, twinkling like so many stars. Sarah thought Los Alamos, the city where the Atomic bomb was nurtured, was a person of some kind. She always said, "Nighty-night, Alamos" before she went to sleep. Now she was off hunting owls while I dumped the black plastic garbage bags. There, done. I called Sarah. She didn't answer. "Sarah, we're leaving."

It was getting dark but still that time of day-between-night that Geronimo called the "time of deception." Loose papers rattled in the wind. It was almost completely dark now. A thin hunter's moon was coming up. In New Mexico any moon means light you can read by. I could see the small sneaker tracks of my daughter as they wandered among the owl holes.

I called for her again. "This is no time to fool around, Sarah. Where are you?" No answer. I took off after the tracks that wavered in and out of the hills of trash. They wandered down behind the owl strip into a narrow arroyo. A kind of desperate fear that I had commanded to stay at the bottom of my thoughts rose up. It was a panic that overcame reason. I did a fast sprint down the arroyo.

Then, some fifty feet ahead of me I saw Sarah sitting in a blue gray pool of moonlight and juniper shadow. She was scooping sand with her hand, playing innocently by herself. I ran up to her, she hopped to her feet and gave me a great vice-grip leg hug.

"Daa! I saw that owl."

"Why didn't you answer me?"

"There's a mommy cow," she said. "And a baby cow. And a daddy cow."

"I don't see any cows."

"Daa, do cows have eyes?"

"Of course they have eyes."

Then I saw something. But I wasn't sure what it was.

"Up we go," I said, picking her up. "No more cows or owls, let's go home." An owl skimmed by my head so close I could feel its wings.

"There's that owl," Sarah said. "The daddy cow is sleeping now. He turned off his eyes. But he turned them on for me, didn't he, Daa?" I put Sarah in the front seat of the pickup, closed the door and got in on the other side. I backed up, turned around and headed up the hill towards our Tesuque house.

"Cows don't have eyes," Sarah said, "but they do."

I put on the brake. Pulled the emergency. The truck was on a little rise and the moonlight revealed a big dead cow just a little bit behind where Sarah had been scooping sand. A few feet away from the dead cow there was a huge snow white dog that looked like a lobo wolf. It was sitting obediently in back of the cow. I got out of the truck and stared at the dog. Then I glanced at Sarah and when I looked back at the dog it was gone. I stared at the dead cow. Then I got into the truck and drove towards home.

What had I seen? I couldn't be sure. I couldn't be at all sure. Just a dead cow and a white dog?

"Fireflies come out of his eyes, right, Daa?"

"Yes they did."

"Out of his mouth too."

"Yes, there too."

"But he didn't have a tongue. Poor daddy cow, he couldn't say words without a tongue. So the fireflies talked for him. Didn't they, Daa?"

"Yes, they talked for him."

All the way home I kept seeing that white dog, the translucence of its fur, the light coming off it and out of the open mouth of the cow—the same light.

The two of them exchanging bodies of light; the living taking from the dead. Or the dead from the living, which was it? I knew then that my best bet was to keep this strange thing a secret.

Chapter Two

I was not good at keeping secrets. I liked to talk, to tell, to write.

It was my way of forcing my hand. Busting loose under pressure. Maybe that was why I had become a writer—to be like the canary in the mine.

Somehow with the birth of our second child, Sarah, I got the urge to move, get out of the East and take up a whole different kind of writing. Exactly what kind I did not know. But in a short amount of time I finished a book project and began to spend more time meditating than writing.

My wife Laura and I started to plan our move to Santa Fe. This was not accidental. She was from the Southwest and we had met each other at Highlands University, which was not that far from Santa Fe. We had some money saved and we bought a two-seater Ford pickup. We sold our house, hit the road with one-year-old Sarah and six-year-old Mara, plus two dogs and three cats.

This was the summer of 1976 and the Southwest was unnaturally hot that year. We smuggled our cats into every Howard Johnson's we stayed at, and they crawled up the curtains to secure perches above the windows where they glowered at us until dawn when we hit the road again. I'll never forget the cats and the curtains and the panting dogs and the heat but the kids were good and Laura and I were happy remembering what one of our neighbors had said, "Move? How do you do that?"

In a fairly short amount of time we bought some land in Tesuque, north of Santa Fe. I phoned my brother, who was making a living as a studio musician, and my cousin, who was working as a contractor and they pitched in and this was how we built an adobe house in the high desert. A family effort. For the rest of the summer we made and laid adobe bricks, had a hill carved out, and put a foundation into it. This was going to be a passive solar home, small but nonetheless two-floored, reaching up to just about the level of the hill, say, about twenty-five feet or so.

Eight months later, we were living, or rather camping, in the house we had built all together. Well, we had some help from a Mexican family who bolstered the second story, made bricks better than ours, and made the tossing of them look easy, floating fat, heavy adobe bricks straight up into the air where they would sometimes catch them from behind. They were downright acrobatic on their narrow planks that bowed under the weight of men and bricks. Plus they were really fast.

The first few months in the new house were a little rough though. The floor, which was to be black brick, was not in yet. So the bottom floor was just arroyo sand. The solar windows in front were not installed and we nailed heavy-duty clear plastic to the frames. The wind played these like a harp from hell. We got used to that weird willow-whipping song of theirs and learned to sleep through it.

So the house was livable, and we loved it. But we had no money, we had spent it all on the house. I set out to find a job, or I should say, jobs, because I took whatever was available, and more than one was advisable. I hod-carried for an adobe crew, edited a magazine on Southwestern boomtowns, wrote for *The New Mexican*, did stock report edits for Texas based gas and oil companies, and just generally made myself available for anything that paid wages. None of these jobs got me any high marks but, added up, they paid the bills. And then, finally, a real job. I got hired by *The New Mexico Review*, a popular weekly magazine that was managed by a clever man with slow southern manners. He was quixotic and mysterious and he had a reputation for hiring and firing on the same day. I did not care. I needed a regular paycheck to complete the house—we still did not have any electricity.

I took the job. Jack Andrews was now gainfully employed.

Chapter Three

I got my assignment that same morning and went to the microfilm archive at *The New Mexican* in the hope of turning up an angle or two, an interview or story that might throw a beginning my way. My assignment bordered on the dead cow and the great white dog . . . mysteries of the dump, so to say. But, really, a sortie into the madness of the latest New Mexico mutology stories. Actually the word mute was the one in fashion with the press. Everyone was getting into the fray of mutilations: animal and human. But it was easy to make fun of this stuff in the light of day. In the night it was different.

The cases I was reading about in the archive stretched back in time.

There was nothing new about it. Supernatural events were carved into the walls of caves. But what was supernatural? There was a comic book reality to some of the mutilations I was examining on microfilm. Beyond that, there was the so-called "alien quotient". Put that in there and you have the ultimate mystery. The one that people like to read about in the papers. Outer space, aliens, underground tunnels, highways to Hades.

I read on . . . until I came to the part about there being no witnesses.

I roved among miles of microfilm, immersing myself in a virtual beeswarm of microdots. I traveled in silence into those shapeshifting black dots of print where the only sound was the hum of the screen. After a while, though I fought to stay awake, I fell asleep with my eyes wide open.

"Sorry to disturb you," a voice said in the silence of the dreamtime. In the semi-darkness of the microfilm library, I woke with a start, peered at a tall form swaying two feet away from me.

"Who's there?"

"You look like a drowned sailor," came the reply.

I recognized the weary sardonic tone of a freelancer whom I had recently met at *The Reporter*. Robert Grundig came up and leaned over me. He stared at the clipping I had been looking at. One of those vintage shots of a mutilated heifer down by a Pueblo creek bottom, with two Indian tribal agents peering into the dead animal's vacant mouth. The white teeth were exposed, the muzzle was partly removed, carved as if by a laser. There was a haze over the cow's head—a nimbus of expired breath, I imagined it to be, but, really now . . . wasn't it just a blurry photograph?

"Cheap trick," Grundig said. "Nothing to it."

"What do you mean?"

"Well, I know you're new to this thing, so I'll explain. Elaine Eldridge took that photograph. Poor exposure. Don't tell me you find that image revealing of some, shall we say, mystical truth?"

"It's interesting. Something about the way the men are communing with that mutilated animal."

"You mean *seem* to be communing. Our news bureau chief won't let any of us go near this kind of dead news, forgive the pun."

I smiled, said nothing.

"Go ahead," Grundig said, "tell me you see the light wafting off the cow."

"There actually does seem to be a light wafting . . ."

"Oh, sure. Remember the Druid bunch up in Taos? Or maybe you weren't here then. Man, those guys saw the Second Coming spurting all over a frigging gravestone."

"Nicely put."

Grundig huffed once and then scuffed down the hall. I gathered up my things, slung the leather pony express bag with my papers and pens over my shoulder.

I got up, yawned, went out the door.

***

That night I sat at home, as I knew I would, in front of a piñon fire that popped with sap. Laura sat beside me, the kids were in bed. The house was quiet except for the fire eating at the wood and the wind blustering around the adobe walls of our half-buried house. All but the front was shelved into the hillside. No cave was more secure. On such a night you could really appreciate an earth house made of adobe brick and sunk into a hill of sand.

I went outside to get more knotty chunks of piñon and the wind gave me a good bump. I stared in the big front window at the cozy scene inside. Laura sitting before the fire pulling burrs out of the fur of our ten year old collie, who lay at her feet, paws stretched before the fire. If dogs did purr . . . I loved the look of the house, the black brick floor with its zigzag pattern, the kiva style Pueblo fireplace set into the wall so that you could sit below it with the flames toasting your body and the whole wall, an oven-like extension of the fireplace. I would have given anything that night to just give up and get out of the newspaper job, write a thousand poems in front of that fireplace, do nothing but write poems and read them aloud on windy nights to my wife and the dog both of whom pretended to love the sound of my sonorous voice.

I knew well what was happening. A familiar chemistry. I had been in it and through it many times before. And Laura knew it for what it was, too. I came in with the wood and she said, "You've got that look again. Don't tell me you don't, it's in your eyes and I can see it."

"I saw Grundig today. You know how that guy gets under my skin. I don't hardly know him but he annoys the shit out of me."

"What did he say this time?"

"It's never what he says, it's how he says it."

"So that was the look you had when you came home. Nothing to do with Grundig. Just you. I bet I can guess what's going to happen next."

"What?"

"You're going to try to see a mutilation. You're going to try to be a witness."

"Do I seem so desperate?"

She gazed into the fire, nodded.

"I suppose this stuff gives me the chills," I said.

"What's to be afraid of?" she asked, then added, "You always get like this so I guess I should be used to it by now."

"Used to what?" I asked.

"You get so self-involved. It gets a bit tiresome."

"Sorry."

We were silent for a while, fire-gazing.

"Did I tell you what Durwood said?"

She shook her head.

"He said I'd hate the blood and guts. "But . . .""

"You can't blame him. You're on assignment. By the way, you're the one who gets obsessed. Would you rather be covering the local gallery opening? In that case, you'd be complaining right now about being bored."

"You're right about that. But it's easy to get creeped-out when you see so many mute photographs. I saw one today that I can't get out of my head . . . you know, if you remove the cow's lips, all you see are predatory teeth. They don't look like innocent grinders of grass, more like the teeth of a monster."

"Not like the cow that jumped over the moon?"

"Ask Sarah, she saw a mute at the dump. Does she talk about it?"

"She mentions only the moonlit mist, or whatever, that came out of the cow's mouth."

A piñon branch scraped against an upstairs window and we both jumped. Even in a fortress house buried in a hill, you can feel the force of nature conspiring against you. The eerie grinning face of a mutilated cow will do that to you.

Chapter Four

There is a men's club in Santa Fe that dates back to the old days, those times of innocent literary loafing, when Witter Bynner or Hal, as he was known to his friends, was working on the *Jade Mountain Anthology* of newly minted Chinese translations. D.H. Lawrence was writing about the plumed serpent.

Other writers were chopping down telephone poles because they blocked the view of their favorite saloon. There was even a bear who joined them in their pranks. A brown bear who elbowed up to the bar and drank draft beer with the best of them. In fact, the bear was such a regular at the La Fonda Bar, and such a smelly one at that—someone poured a bottle of lavender water on its head. The bear didn't seem to mind as long as it had its paw around a beer mug.

This men's club I mentioned was called La Vida, and that is the name it still holds. The members of its distinguished roster are few, but each has made a contribution to the world of letters. I would, when invited, attend La Vida gatherings with a venerable old doctor, who as a kid ran bets for Hemingway in Paris. He was one of La Vida's founders.

I enjoyed talking now and then with Jack Shaefer, author of the classic western novel *Shane*. We were in an adobe mansion built atop a high hill overlooking Santa Fe and the usuals were there. Jack stood out because he was such a small man. A regular little gopher (a fill-in for the bear of yester-year?) Each of us had a tumbler of whiskey.

"What are you writing these days, Jack? I asked.

He raised his glass. "Nothing," he said. "Nothing at all."

How lucky can you get, I thought. To write so well you don't have to write anymore.

"Are you thinking about writing?"

He chuckled, finished his whiskey. "I am always thinking about writing."

"Anything in particular?"

He squinted and said, "I'm getting a little low."

"On words?"

"On whiskey."

I ordered him another one, and one for myself.

"That's better," he said. "I have been thinking about a pocket gopher I know quite well."

"Does he write?" I asked.

"No, but he thinks like I do. So I'm thinking I might write a little book called Conversations with a Pocket Gopher. You steal that title and I'll kill you."

La Vida was, for me, like going to the movies.

After talking to Jack I took my drink out the back patio door to admire the view of the distant mountains sparkling in the twilit smoke as the sun went down, and there beside me with the same tumbler of bourbon in his lank crooked paw was old Grundig.

"I thought this was a private club," he said drily, "but I can see they let anybody in who can slink up to the bar."

"Yes, that's right, anyone who can write ad copy and call it editorial can become a member nowadays."

"Well, don't let that discourage you," he said clattering the ice in his glass, "you'll write something yourself one day, and then you too will be invited to join."

I was about to make fun of his tie or his nose when I felt another presence and turned to see an erect older man, somewhere in his early fifties, admiring the view with us. He was not drinking, or at least he had no drink in his hand, and that surprised me. I decided that he was a guest just like us but unlike us. He didn't feel compelled to imbibe. He stood next to me staring into the sunset, a whisper of a smile on his lips.

"Twenty thousand people once lived on the other side of the river over in that valley," he said abruptly. "And now they're gone and the only trace of their existence is a potsherd or two."

"A splinter in the world's thought. . ." I said.

"Yeah," he said. "Hey, who was it said that—Jeffers?"

"Yep." I got a chill, not from the advancing darkness, but the touching of two minds. A quotation will do that when nothing else can.

"Ever been over there?" he asked.

"No, not that exact location, but I've seen my share of ruins."

"Well, he said, "twenty thousand's a good number of people, and they had quite a civilization going for them. Peaceful folk, as you know. We have no idea what made them move off, or where they went. They seemed to have vanished."

"My name's Jack Andrews," I said. "I live over the hill in Tesuque."

"Carlton Murdock, Los Alamos."

We shook hands. Somewhere off in the gathering gloom, in the corner of my eye, I spotted Grundig fishing for another sardonic conversation with a couple of writers. The rim of fire on the horizon was like a laser beam of lost light, and it made me think of a book I had just read about Los Alamos called *Fire on the Hill*.

I asked Carlton if he'd read it. "Can't say that I have," he answered, "but I don't read books about the present, just the past."

"What do you do over there?"

"I'm in the laser lab most of the time."

"That's something I'm interested in."

"Who isn't? But I'd rather chat about the Anasazi, myself. There's plenty of mystery in that subject. Why they left, where they went, and mostly what they knew. It's all a mystery. Lasers, on the other hand, are a topic of finite dimension for me. Most people don't realize just how finite they really are; if they did, *Star Wars* wouldn't make very much sense."

"By that I guess you mean the special effects were so over-dramatized, they were scientifically laughable? I enjoyed the movie, whatever its incongruities might have been."

"We're trained to think of what is possible or probable, based on what is available at a given time. All I can tell you, quite honestly, is that portable lasers, the destructive kind, are so far beyond our present capability that we can't give them credibility as a futuristic dream. Or science fiction nightmare—whichever one you prefer. I'm not saying it couldn't happen. But it's less likely than our finding out the DNA of the Anasazi."

"Dinner is served," a voice called from the patio, "Come and get it, boys!"

Dinner was *posole* and pork, full blown watery cooked kernels of corn steeped in chili and pork overnight until the white popcorn-looking corn kernels explode with the flavor of meat juice and soupy gravy. There were also side dishes of *carne adovada* or chili beef, only the finest cut in a rich red chili sauce that is flecked with little stars of burning red pepper. Tortillas and sopaipillas completed the menu.

Some people ate outside. I felt like staying in with the old men. They were interesting. I looked for Carlton and found him seated opposite Grundig, damn. That in itself demanded a trip to the bar before I took a place down from them at the same table. Altogether there were four of us there. I recognized the columnist who had been writing a memoir for most of his life.

He was rich in white beard and green currency. Like some of the others who had made it big he didn't have to write unless he felt like it.

"So what the hell do you do for a living?" he asked me.

"I'm a cartographer," I lied. It was the whiskey talking.

"The hell you say! You' re another damn writer like the rest of these bums!"

I shrugged. "If you say so."

"Seriously," he said.

"Well, I work for *The Review*."

Grundig added, "Andrews is head of the mute probe," he said with not a little sarcasm.

"Truth is," I said, looking at Grundig. "The whole thing is about to get wrapped. We're maybe one week away from resolution."

Grundig gave me a funny sort of grimace. More people seemed to be magnetized in my direction. In fact, several tables had fallen silent to hear what was coming next.

"A couple of technology wizards from Kansas have admitted to being part of a nationwide conspiracy to overthrow the government by attacking the meat industry. They, and others like them, have admitted to mutilating cattle using pocket lasers that look like flashlights. Members of this secret task force have been picked up in Kansas, Nebraska and Missouri and even parts of New Mexico. There's a couple down in Belen awaiting trial and my interview with them is going to appear in print early next week. "

Carlton Murdock was staring at me. So was Grundig and the rest of them.

"You're serious?" Jack Shaefer said from a nearby table.

"Not really," I said. "Just kidding."

You could hear the whole room let out a mutual sigh.

I repaired to the bar. Suddenly Carlton Murdock was there beside me. "I'd like to have a word with you. Outside. Okay?"

We went back to the place where we'd conversed earlier. The low adobe wall over which the hillside pitched headlong into the great blue night valley of the lost Anasazi.

I thought he was annoyed with me. Maybe even furious. Pocket lasers! I'd actually said that, hadn't I?

He eyed me carefully.

"Well?" I said.

His face softened. He burst out laughing.

"That was wonderful, what you said in there. Really funny. For a moment you really had me, too. I bet those geezers will never look at you the same again. You really pulled their leg."

"Maybe so."

"No. Good show. And what made it all believable was your remark that the whole thing was the effort of a bunch of psychos going to kick over the government. Well, that's one thing these guys like to hear. They may seem like loveable old rascals, or even love able old radicals, but I'll tell you what—these La Vidians are conservative."

He looked at his watch. "Time for me to go. Tell you what. Since you have already linked the mutilations to laser beams, and it's a proven fact, how would you like to see for yourself why it can't be so? Here's my card. I don't work tomorrow, but I have to be in my office to do some paperwork so why don't you call around ten or so and I'll meet you in town and buzz you in at the security gate so you can take a look at one of those little lasers for your-self."

I was surprised. The Los Alamos laser facility was impossible to get in to. Reporters from *The Review* had been trying for years. So this was my first behind the scenes newsbreak. But I was too tipsy to fully appreciate it. On the way home I whispered to myself, *I'm going to the Emerald City!*

Chapter Five

Like most of us I'm a slow-starter when it comes to waking up in the morning. I need a strong cup of hot black coffee. After which I become, by degrees, conscious. Still, I like to get up with the sun because in this land of fire and thorn where the fire and turquoise meet in the sky, well, it's like the spiritual center of my day. All of our dogs met me at the door, jumping up and sending ghostly plumes of breath in my face. They're big dogs and they guessed right—I was going for a run. I finished my coffee, headed down the arroyo, dogs fore and aft, in the white morning sun.

After passing the fifth ponderosa, my mile-marker, I followed the ridge above the arroyo. I could see most of the Tesuque Valley and good portion of the Pojoaque Valley. Off in the distance was Los Alamos and below the city lay the anvil-beaten mesas of the San Ildefonso Indians. The sun was burning off the shroud of gray that made Los Alamos look like a satellite twinkling rosily on its pedestal of sand and stone. You couldn't look at it without thinking that this innocent-looking hill city had spawned the atomic bomb.

As I ran along the ridge, my thoughts turned to Carlton Murdock. He had denied the possibilities of lasers being used in mutilations. But in my mind I couldn't rid myself of the idea that they were in clandestine use by the military.

There were so many things we had seen living at this elevation and so near what the UFO folks called the 37th Parallel, that line from east to west that is a meridian of Air Force bases, hidden laboratories, and 'alien' sightings.

One night I saw a globe, like a glass blower's goblet, rise up from the snowy peaks back of Los Alamos. It had shaped itself, grown large and orange as it rose into the sky. It swung to the south and disappeared. Things like that happen in Los Alamos.

Not too long ago, two men cleaning a large vat in one of the labs were asphyxiated. The news on that was kept on the down low. Scientists, from time to time, committed suicide. A maximum security check of a year's duration was required for any employment position on "the hill", as they called it.

But the overriding fact of the city was not its secrecy, but what it had bequeathed to the world. In the midst of some of the most beautiful mountains on earth, surrounded by pueblo people who still believed that the earth was the mother and the sky the father, a nuclear bomb was born with the capability of destroying worlds within worlds. That incontrovertible fact was there and it bore into one's consciousness.

You can't reconcile Los Alamos. It is a shivery, glittery mystery city burning at dusk and dawn and it represented what its "creator," Robert Oppenheimer, said when he quoted Shiva in *The Bhagavad Gita*: "Now I am become Death, the destroyer of worlds."

I wasn't going to give up on the laser technology either. The leap that lasers and mutilations were linked. The concept of a star wars weaponry that few knew anything about. I wasn't so far out with this idea—scientists as well as sci-fi writers had made such claims. In fact a few days ago, a law enforcement officer covering the mute scene had hired a chemist at Sandia Labs to analyze some residue from an alien landing site at San Juan Pueblo.

The cop said there was evidence that the residue did not contain elements known to the chemist at Sandia. "Something unmet in the 20th century," he said. "These things that are turning up—cows with artfully carved-up outsides and centrifugally pumped-out insides, none of this stuff I'm seeing bears any resemblance to the science we have available at this time. The cloak and dagger days are over. We're now encountering highly technical removals of organs and external hide and skin, and the strange thing is that it appears to be non-violently lifted. When asked what that meant, a forensics expert testified that the animals in question showed no sign of being molested or tortured."

Furthermore, the forensics man went on to say that "The only time I've ever seen such high-temperature, precisely placed burns was at the laser lab at Los Alamos."

I tracked down the cop's chemist and the forensics expert who made various statements to the newspapers, but I had no luck getting either of them to return my calls.

However, I did find one more statement that was interesting. A medical practitioner who was called in to view a mute case at Sandia Pueblo commented that "The incisions we examined seemed almost self-healing with no blood leakage and an absence of scar tissue."

Jogging home, my thought circled back to the dump night with Sarah. The facts spoke for themselves. I'd left the scene before I could focus on the thing clearly. It was as if I didn't want to know more than I'd glimpsed. Yet what met my eye stayed with me. The glow that came from the dead cow's eye sockets and also from its mouth was more disrupting than I could say. Lines of light as thin as spider's silk emanating from orifices. What could be weirder than that?

***

I got to Los Alamos by around nine-thirty and phoned Carlton Murdock from a diner at the edge of town. I had been to the City before, if you can call it a City, it is really a cluster of prefab, postwar and wartime hastily constructed. Most of the buildings were military grey in appearance. There is a sterility that enters the soul upon reaching the outer limits of Los Alamos.

My call to Carlton went through a couple of extensions which finally caught him at his desk. Although the connection was good, he sounded like somebody else. I asked if I were speaking to Carlton Murdock and identified myself as the reporter from La Vida. He directed me to wait and he would return my call. "I repeat," he said, "stay where you are until my return call."

I sat at the counter of the diner, looking over my shoulder at the pay phone. I waited about ten minutes. Halfway through my second cup of coffee the phone rang. I walked over and lifted the receiver. It was Murdock. "Stay put," he said, "someone will meet you in a couple of minutes. What are you wearing?"

"Red ski vest. I'll be outside in the parking lot, okay?"

18

"I'd rather you stay in the diner, if you don't mind."

"Alright. I'll—"

He clicked off.

I returned to the lunch counter, ordered a refill. The only thing that puzzled me was Murdock. Didn't sound like him. Then I realized that my first impression was that he seemed more of an archaeologist than a scientist. I was thinking about this when I felt a gentle hand on my shoulder. A large man wearing green hunter's pants, an orange quilted jacket and a duck-billed cap was standing over me. He had a friendly, outgoing face. Big hands and big ears. "I'm your pick-up," he said.

Once outside in the lot, we got into a grey Ford with LASL, United States Department of Energy stenciled on the doors. Below that there was a contract number of about six digits with a code in letters.

I relaxed in the company of my pick-up man, who hadn't given me his name. But I assumed that I was just one of many routine pickups he made in the course of a day.

"Nice weather," he said.

I got right to the point.

"How classified is the place where we're going?"

"It's classified. That's why they sent me to get you."

"What level?"

He chuckled. "If it were real classified even I couldn't go near it. No one goes near that building, for instance."

We had already passed into the main complex of LASL's heartland, and as yet, no screening areas. On the right hand side of the road, where he'd gestured, there was a cinderblock structure with a high wire fence.

"What's in that building?"

"Couldn't tell you. I mean, even if I knew. Which I don't."

We came to an intersection. A guard stood in a little booth beyond which was another fenced-in parking lot. Inside and at the end of the lot was a bunch of modern brick buildings, nondescript and mixed in with a variety of newly started foundations and half-finished, cheaply designed duplexes that had the usual asbestos shingle exteriors; basically two story affairs, squares on top of squares, uniformly grey.

The guard at the main gate nodded to my driver who showed his plastic-coated pass. The guy in the booth took a good look at me and then nodded to both of us. What if I had a bomb in my pocket, I wondered. Would the guard have seen it with his x-ray eyes—was he a bionic guard, or only an android?

I was thinking about what a loser I was as an investigative reporter: too imaginative, too silly by nature to take things seriously until they turned out not to be in my favor; then I was all chills and fevers. Oh, well.

We were in the lot and we came up to a white mobile home seventy feet long which had another of those security fences around it. On the steps of the trailer was Carlton Murdock. He looked pretty much the same, but clipped to his lapel, he had a plastic pass with his mug shot and serial number. He was standing stiffly, exactly like his voice on the phone.

I decided not to let appearances, in this place of places, lead me astray. I would keep my cool, even though it might mean acting like an ingénue. It was a role I often adopted under similar circumstances.

I greeted him with my mellowest hello and warmest handshake. He returned it with a cold nod and a brief touch of skin, the old deadfish, as it is called. He was not, definitely not, the same man. He escorted me to the inside of the trailer, which was appropriately paneled in fake wood with rows of secretarial desks and filing cabinets making the narrow office seem a wind-tunnel.

"Come into my office, please," he said, still affecting the neutral look he displayed at the door. His office told another story altogether. On the walls were posters from the Sierra Club, photographs of redwoods and lichen by Eliot   Porter. That was the man I had met at La Vida, not this robotic diplomat. He took a seat behind his desk and I sat opposite him.

"Coffee?" he asked.

It was his first friendly gesture.

"Thanks, I'm coffee'd out. Some party last night, right?"

"You'll have to excuse me," he said, rubbing his eyes, "I didn't sleep at all last night. I was under considerable fatigue just being at that party."

"I meant to ask you what La Vida member you came with. . ."

"No one invited me. I came uninvited. With permission, of course."

He looked greyer and older in the harsh light of this Los Alamos day. I asked him if the party attendance was an assignment.

He gave me a half-hearted smile.

"We appreciate your making this trip to see us," he said. "And that was my purpose in attending the party. It was, there's no getting around it, an assignment. To bring you here. Of your own accord."

"Well, I'm here and of my own accord, so what's this all about?"

"You're new to the field, I take it? And I believe your paper is also rather new, isn't it? Your boss is a southern boy, isn't he? Well, those things are neither here nor there. Our purpose is to show you what lasers can and can't do, and, most important, what we'd like them to do in the future."

He gave me a searching look that almost returned him to the person he'd been out on the terrace talking about the Anasazi.

"I didn't mean to scold a moment ago but I had a hard time controlling myself last night. You were very much out of hand, were you not?"

"I was a bit drunk, there's a slight difference."

"That's no excuse for unprofessional conduct."

"I wasn't aware of any."

"Maybe we should give it another name. Let's say, your lack of discretion with regard to your profession. You made some rather foolish remarks—a discredit to your paper and yourself. You could have caused public embarrassment for some people."

"What people?"

"I'd rather not delve into specifics. But I would like to warn you and at the same time acquaint you with what we do in this department. Am I being clear?"

"Why not get to the point?"

"All right. I was asked to bring you here and I have done that. Someone else will inform you about our top secret laser program."

I watched him go out the door, thinking he was going to return, but instead another man quickly took his place.

"Hello, Ronald Ambersand here." He spoke softly, adding, "I'm going give you a little tour this morning."

I nodded, smiled.

"Mr. Murdock, whom you've met is our local information officer—under my jurisdiction. I run the public information releases for the different divisions of LASL." He pronounced it as a word rather than an abbreviation.

"Sorry I was a nuisance last night. Mr. Murdock seems to think I stepped over the line."

"Well, it's fair to say that's what you did. But I don't feel any harm was done. As for my subordinate, I think he often feels annoyed accepting these little assignments, you know, like the get-together last night. Murdock's quite a loner, really. Well, let's get off this, shall we? Let me take you on a small tour of our facility. Then if you put something together for *The Review*, and I approve it, we'll let it go at that."

"I thought all of this new science was top secret."

"Not all of it, but you have to get the science right. The trouble is, most reporters don't."

The tour, as I figured, went from one experimental laser lab to another. After showing me through several laboratories, he drew my attention to a device that resembled a dentist's x-ray machine.

"What we're working on here," he said, "is the potential of using lasers to fuse atomic nuclei in a controlled manner to release energy. You see, the energy of the sun itself is the result of thermonuclear fusion—two light elements colliding, fusing to form a heavier element, and in the process, creating a release of energy.

"Now, the idea behind laser fusion is to manufacture a small sphere, a pellet of glass, or we can call it a microballoon. It is actually 100 to 200 micrometers in diameter. To make that a clearer visual image, you can sit a number of them on top of a hair follicle, which magnified, would look like a log. Am I making myself clear to you?"

"I've read about micro-balloons," I told him, "and according to what I read in *Scientific American*, each balloon is filled with a deuterium + tritium mixture, an earthly equivalent of the reaction taking place on the sun."

"Well, I can see you have done some homework, very good. Most reporters couldn't care less about these things."

He was right there, but for a different reason than he suspected, or would ever suspect. I didn't care either, except for the sci-fi thriller that I was at that precise second writing in my head. I could engage my imagination in such a way as to actually live on several planes and I might never write a word of this down, but still it was happening inside my head in a certain way, a kind of Walter Mitty moment with lasers, center stage. I imagined lots of little men like Ambersand blowing kingdoms into kingdom come. I had a good seat up front for the whole show.

". . .a short pulse of laser light," he was saying.

I envisioned a great dome of inner space rolling through the starry void.

". . . this short pulse of light takes only a nanosecond, strikes the fuel pellet, and is absorbed by the outer layer. . ." He paused for a moment to see how I was taking it in. I nodded.

"So, this absorbed light," he continued, "causes the outer layer to vaporize and blow away as a hot plasma. . ."

I saw in my mind's eye the pulse of a new age. The beginning of laser technology that would take starships to Mars.

". . . an inward rocket-reaction force compresses fuel in the center of the pellet and heats it to the fusion reaction temperature, and the DT fuel undergoes fusion burn. . ."

Again he glanced at me to see if I was getting it.

And, again, I nodded.

"If you've been following me each laser pulse might contain a single mega-joule of energy. Do you know what that represents?"

"Not really."

"Well, let's say it's enough to run a color television for one hour."

One whole hour?

I tried to sound impressed but in my imagination I'd seen iterations of the Big Bang, and here he was talking about running television sets.

"Is there an application for military use?" I asked.

He tilted his head and looked to the side. "I really thought you were following me. I was ready to permit you to see our Antares Project."

"Sorry. I have to admit some of us see all of this in terms of the Pentagon."

He wasn't buying my excuse.

"You have to understand something," I went on, "I'm from another generation. I grew up on Flash Gordon and Buck Rogers."

He gave me a weary look.

"There is national interest in what's going on here," I told him. "People want to know where it's headed. Are you saying there is no military application in sight?"

"All right, he said. "Let me show you why that's out of the question."

He hurried out of the lab with all the experimental hardware in it, and we walked at a fast pace out into the sunlit parking lot. Across from us was another building made of cinder block. An American flag flew on its roof and the stairs leading up to its doors were wide and spacious. We entered through glass doors and a uniformed, armed man met us at the main desk. Mr. Ambersand showed his badge, and jotted down serial numbers on a clipboard.

"Would you please make out a temporary visitor's pass for this gentleman?" Ambersand asked.

The officer asked for my driver's license. I took it out of my wallet, he looked it over, stepped behind his desk and put the license into a copier, pushed a green button and instantly, I, too, had a badge of entry to the secret most cellar of Los Alamos. We entered an elevator on our right, and descended into the depths of the building. We landed in a cavern swollen with great bulbous pipes and vast intricate weavings of colored wire.

All around us there were characters out of *Dr No* wearing puffy orange playsuits with plastic boots. I felt unusually uneasy in this high tech subterranean chamber.

"Please put on a pair of those overshoes," Mr. Ambersand said, "they help keep dust and foreign matter out of the laser facility."

I did as he asked and then we walked into a smaller laboratory chamber, but this one had more and larger laser equipment.

I noticed a series of lathes lined up on a metal table interspersed with mirrors, which I supposed were used to bounce the light pulses where they were directed to go.

"This whole thing is operated upstairs by computer," Mr. Ambersand said. "And there it goes!" he added.

There was a buzz followed by a loud click, and whatever it was, was over.

"We have an eight beam system," he explained. "The most powerful CO_2 laser in the world. Our goal here is scientific break-even. What we mean by that is, the energy released by the pellet fusion reaction equals or exceeds the laser pulse energy that strikes the pellets. With this in mind, as a future reality, we may be able to invalidate our whole concept of electricity. In fact, you may be looking at the power source of the future. I believe this to be true. Now do you see why this application is non-militaristic? Come here, just a second, will you?"

He led me out the door we had come in and down a corridor and through another door into a cavernous place that suggested the interior of Carlsbad.

Tubes leading to the biggest cylinders in the world dominated the space upwards of eight feet from the floor. There were circular stairways leading up to platform stations where lab technicians were poking into the cannon-like mouth of one of the reaction chambers.

I heard one of them say: "Some of these pellets are dead." But I couldn't make out what his partner said. It was impossible to be in this cavity without wondering what it all meant, and whether Ambersand was right about the future of our best known power source. Moreover, it was equally impossible to comprehend that within the immensity of the reactor chambers, there were hand-made pellets or microballoons, so small that one of them could fit into the eye socket of the eagle on a quarter.

As we left the building and got back into the bright New Mexico sunlight, I looked away from the parking lot off the mesa that was Los Alamos, and far away to the piñon-spotted hills below the Sangre de Cristos.

Lower in the valley it was a labyrinth of arroyos. Our own adobe home was down in there—so close, so dreadfully close to all this impersonal supersonic pellet madness.

Too close, I thought as I shook Ambersand's hand, said goodbye and got into the transport vehicle that had been arranged for my return. Ambersand seemed so delighted with himself for having blown off the top of my head with the Antares Project that I wanted to deflate him in some way.

"There is one thing I want to ask, if you don't mind."

"All right."

He looked apprehensive.

"Why does the fact of Antares negate military application?"

His face fell a little bit, but then he remembered his mission.

I suppose he saw me as yet another hopeless case, a writer bent on pushing a science fiction script into an inflammatory news story.

"Listen," he said. "If you could find a way to install a unit the size of Antares in an aircraft, you would then be in a position to put a battleship into a handgun."

"I think that answers my question," I said.

Chapter Six

Taos is sort of like an adobe version of New England with all its meadows and leaf trees. For a great many years it had been the enclave of counter-culture, more so than Santa Fe. For the old rebels—the ones who came to Taos in the 1920s—the arrival of the bearded and barefooted 1960s newcomers, hippies of Haight-Ashbury, it was a bad sign of the times.

I had driven to Taos to interview two of those earlier artists, Phil and Gene Kloss. Once upon a time they shared the company of D.H. Lawrence and Frieda and Mabel Dodge Lujan. They knew Robinson Jeffers before he came to Taos and they'd been friends with Georgia O'Keeffe, Steichen, Fechin, Blumenschein and the other Taos masters. It seemed to me there might be a link between the druids of the past and the new breed who had been accused of sacrificing animals and perhaps mutilating them.

Phil Kloss, author of *The Great Kiva* and many other books, had a lot to say about—practically everything—including neo and olden day druids. He'd seen the coming and going of the Anglos who lived in tipis on the other side of the Rio Grande Gorge.

"Now you see these sullen types," he told me, "mostly unkempt and uncaring. I miss those choirs of blonde beautiful people and their cherubs that you saw shopping and kissing in supermarket. This new lost generation is quite different. But then again this is the drugged-out end of the 70s not the back-to-the-earth days that were far more innocent."

Phil had met me at the door of his split-level one story house and he was already talking up a storm. He was small of stature with a thatch of snowy hair. He dressed in the Taos fashion of the thirties when artists wore knotted tie and nicely ironed colored cotton shirts.

I'd interviewed Phil and Gene before and they were very easy to talk to, full of opinions and extremely observant. Phil walked out and met me on the flagstone path to the door. He stood smiling in a minefield of sagebrush on all sides.

"I bought all those extra acres over that way, so I would have an unbroken view of the mountains, he told me, "but look what they've gone and done—built that damn tennis ranch other there."

He took me by the arm and led me inside to where his wife was sitting by a big oak table. She was wearing a blue print dress, such as women used to wear, and it accentuated her straight-backed posture. Here was a woman who had, like her husband and the land itself, resisted every effort to change.

Gene rose from her chair and gave me a strong handshake.

"I think we'll be more comfortable in the studio," Phil said, "the light in there is conducive to talk."

The studio was not his, but hers, and it was full of paintings and etchings, copper etching plates piled up in a corner, a large worktable covered with sketches for future etchings.

Gene Kloss was one of America's greatest artists, an etcher who was a member of the National Academy and whose work was highly sought-after and very high priced. Over the years she'd received the world's honors without a narcissistic nod of appreciation. She lived entirely in her world of canyons, pueblo dancers and glowering skies. She was, some critics said, an artist whose work was as good as O'Keeffe's.

"Well," Phil began, looking down at his feet, "a friend once asked me how it felt to be married to the world's greatest etcher and I asked him how he thought she felt being married to the world's worst poet."

Gene laughed. Phil said, "Neither statement's accurate. We do what we do, that's all."

"You've both seen some changes up here in Taos," I pointed out. "From the days of Tom Mix cowboy hats to today's baseball caps."

"A good bit," he said.

"Heavens," she said.

"You were here with Lawrence."

"Well, you mean," Phil said, "Was Lawrence here when *we* were here? The answer's yes, he was. We didn't see too much of him but not because we didn't like him, but because we didn't come to Taos in nineteen-twenty to *see* people. We came to get *away* from them."

"Escaping from people is almost impossible now," I said.

"Isn't that the truth," Phil said. "They're building too many houses."

"We can still see Taos Mountain," Gene said. "That's all I care about."

Phil said, "You know there was a Taoseno here helping us do some plastering and Gene saw him looking up at those peaks over there, and she said, 'We've been there.' And he gave her a look that said, 'What would a seventy-five year old white woman be doing on top of Taos Mountain?' And then he said, 'What did you see on top?' And Gene said, 'A nice stretch of pretty grass' and he smiled and went back to work. But I heard him say to one of his friends: 'She went up there all right.'

"Taos Mountain is off-limits to anyone but a Taoseno," I said.

"Correct," Phil replied.

"So . . . what's the strangest thing you ever saw in Taos?" I asked.

"The strangest thing I ever saw . . ." Gene smiled. Then she lapsed into a sort of daydream.

"What was it?" Phil asked, interested.

"That day you killed forty-eight rattlesnakes, one after the other."

"Oh that was way back when . . . you killed a lot of them too when it got hot. The snakes came out to drink at the irrigation ditches, and that's where you'd get a good lick at them with a shovel. Gene couldn't bear down on it hard enough, she'd just kind of lay that shovel on 'em—whack—but it wouldn't hurt 'em at all, so I'd come over and chop the head right off, then lay the limp body alongside my fence. Well, one day a Taoseno friend of ours saw all those rattlers laid out in a row and he got to worrying, because you know the Indians think differently than we do when it comes to poisonous snakes. And he just came right out and told me not to do it anymore—I needed to learn to live with snakes, he said. That was how he put it."

"Maybe we need to imagine they're not as opposed to us as we are to them," I suggested.

Phil smiled. "The other thing is not to step on them."

I asked if he minded it when the hippies came to Taos because they came in droves. They were still showing up and we had small communes in and around Santa Fe, too.

Gene said, "At least they kept pretty much to themselves."

Phil added, "There was a time when you couldn't walk in Taos without bumping into them though. We moved back to California when it got really bad."

"When was that?"

"About 1969."

"Oh those were *terrible* times," Gene lamented. "Babies born out in the sagebrush and no one to care for them."

"Really? I find that hard to believe since the whole hippie thing was based on sharing and caring, and family."

Phil rolled his eyes.

"They were poaching all the time, those kids. You know, our generation may've been a little crazy but we respected nature and took from her just what we needed to live. We learned our ways from the Taos Indians. You know the book *The Man Who Killed The Deer*"? The author, Frank Waters, is a good friend of mine and I also knew Martiniano, the fellow who kills the deer in the novel. I knew him quite well actually. It wasn't a sin for an Indian to hunt out of season if he had to feed himself or his family, but a pueblo works as a single unit.

"There aren't individuals in a pueblo just a group. As you know, that's what that book was about and that's what got our friend Martiniano into trouble. But this other thing, this hippie poaching problem we were talking about. That's another story. Lots of hippies came into the Mora Valley. You know what it's like over there, Jack, very ingrown among the Hispanics. The hippies set up their communes and I remember seeing a dead person hung out on a fence just like a coyote. The Mora police wouldn't do a thing about it."

"Let's not talk about that, dear," Gene said. "Let's just be thankful that it's passed."

"But it hasn't," Phil protested. "Now we've got these damn mutilations and I've been saying all along that it's leftover hippies doing it."

"If so, they have some pretty sophisticated equipment," I told him.

"Some say it's government, some say military, and some swear it's aliens from out of this galaxy. It's all nonsense. Look at that druid business. Just a new breed of hippie. Don't get me wrong, I know about druids. I studied druidic mythology at the University of California. The original druid people were led by holy men, priests, mages, whatever you want to call them. Now the Greek word for oak was *drus*, these were oak priests who led rituals under their sacred trees in Great Britain. I know all about druids. Yeats himself was one."

"Our so-called modern druids . . . what were they?" I asked.

"Hippies! Or ones tired of being hippies. Or ones too drugged to know the difference. Anyway—have you known any of them? I have. They're delusional, just a bunch of nut cases. They've got a smidgen of misinformation about druidry rattling around in their heads. That's about it. But I know they're behind some of these ritual sacrifices."

"What's that about anyway?"

Phil shook his head, shrugged. "Nobody knows that much about the original druids because they're part of our mythology. They were peaceable folk, as far as I'm concerned. No sacrificing of children though I do believe they let the blood of a lamb flow into a stone cup and just as the sun came up they drank it, or some such."

Gene spoke up. "What about the kids out on the Navajo reservation, Phil? Near Ramah."

"That's the part of the Navajo tribe that even the Navajos don't want any part of. Well, these Ramah kids were mutilating animals, cutting off dog's heads, drinking blood and all manner of idiocy until they were finally caught at it and thrown in jail."

"They were sentenced for animal cruelty."

"No, that wasn't it," Phil said, shaking his head. "They were thrown in jail for killing an infant. Sacrificing it to their deities."

"Do we know that, Phil?" Gene asked.

"I have some pretty good Taoseno sources that say so," he replied.

"What makes you think hippies are responsible for mutilating cattle in this area?"

"Well, if those Ramah kids could kill a baby and drink its blood, then our own Taos hippies could certainly do the same to a cow. Come with me," Phil said, rising from his chair. "Come along, I want you to see something."

He led me outdoors and we walked around to the side of the house. There was a tool shed and a well-cap, and nearby he had made a collection of stones. It was like a Japanese garden, all laid out in circles and rows according to size and color and shape. He bent down and took a bunch of small black flint chips.

"I want you to have these," he said.

I looked closely at what he was offering. They were not flints but something else.

"The Spanish call these black crystals *Lagrimas de Cristo*. You can find them buried up there in the hills where the ponderosas start. I used to go up there all the time. All we did was hike in the old days. Not so much anymore. But here they are, I want you to take a bunch of these and keep them in your pocket for good luck."

I held out my hand and he put a goodly number of the little stones in it.

"Each one of these is a cross!" I said in surprise.

"Yes, he replied "a perfect cross. Hard to believe nature could make anything so exact—just like a sculptor's hand. See, just like it was cut with a chisel. Keep them to remember me by."

For a while we didn't say anything. We just looked at the long, level, endless sage meadows that stretched to the south. A dusky gold light filtered off toward the mountains.

"Right over there," Phil said, "is where the Watchers would go." He pointed to a triangular shaped mountain on the horizon in the direction of Santa Fe.

"The Watchers?"

"Taosenos. They'd be up there at this time of day looking for Navajo raiding parties because from that height they could see as far as heaven in any direction. The Pueblos were a peaceful people, but they could fight like hell if they had to. The Spanish learned that the hard way. But there they sat, I can see them cross legged in the gathering dusk, the Watchers, keeping an eye out for any evil stalking the plains. The Navajos were a hard bunch. If you wanted to checkmate them before they attacked, you had to get up pretty early. That's what the Watchers were there for."

Chapter Seven

The image of druids praying on the red sands outside of Ramah appealed to my sense of incongruity. To what did they pray? Clouds, sandstone cliffs, ravens? Surely not to the stunted oaks that cling to life stubbornly and barrenly in their arrangement of leaves and insignificant shade.

It was difficult to call to mind those hooded figures, who kneeled or stood or prostrated themselves under massive Irish oaks three hundred years old, or even under the cool stone slabs of Stonehenge. These kids were different druids, and they demanded from me a little more than the casual questioning of Phil Kloss.

At the county courthouse in Santa Fe, I unearthed the records of a trial in which the druidic band had faced a murder charge when it was discovered that one of their members had buried a six-month-old infant. Until that time they had been allowed to camp and live where they wanted to, though their base camp was outside Ramah.

Santa Fe with its soil blessed by ancient rites, curses and miracle seemed to have attracted them for a period of several months out of every year. Their means of travel was a big old school bus, decorated on the outside with symbols of the *Rom* or Gypsy movement, little hexes and crosses meaningful to those dark-eyed bands whose people lived in Rumania, Hungary and the Czech Republic over a hundred years ago. These symbols and signs told a wanderer where he might find shelter or food, where the weather was bad or the people inhospitable, where the mountains were uncrossable, where a bridge was washed-out or rebuilt.

The bus was seen parked under a copse of cottonwoods on Tesuque Pueblo land. A fenced area guarded a deep green water tank around which the druids sat and stared at the Indian cattle that roamed freely around the well-watered, willow country surrounding the tank.

And then the bus would be gone and its ragged, pariah-faced passengers would leave nothing behind except a pair of coveralls hanging from a low limb of one of the great cottonwoods, and the Indians who owned the lake and parked their pickups under the shade of those trees, stuck copious numbers of beer cans in the pockets of the coveralls and a bottle into the open fly and this scarecrow-leaving of the vanished druid band hung on there for quite some time.

It was after one of the vigils at the end of a long hot summer that a Tesuque Pueblo Indian fishing by the lake discovered a small burial mound, and moving the earth from it, found underneath the small form of a fetal-crouched infant of about six months.

The trial that followed the capture of the band, six adults, male and female, and several half-grown children proved only that they had, in fact, been camping near the lake shortly before the time that the dead child was discovered.

There were no witnesses to swear that the druids had a child of the buried one's age in their company, and by their own admission, their group consisted of exactly the number that had been brought to trial. No brothers or sisters were missing and there was no way to indict them for camping, and in the end, bored with the proceedings of several weeks of questions that got nowhere, a Santa Fe judge banished the bunch from the state of New Mexico, whereupon they announced that they would resettle in Australia, and that was what they did.

They left in the same secrecy that complicated their New Mexico encampment. The dead baby was, of course, autopsied and the results showed that it had died of influenza. Born of Caucasian parents, there were no other conclusive facts about its short faded life. Just that it was born, lived six months, died and was buried by the Indian lake.

The Pueblo reaction to the druids was hard and fast. Signs went up everywhere where no signs had been before and other northern Pueblos instigated laws so that non-Indians would have to get special permission in writing from the governor of the Pueblo to pass through Indian land. And this battle still goes on in the courts today—members of the Spanish and Anglo community complaining that if certain access routes were cut off, they would then be forced to drive up to a hundred miles out of their way to get to work every day.

The druid trial caused other outbreaks of violence, threats and counter-threats. Among these were an attack by local Hispanics on the nearby white settlement of Sikhs, the religious organization centered around an original Sikh caste in India.

This group had been peacefully (somewhat) ensconced in the Rio Grande Valley for about seven years, and dress-code notwithstanding—they wore snow-white loosely skirted garments and turbans as well as scimitars, women included—they seemed to have made an uneasy, yet durable, alliance with the local community by fixing cars, selling produce and health products, rug-cleaning, doctoring, lawyering and anything else you might imagine in a trade or professional program that might be viable economically.

But after the druid affair, attacks were made on the Sikhs by some local boys from Chimayo with the results that the locals were beaten within an inch of their lives, brought to trial by Sikh law and publicly rebuked and punished by having to toil on Sikh farmlands. And that ended depredations on Sikhs for it became known that the Sikhs would protect themselves without the out-side aid of regular law enforcement. The Sikhs were left alone, except that certain Santa Fe businesses found the Sikhs were excellent night watchmen.

Sometimes you'd catch a glimpse of one or two pacing in front of a su-permarket after hours, with a long nightstick. Often these were extremely tall men swathed in white cloth with a turban and black beard. So the druids might have been forgotten altogether, if two of the group hadn't defected from the ranks in Australia and come back to Santa Fe. Along the way—they returned to the states using Miami as a port of entry—they traveled leisurely across the country in a microbus which ended up broken down in the mined-out hills south of Cerrillos twenty miles or more outside Santa Fe.

This part of the druid saga really interested me. Why did they return? I decided to find somebody who knew something about it.

***

Tom Ahern was a fiddler, not in the lazy, but musical sense, and he had come to Santa Fe from the *San Francisco Chronicle* where he'd covered a crime beat for five years. In Santa Fe his love of music overcame his love of words. He played fiddle in a band and gave up writing unless he needed extra money, in which case he knocked out a quick two thousand word piece for the *Santa Fe Reporter* or the *Santa Fe Sun*. It was through his covering of the druid return that I was able to find him living in a beat-up trailer in Cerrillos.

Tom and his wife and adopted Navajo son lived in the trailer. But he also had a writing, fiddling and painting studio out back. The studio was cleverly ensconced in a hill was actually a cave. Inside were nicely plastered walls with pictographs done by Tom and his son. The entrance was hidden. I had to creep through a maze of feathery salt cedars. On the other side of these I found myself in a world set apart from the Cerrillos sun.

And there, in his subterranean studio, was Tom. He was putting on a new string when I came in. For a while I forgot about my assignment, and just sat with Tom in the coolness of the cave. Surprisingly, he had a standing pipe with water and a beehive fireplace made of natural stone with a pipe that went up and disappeared into a cleft in the rocks. Tom ignored me as he re-strung his little heart-shaped fiddle. His son sat beside him.

Tom was a large man with large hands that seemed too big to play the fiddle. But I was wrong in thinking this, because as he tuned up, I saw that his fingers were like hummingbirds, and the high trills of the fiddle were like the honeysuckle vines that hung around the entrance of the cave mouth.

"What'd you want to know," he said in a grumble voice after a few minutes of idle trilling.

"That was fine fiddling," I said.

His eyes glittered in the blue gloom of the grotto.

"Wish I could make a living with this thing. Can't though. What'd you come for?"

"I work for the *New Mexico Review*. I'm doing a feature on the cattle mutilations and somehow I got into the druid trial and saw your piece on them."

"They killed cows," he said.

"I haven't been able to find much on it."

"That's because there's nothing to find. And I won't add to the smear that's already in print. My article was bad enough, no need to make it worse with more shitty, irrelevant details."

"You knew them?"

"The boy was a little slow, but they took care of him okay."

"Did they ever speak to you about killing cattle?"

"That was in the papers, but I didn't write it."

"But as far as the cattle mutilation thing goes. . ."

"I don't mean to be rude because I know you are just doing a job, like I do when I have to. But those people were all right, they just happened to have some far out religion. If they killed a cow or two, that was between them and the rancher that caught them at it. And to tell you the truth, I don't really know any more about it than you do. All I know is they stole some stuff, a saddle, I think it was, to pay for some food and they were caught, and then, because they were suspicious characters in the eyes of the law, they got the book thrown at them. And there were all kinds of rumors about cattle mutilations being attributed to them. Personally, I think that was just a lot of scapegoat bullshit."

"Their being in jail hasn't stopped any mutilations," I said. "You knew the husband pretty well, so I heard anyway. What was he like?"

"Like you or me. But he didn't seem to have any sense when it came to making decisions, like how to get bucks together to pay for the daily bread and all that. They were both incapable of earning a living."

"Why did they return to Santa Fe?"

"They could have stayed in Australia the rest of their lives, because they had an angel of some kind taking care of them. But they wandered back without any real reason except they were tired of it over there, and they liked Santa Fe better. So they came back."

"Your published interview with them described some pretty hard times."

"Yeah. They were cold-blooded folks. Kinda like lizards. They liked to lay around on the rocks doing whatever it was they liked to do—talking to God, I guess—and when winter came in all of a sudden, you remember those

October snows, and all the mud, well, they just holed up in Madrid, and they moved from one deserted mine shack to another, bumming food wherever they could, huddling in the cold, wrapped up in sacks. They stayed in one shack around the time I first met them and the thing had no windows so they put some cracked tarpaper over the window frames, banged nails in place with a rock and sat in front of an old coal stove that had been abandoned in 1933. The place was so smoky it made you cough just to stand at the door. That's how they were. Completely lacking common sense. But otherwise sort of harmless."

"What happened after the saddle incident?"

"You probably know as much as I do about that. They were starving, even though there was a bunch of us feeding them with whatever we could spare. Anyway, they busted into the Woolcott Ranch tack room; there was nobody there but a night watchman who was asleep at the time, and they stole a saddle and tried to sell it down the road to a rancher for a couple hundred bucks. And they were caught right away. Then because they were druids, they had all this other stuff heaped on them, and now they are put away and our city's safe again."

"What happened to the kid?"

"Ward of the State. Well, now they can't hurt themselves. Or that boy. He'll get better care from the State. Hey, man, I'm tired of talking shit. Are you done with the questions?"

I nodded, shook his hand. It was rough and calloused and big as a bear's. I wondered how he played the fiddle so well with those big hands. That was one mystery, piled on all the others, I wasn't going to solve.

But as I walked down the road that led back to the trailer where I had parked my car, I heard Tom's sweet little fiddle. The song he played had an Arabic quality to it, a Moorish feeling. It reminded me of the singing of the Penitentes on Holy Thursday. It was the same ancient sound that had come from the coal-miner's cabin down in the valley. The same wind-chilled December song before the Christmas of the stolen saddle.

Chapter Eight

By the third week of the mute probe, I had little enough of anything, but maybe some bit of something to write an op-ed piece on the questions all of us were asking. I'd asked lots questions and had gotten few enough answers. I called my essay *The Manic Panic of Mutology* because by now all the papers, magazines and news programs were covering the mutes and everyone had questions and as usual no one had answers.

Why this meltdown over mutilated animals?

My answer, perhaps naively answered, was that humans are fussy about their food, protective of their property, and always worried about primal predators they don't know about. This includes everything from Bigfoot to Jack the Ripper. And it all goes back, I think, to the cave dwelling storyteller who, standing before a fiery blaze, told of fur-raising events that lay beyond the light, waiting for the unwary in the shadowland of our deepest, creepiest limbic-centered fears. Druids, miscreant skunk apes, belligerent hairmen, murderous hippies, freaks from the sky—multifarious gifts from the same archaic and arcane storybag. Summed up and clearly stated by the Navajo elder nicknamed Stargazer by those who knew him— "Things are coming out of a hole in the sky and we don't know what they are."

So are we the progenitors of the mute mystery?

Are we the phantom surgeons of the night?

It was indeed Kurtz in Conrad's *Heart Of Darkness* who cried out in the night: "The horror, the horror." Kurtz, the murderer, who, sanctioned by universal human war knew the genesis of mute horror better than anyone.

So if not from us, where? From the sky? Was there really a hole, a rent in the heavens?

How much easier to imagine extraterrestrial agents of evil creating all kinds of cosmic mischief. Or perhaps, as some suggest, members of our own race thus transposed in time, warning us, telling us that it is not too late . . .

yet the time was nigh. The moment is near . . . take your pick, cosmic good guys or cosmic bad guys . . . either could be us in a future phase.

Mostly my article asked questions about such things.

In three weeks I'd heard no likely answer to any of my unlikely questions.

I was hoping, no, *praying*, for a witness, even a crazy one, but so far none had showed. Not one person had seen a single perpetration, penetration, exsanguination . . . whatever you want to call it. No witness.

***

Within an hour of the appearance of my front page story, the phone at *The Review* began to receive callers. I was a little surprised at the number of adamant, outraged, and annoyed readers who said they were fed up with these lame, or clever, questions. They wanted answers. Why weren't the police, the authorities, doing something about these egregious crimes against humanity?

Where were the FBI when we needed them? "If space creatures were responsible, why haven't we declared war on them?" And, one of my favorites: who the hell is this Kurtz guy and why isn't he safely behind bars?"

Late in the day a call came through and on a whim I took it myself.

"I'm a cattle rancher in Springer," a gravelly voice said, "and you're so full of shit it's coming out your boot tops!"

That was amusing, so I took some more phone hits.

All in all, it seemed that I'd hit the funny bone of the low-information people. And all of them used the excrement word in different but similar ways. I was named a "shit-faced hypocrite" and a "shitcrit", whatever that is. I guess it's short for shitcritic.

"I know where you get that stuff," a crinkly, old lady voice said, "it comes right out of your ass. I laughed at that one because my dad used to say when I got wound up on a talking binge— "Wipe your chin the bullshit's rising."

My boss Durwood loved this stuff. As a Christian Scientist, his view hove to Mary Baker Eddy's belief that our base thoughts originate in "mortal mind" or what Durwood said he heard a little girl say at CS church— "So all this bad thinking just comes from a mean little woman named Myrtle Mine?"

Durwood and I met at the coffee maker in the shipping room of *The Review.* It was a good place to talk. No one bothered you there and the phones were up front and you could not hear them. "I think you've got their dander up," he said pouring himself a large mug of coffee. "Frankly, I'm surprised. Not since The Shadow have we had so much wackiness over a little bit of storytelling. Nice work. We're selling lots of papers at La Fonda Newsstand and all the bookstores in town."

I poured a cup of black coffee and sipped some.

"I never expected such a wide margin of idiocy."

"Next piece, nail down a few facts. Some of the idiocy might go away."

He flashed his solid salesman's ivory smile.

"The facts aren't there, Durwood, and even if they were the nails would bend."

He chuckled, shrugged. Then, "Do you believe any of these mutilations are extraterrestrial in origin?"

"Not as much as I believe in the boogeyman."

"Well, J, I come from the South where people *really do* believe in the boogeyman."

I shook my head. "Sometimes things we can't explain have no explanation."

"What if it's being done by some kind of modern day Jack the Ripper type? That would be the psycho theory, wouldn't it?"

I said, "The closest I've gotten to anything scientific is a hand-held laser gun."

Durwood laughed. "Who's holding it then?"

I shrugged, sipped some more coffee. Durwood was a piece of work. Sharp as a tack, quick as a knife, handsome as hell, and sweet as sugar if he wanted to be. His nicety came to the fore when we were making money. He loved teasing people into efficiency. Usually it worked.

"I think you're miles ahead of your reading audience," he said with a sigh. "And that's what all the buzz is all about. I'm very pleased with what you've done, what you've set into motion. Just don't get lazy or loose on me. Stick with it and hit it hard."

"Which way do you want me to roll?"

"I want you to tell me, J, what's going on out there. Drop the mythology, the philosophy and tell the public what they want to hear. They want a predator, find them one, but make it true to form. No sci-fi, OK?"

"So you want me to *witness* a mutilation and then write about it?"

"Hey, man, take some risks. Walk on the dark side . . ."

"No one's ever seen a mutilation in process. Only after the fact."

"That's right. But I want you to be there when it happens."

I almost gagged on my coffee. "You just said no sci-fi, now you want me—"

Durwood grinned, winked.

"Well?" I said.

"I want you to see the truth and tell the truth."

"—*And* you want me to be invisible."

Durwood poured himself another cup of coffee. "This thing's getting low, he said. "Are you ready for another?"

"Might as well."

He refilled the Mr. Coffee with French Roast and flicked the switch.

"Easy," he said.

"What's easy?"

"Flicking a switch."

Before the coffee maker had run its full cycle Durwood removed the glass carafe and replaced it with his own cup. The fresh brew perked and dripped, he filled his cup and then refilled mine the same way without spilling a drop of coffee.

"As simple as what I just did," he said. "Just a matter of timing is all. You got to have your cup ready, and then it's—quick-quick, get it under fast with no hesitation. Trouble with you is you're a hesitator. Damn good writer. But a worrisome hesitator."

"I don't like to get my hand burned. if I don't have to."

"No problem. *Be there*."

He left the shipping room. I could still smell his lime aftershave. *Be there* was one of his favorite expressions. It was short for be-in-the-moment. He meant be there before it happens, and you're *really* there. Ah, that Durwood.

A little later I was ready to leave. Durwood was at his desk. I walked past quietly hoping he was actually reading the magazine he had in front of him, but he heard me creeping down the hall and said, "Now go on out and really *see* something. If you don't exactly see it, tell us what you *think* you see, and if you don't know for sure, tell us anyway, make it good and scary. You know, take us to the site of that good old raw-hided bloody bone."

Durwood sat there at his three-cornered desk, looking for all the world like a southern politician. A slim, trim, Huey. Which was weird. Because actually Durwood was part Choctaw, part black and some little smidgen of coon-ass Cajun, as they say, or as he said himself. He was so ridiculously sure of himself that he made the rest of us unsure of ourselves. There he was in his shirtsleeves, the ones with frilled gambler's cuffs and silver cufflinks.

"I'll get you that bone," I said. "and put it on your desk, gristle and all."

He turned serious on me. "Believe me, I'll back you and anyone else on my staff the moment you or they are in trouble but you are going to have to trust me to know when that time comes and it isn't now. Far from it. You're feeling the calm before the storm and it's a nervous calm and that's all right for now but get me that bone, will you, J?"

His cold prophecy rankled. He would, I knew, tease and prod at me until he got what he wanted from me and that meant more weird stories, more sales, more controversy, more money and lots more frayed nerves.

"Remember," he said, as I nodded goodnight, "Define your varmint. Call it out of the darkness. You yell loud enough it'll hear you!"

"I'm going home," I said.

"Good. I want you out of here for a while. Git."

As I went through the front office, Marsha, the typesetter, called out to me—"Sorry, honey, someone on line three wants a word with you. . . Should I say you're gone for the day?"

"I'll take it."

I heard Durwood yell from his office: "Good Boy!"

I picked up the phone and pressed the white button.

"You're a real hotdog," a crusty voice said.

Somehow I knew the voice but couldn't place it.

"Who is this?"

"You'll be getting a call next week from someone I've given your article to. You might even get a confession who knows."

The voice clicked off without saying goodbye.

"That was most impolite," Durwood said from the next room.

He'd been listening on his extension, a fact about his operative tactics that used to bother. Now it seemed normal. He would rarely comment but he enjoyed an earful now and then.

"Who do you think *that* was?" Durwood asked, leaning back in his leather office chair.

"Someone I know but can't quite remember."

"Grundig," Durwood said. "He's always killing someone with kindness. Now he'll throw a carcass at your feet and want something from you in return."

"Maybe," I said, and walked through the front office and stepped out into the late day's sun. I drove out of *The Review* parking lot in my old, newly remodeled '56 Chevy. The one I had been restoring for the last six months. Buying windows at junkyards and having the floor replaced with three quarter inch steel, and even having an electrician put in custom back-up lights. The interior too. Specially fitted naugahyde. It was a sweet car, a station wagon with a 382 rebuilt engine I'd never really put through the paces. Maybe now was the time.

I stopped at Burt's Burger Bowl going out of town on the Paseo and ordered a French Coke. What a decadent soft drink—half cream, half Coke. Very '50s, I thought.

The elixir quaffed, I headed home.

And gunned it on 285 North right at the point where you see all the white military crosses on the green cemetery lawn. The little crosses keep growing but the people under them remain fixed. I floored it. The engine sprang to life

. . . *barrrooommm*. Four barrel carburetor kicking in, highway streaming underneath my new Firestone tires.

I was driving defiantly away from mean reports and stupid reviews. I was burying the needle. It went all the way to 110. And then I heard a voice that said *Slow down, pal, there's roadblock up ahead*.

I took my foot gently away from the pedal and let the Chevy crest the hill and begin its descent as I applied the brake. Halfway down, there was, in fact, a huge roadblock. "Prison break," the cop said as he waved me on. Then, "Hey, bro, nice car!"

I crept off the Tesuque turnoff and drove like an old woman until I got to State Road 22, the road to our home and beyond that, Chupadero, and then I drove like an old man, at least 10 miles faster. Before I got to our turn I heard the voice again, *Slow down, Buster*. I did that.

Right at the turn, I saw another roadblock . . . this time it was a furry train of about a thousand tarantulas. Every autumn it happened on one given day. An army of them all amber-furred and just mincing along, and if such a thing can be called cute, they are that because in truth these animals are beautiful creatures with as much sensitivity and better eyesight than your average dog.

They crossed and I made my way down the dirt road. I was just about to the last upward bend where I could see the roof of our house and the hill above when I glanced to my right and saw a man duck behind a piñon tree. Prison breaks make for jumpy nerves. This time there were a bunch of guys on the loose. I drove my Chevy over by the tree, turned off the engine and got out. And found myself looking into the eyes of the tallest pueblo man I've ever seen. He had hair down to the middle of his back and resting on his shoulder was an axe.

"Hey, man, what are you doing?" I asked.

"Cutting down this tree," he said.

"That's my tree," I said.

"Does it have your name on it?" He laughed as he slipped the axe off his shoulder and let it easily slide to the ground so that he sort of leaned on it a little while he looked me over.

I laughed uneasily. "You're here . . . for what reason?"

"To cut down this tree for firewood."

"This land belongs to me," I told him.

He squinted at me. He had a very handsome face, like an actor who was now acting in a grade B movie that was beneath him but he had to do it. He said nothing.

"Sorry," I said. "But I own this land."

"No man owns the land. It belongs to Mother Earth."

"I am a tenant of Mother Earth."

"And I," he said, "am her custodian. But right now I need some wood."

"Okay. You can have this one tree. It's yours."

He looked into my eyes for a moment and then his eyes roamed around the many acres of open piñon country that stretched all the way to the Santa Fe National Forest.

"I played here when I was a kid," he said. "When I got a little older I cut firewood here and gathered piñon nuts every fall and I played in the arroyo when it ran in the summer and now I am here to ask for some wood. Not just one tree. Some wood."

I didn't much like the movie we were in. But what was I going to do? I thought about it for a moment. We both did, I guess. I wasn't about to fight him. Besides he had an axe. So I said, "Go ahead, cut your wood. I don't care."

He looked me hard in the eye for the first time.

"No worries, man," he said. "Maybe we'll meet another time."

I watched him walk down the arroyo, his axe balanced on his shoulder, his big hands moving forward and back at his sides, his back arrow-straight, his long hair glinting in the sun. After a while he disappeared around the bend.

A cool wind came down the canyon. I let out a deep breath.

Chapter Nine

Her name was Winnie, but everyone called her the Snake Lady. She had a sprawling adobe ranch house on the Tesuque river outside Santa Fe, and she raised, among other things bullsnakes, with whom she had established an otherworldly rapport, sometimes permitting her to appear at a social occasion in a skintight emerald snake's dress with a jewel on her forehead and a bullsnake loaded into her bosom.

She was famous not only because she thought of herself as famous, but because during the World War II she had achieved true fame as a bombardier and was rumored to have been the only allied female fighter pilot, who had accomplished more than a few successful missions over Nazi Germany.

My reason for wanting to speak to her was that Winnie's name often came up in connection with one of New Mexico's most notorious land scams: Mountains West Realty.

Property owned for hundreds of years by Tesuque Pueblo was somehow leased by a party of profiteers made up of bankers and lawyers who, bending the laws to match the illegality of their wishes, tried to sell subdivision lots to unsuspecting buyers.

In the end, a tug of war between Indian and Anglo over ownership of water rights—to name only one of the issues—a battle between the old and the young on both sides was finally brought out into the open when someone tossed a Molotov cocktail into the Mountains West Real Estate office one night and blew it up. What remained of the mess was a Custer's last stand in the courts of New Mexico and a great pile of redwood siding, broken into bite sized pieces for the warming of many pueblo hearths.

And where, if anywhere, did Winnie fit into this charade, and how did any of it affect the mutilation of cattle in the state, or anywhere else for that matter? Again, rumors. But some say, insist is a better word, that an elderly woman on an unlikely mount—a 1918 motorcycle with sidecar—was seen cruising down the Taos Highway just before the blow-up occurred. And was it merely a coincidence that Winnie herself had been actively blowing up highway signs, or any blight on the landscape for twenty years, and had an avowed penchant for turning political schemes into piles of confetti precipitated by an ancient love of explosives?

I was also not about to discount the possible tie-in of mutilations on Tesuque Pueblo land with the Mountains West land scam itself—were the mutilations a maniacal plan to further land values? An ingenious quasi-mystical means of scaring Pueblo leaders into an auctioning off of properties which they had once mistakenly leased and then triumphantly seized back again as rightfully theirs?

The most effective way of undermining any unified group of people is an attack on their spirit, their religion, their center of being.

And this was what certain cultural anthropologists were looking toward in formulating a theory of the more obvious mutilations, the ones where helicopters had been sighted or skid marks located near a mutilation site.

What do you say upon meeting a woman of seventy who looks forty, and who reaches down like an acrobat to scoop a handful of dog poop with her bare hand while explaining the acceptable method of freezing stillborn rabbits for the nourishment of snakes?

You say nothing.

You listen.

"I have every snake stool of this year calibrated and collected for future reference and use," she explained enthusiastically. "Did you know," she went on, "that when you feed a color-tinted chick—you know those Easter colors they use in the pet stores—to a grown bull snake, the stool will come out the purest pink you've ever seen? Beautiful, a real work of art."

She led me to the room off the kitchen where her darlings were housed in immense glass terrariums. Heads, yellow and black rose inquisitively at the vibration of her voice.

"There they are, my sweets. Look how they come to me just like puppies."

It was true, the snakes flickered and curled like mustard colored flames. Great loops of them, uncoiling sinewy and slack, the eyes either beaded and sharp or clouded over with haze.

49

"Those dearies with the misty eyes are shedding their old skins now. They can't see you, but their tongues can pick up who you are and what you're about probably better than any human can."

"I'd enjoy holding one of them in my hand," I told her.

"Well, bless your heart. Let me fetch Herman for you. He's a sleek one, he is."

She reached into one of the glass cubicles and I watched as ten or more snakes lifted their heads and pressed themselves into her open palm. It was like seeing a twisted version of St. Francis as he beckoned his winged friends from the air; serpents twined in a rapture of loving ease all about her palm and up her arm.

"Only Herman this time, sorry Angela, dear. Donald Do-Bite, where are your manners?"

On command the unwanted reptiles slunk from her arm, snaked down low like whipped mongrels, nosing themselves along the lowest snaky level of their existence. One snake remained and this she swept up to my face for a closer look.

"Here's my precious Herman," she said, her eyes sparking like sapphires, "treat him as you would a baby, he won't hurt you."

"I like snakes," I told her. "I've never feared them." It was then I realized I had been accepted into the inner sanctum of Winnie's private heart.

She would, I could tell, give me the answer to any question I might want to ask. I took a seat on a kitchen chair with the snake twined around my arm; its cool length, smooth as marble, the belly scales rippling with muscled balance and agility. No smoother thing had ever been on my arm and I didn't mind its being there—nor did it seem indisposed to attach itself to me—a fact that was not lost on my new friend, Winnie.

"Didn't you mention there was something you wanted to ask me?" she said pleasantly.

Herman raised his somnolent head as she spoke, and he directed it toward the vibration of her voice, shooting his little red splinter of a tongue quickly in and out as he moved in slow motion.

"That's alright, Herman, dear," she whispered, "We're among friends, you can lie down now."

The bullsnake seemed to appreciate the intonation of her words because it flattened its three foot length along my arm, returned its head to its tail and insinuated itself into the crook of my arm, pressing its hard flat head deep into my skin.

"Oh, he likes you," she purred. "Do you know that a bullsnake has two penises? I have a picture of them in action, would you like to see it? They're called hemo-penises and I don't know why Herman has to have two of them, but I am sure they must double Angela's pleasure. She is pregnant, you know. What lovely spring eggs we're going to have. So, what was it you were going to ask me?"

No preamble of introduction was necessary with this woman. I came right to the point, speaking as directly to her as she spoke to her snakes.

"Do you think there's any connection between the cattle mutilations and the Mountains West land deal?"

She gave me a long silent appraisal that seemed to ask whether I was friend or foe.

"What's this for?" she said sharply.

"For me," I said.

"Will this appear in print somewhere?"

"Not without your permission."

"I don't want to be quoted. There's enough nasty rumors going around. Why, someone even spread word that I was the one who burned up that real estate office. Well, it was an offensive projection of the male ego, but I wouldn't burn it up on that account. Besides, the Pueblo has already taken responsibility for it. Some angry Indian kids did it. But who knows—who knows for sure? Maybe one of the realtors. . . Coffin himself might have done it . . . for the insurance."

"Hardly likely. An insurance claim couldn't have begun to cancel his debt, it's up in the tall millions."

"Well, my snakes could learn how to be sneaky from that man, but to call him one would be insulting to Herman."

"I'm curious about the motive for mutilations—someone getting even with someone for something. I know it sounds comicbook, but does it make any sense to you?"

"Everything makes some kind of sense if you look at it a certain way. I deplore cattle. They're not nearly as intelligent as snakes. But I also deplore people who cut up cattle for no good reason.

"But the Indians don't make it any easier on themselves: at least once a week someone in Tesuque has to round up the Pueblo cows after they've trampled a nice garden or destroyed a corn crop or something, and then the Governor's incensed when one of the cows gets hit by a cowboy in a pickup truck. If they leave them wandering all over creation, what do they expect? But look at it this way: all this land belonged to Tesuque Pueblo once upon a time, or one or more of the many pueblos scattered about these hills—did I tell you I found a child's skull, six hundred years old, teeth bright as diamonds. There it was in my back yard."

"Do you think Coffin or any of his cohorts would have reason to harm the pueblo cattle?"

"He'd do it for the fun of it, and it wouldn't cost him a penny."

"Why not?"

"Don't be naive. The man was a senator. He has connections like taproots all the way to New York. How do you think he pulled off Mountains West in the first place?"

"I don't believe he did. He was caught and now he'll pay the price."

"We'll see about that. We'll see how he worms out of this one; and please observe, I would never say, 'Let's see how he slithers out of this one.' That would be treason, wouldn't it, Herman, dear?"

Herman poked his head out of the crook of my arm, tongue flashing incendiary messages from across the table.

"Come to Mama," she said, and the big limp coil slid down on to the table top and made for Winnie's chest. She sat there in perfect stillness as he dropped down her shirt.

"Does he always do that?" I asked.

"He takes cover whenever he hears Coffin's name come up. Let me tell something you're not going to repeat. All right?"

I nodded.

"Take it for what it's worth. If someone wants to attack the Pueblos, they come at their religion. Because that's what's kept them together these many hundreds of years."

"Are you talking about witchcraft, voodoo, what?"

"The Pueblo Indians have their own forms of that kind of thing. A good cattle mutilation is another matter. All of the tribes have cattle. Bizarre mutilations, like a cow with its tongue removed surgically, and no trace of a wound. No blood. Other body parts missing. No tracks. No way to find out who or what did it. I know of one case where the whole cow vanished over a period of days."

"Just disappeared?"

"By degrees. First the animal turned whitish. Kind of ghostly. A colored mist came out of its mouth and then it wasted away until there was nothing left but bones. And then the bones disappeared. No tracks. No blood. No nothing."

"You think this was the work of a witches' coven?"

"Some say so."

"Do you?"

"I don't think so. Too easy of an explanation."

She reached into her blouse and fetched Herman out by the tail. She kind of reeled him in backwards. "The only thing you don't want to do with a snake," she said, "is get him into a place he doesn't want to come out of."

"That applies to many things," I said.

"That applies to many things, even realtors."

"And Pueblo Indians."

"Especially them."

Chapter Ten

Blue Monday. Another of those days designed to undo all that was carefully woven over the weekend, all the accidental sanity bought about by jogging and being at home with the children and seeing sunsets and eating a leisurely breakfast of pancakes and eggs. Only two days, but in that space of time, you can live a couple of lifetimes.

The office had a stale smell which even the coffee brewing in the packing room had failed to dispel. I had an uncanny urge to smoke a cigarette, a Balkan Sobranie, something I had not thought of doing for years—the thick smoke like a mule's kick in the throat. Black coffee would have to do. I sat there and thought about what I would be doing during the course of the week. Politics, in general, didn't interest me, nor did B.I.A. conflicts, but the tension between the pueblo people and the culture at large seemed to go back centuries. Witchcraft, in this context, was interesting, and would make a story if I could find some credible sources. But who? Natives wouldn't talk about it. Non-natives had no right to talk about it. Or did they?

I decided to give the entire subject of mutilations a brief review. There were a lot of recurring mutilations on Indian reservations nationwide, but the largest number was in the Southwest. Many on Southwestern ranches, a smaller frequency on small Midwestern farms. Only a few on National Forest lands. A formidable group of mutologists were claiming that the majority of mutes were scattered in areas of close proximity to nuclear facilities. Meticulously researched maps showed the exact mileage with regard to this relationship.

The people who drew such maps also drew lines of demarcation between "them" and "us." Them meaning the military-corporate-government-aliens and ourselves, the so-called (but not really) innocent Americans. I didn't put much faith in maps and mapmakers. I did, however, place a lot of credibility in the Anglo-Indian disputes I was reading about in the papers. Ill feelings on both sides of that fence could easily erupt into psychic as well as physical disharmony, some of which we could feel merely by living in the region of the Southwest where among other things the mutilations were happening.

Unfortunately, neither side would talk openly. The most I had been able to get out of an Indian friend of mine from Santa Clara Pueblo, who was speaking strictly off the record, was that the mutilations were a form of evil not solely propagated by whites, but this was not ruled out by him either. Primary suspects in his mind were the nearby Sikhs, the Druids, and highest in his personal favor: other Indians. I asked him what he meant by "other Indians" and he explained that so many pueblos had experienced intermarriage and dilution of the old family clans and religious orders that conflicts had arisen between families that had once been inseparable. What he told me was in line with my own thinking. Something broken needed mending. I thought of the ghost dances of the Great Plains, the rituals to dance back the buffalo, all the great fallen magic of the past.

Was something of a similar nature happening again on a totally different scale? It brought to mind the buffalo tongues ripped from the murdered herds of the 19th century. The beavers made into hats, the flamingos, too . . . oh, you could go on and on. The white man sporting events of the past two centuries.

Before that it was the trees that were sacrificed, the beautiful tall columns brought down for ships' masts in the 16th century.

Were the mutes yet another form of sport, albeit highly technical and advanced, visited upon animals? Science out of the lab and on the loose?

The phone rang startling me out of my reverie. The moment I heard the voice, I knew it was my "mystery-caller", the one I'd been warned about. I knew the voice if not the man. I'd had words with him before. He was the best known adman in Santa Fe, the one who'd coined, Santa Fe, The City Different. Which had made Santa Fe synonymous with the good life.

Art Coffin was a loser who wouldn't admit a single loss. Even when public sentiment turned against him, he would shrug it off and come up with more ways to sell The City Different to the indifferent Hollywood elite. He loved pavement but he told everyone he only loved adobe.

He was all for preservation—of money. His own. But now, it seemed he was being sued; public opinion was against him.

"I know what some of you think about Mountains West and my involvement in it," he said on the phone. "How about you hear my side of the story."

"Sounds fair, but I'm on another assignment right now. It doesn't matter to me whether you are personally responsible. I just hope the Indians get their six million dollar reparation money."

Coffin sighed. "You guys kill me," he said, "You don't care about your own people. You're rooting for the Indians. Well, ain't that nice. You forget who pays for your advertising."

"We appreciate your support."

"I don't see Eight Northern Pueblos buying ads. No, just us, the guys you love to hate. The ones who didn't do anything but make Santa Fe a better and more convenient place to live. How about I set you straight and let you to draw your own conclusions. What d'you say? Want some real facts instead of some true lies?"

"I'm on another assignment. I can't do a thing for you."

"What assignment is bigger than Mountains West?"

"Cattle mutilations."

"Well, I'll be dipped in shit and rolled for a doughnut. Look, meet me at the Green Onion in 45 minutes and I'll give you some mute news nobody knows but me and one other member of my staff. Green Onion 45 minutes. Be there."

The phone clicked and a dial tone droned. I pulled open the bottom drawer of my desk and grabbed a folder marked Mountains West Development Corporation. The file dated back to October 1972, the month the rats were caught in their own trap. I read the ad prepared by The Coffin Association:

Live in peace and tranquility in your own custom built solar home at the base of the Sangre De Cristo Mountains in the foothills of the Rockies. Settle back into the affordable luxury you can afford, unlimited views, elegance without the expense that usually accompanies it. Golf course, abundant water, rolling hills, horseback riding and the seclusion you have always dreamed about. And the best part of all—each solar home custom made for comfort.

But less than 11 minutes from the Plaza of America's second oldest, most beautiful city. . .

This was chile-coated chocolate candy that couldn't fail. The copy, that is, until a few little legalities separated fact from fiction. I dug into the same folder where a while back I'd tucked one of our issues. Our big headline ran thus: MOUNTAINS WEST . . . LARGEST LAND WAR SINCE THE PUEBLO REBELLION. Another headline read: POLITICAL RESIGNATIONS AND SUPREME COURT RUMORS . . . HOWARD HUGHES AND MAFIA MEET AT MOUNTAINS WEST TO DISCUSS INDIAN REFORM

Actually the plot, if you were scripting a movie, went as follows. A bunch of good old boys picked up an Indian land lease for 99 years and were all set to turn 5,000 acres of chamisa brush into astro-turf when the Pueblo old timers put on their specs and read the fine print on their contract for the first time.

That was the start of a six million dollar lawsuit, and Indian pleas to the B.I.A. that went like this . . . "You have not assisted us in our needs. It is unforgivable that you refuse to give us useful advice or even guarantee us a competent attorney. We have tried to get help from our guardian, and you have done nothing but betray us."

One of the members of the Mountains West development team was quoted as saying "I'm no Indian census taker. But we're up to our ass in Indians and I feel kind of like Custer."

My forty five minutes of background check was up and I left the office for the Green Onion.

"The whole thing was one great jurisdictional battle," Coffin explained to me over a Bloody Mary. "Even now I don't think there's anything morally wrong with Mountains West Development Corporation."

Coffin had a soft, modulated whisper and for the moment I almost forgot he'd been a state senator. "Everybody wants to be the last s.o.b. to move to Santa Fe," he continued. "That's why the County laws came down so hard. We had a 99 year lease on the property across the road from the Pueblo. The Indians had signed the lease over to us, and it was as legal as Columbus Day. Then the City Council instructed the City Attorney to obtain an injunction against us—on opening day, no less. So we turned around and got a temporary restraining order against the City of Santa Fe prohibiting interference."

"How did you manage to pull that off?"

"We got a district judge who happened to be Senator Manuel's cousin to push it through."

I sipped my Tabasco-laden drink. "And then. . ."

"Well, you probably remember the city got a second district judge to slap a second temporary restraining order which prohibited us from commencing sales. Shit! Next thing we knew the matter was before the Supreme Court. And you know who made the ruling there?"

I shook my head.

"Donald Steppenhouse, former partner in the law firm that represented Tesuque Pueblo. He suspended the second district judge's temporary restraining order and our grand opening was ready to proceed."

While he sipped his Bloody Mary, I ate a jalapeno stuffed with white cheese. "Didn't the Indians claim their counsel was biased? And didn't Mountains West have their own lawyer representing the Indians as well?"

Coffin rolled his eyes which were blue as the sky. He drew his drink to his lips and frowned. "Is there enough vodka in this thing?"

It was midmorning so I said facetiously, "I usually have more this late in the day."

"I do too," he said, with a dour face. "This is breakfast for me." Then he set his glass down, wiped his lips with a napkin, and said, "I don't like to admit to error," tightening his lips and frowning. "But if it has to be done, I'll be frank about it. Tell you the truth, that lawyer crap was a grand farce. We did have a lawyer who also gave counsel to the Pueblo. You got that right."

"Do you also admit to the error of covering up the basic corruption of the scam—selling homes with no water supply, no police or fire protection, no sewage facility, no basic utilities such as gas or electric going in?" Coffin shrugged, gave me an ironic half-smile, said nothing.

"Just think," I continued, "a population of 15,000 in the middle of a cactus garden with no life-lines to support them."

"Let's not be melodramatic. All those things could be had." He smiled, frowned, popped another jalapeno.

"So there were some loose bolts in the foundation. Big deal, right? But it was a very big deal, wasn't it?"

"Yes, it was—and still is—"

Coffin was quiet for a while. He looked thoughtful. "My job was to promote a housing complex that would have brought hard cold cash to the Tesuque Pueblo and to the City of Santa Fe. We were told that since the subdivision was on Indian land, all non-Indian residents could expect the same immunities as the Indians themselves. Only a handful of Indians, the elders of the Pueblo, were unaware of what was happening—the younger ones knew it spelled disaster just as the Indians at Sandia Pueblo knew that a dog track on their land was a basic evasion of State racing and liquor laws. Howard Hughes himself was pushing for that deal down there, along with plans for a resort and casino on Navajo land. Ah, the webs we weave." Coffin jiggled the ice in his drink. "But where do you think the money comes from? How do you think the so-called good life happens here in New Mexico? Good old out of state dollars. That's all that separates us from us from the horned toads . . . and if Howard Hughes or anybody else wants to build or buy a parcel of Indian land for the right price he should be able to do it for the betterment of the rest of us. Land of the free, home of the brave doesn't mean *brave*, as in Indian brave, my friend."

"Can I quote you on that?"

"You may not." He looked into his empty, tomato-rimed glass.

"I thought you were going to tell me something about the cattle mutilations."

"What if I told you that the mutes were directly related to Mountains West?"

"I've wondered about that myself."

"The realty office was bombed by the same people who drew that petition against us, the group called Tewa Tesuque. They carted off every possession on the property—they stripped the land office and then burned it down."

"It was on their land wasn't it?"

59

"The building belonged to the shareholders of Mountains West. The land deal was set to go through with the progressive members of the tribe when the militants bombed it."

"You were going to lower the water table and harm thousands of natives just to water a golf course to please a bunch of developers? I don't see what that has to do with the cattle mutilation problem."

Coffin signaled someone behind the bar to bring us another.

"Not for me," I said.

"I wasn't thinking of you," he said.

His drink came quickly and he lost no time on it.

I could tell the interview, if such it was, was over. I got ready to go when he said, "Wait a minute. I have something to tell you. I have proof that tribal people are mutilating our cows."

"What kind of proof are you talking about?"

Coffin wiped his mouth but some red stain remained on his upper lip. I made a motion with my finger, but he didn't get it.

"Most of the animals that have been mutilated are on Indian land, wouldn't you agree?"

I nodded. "Quite a few anyway."

"Doesn't that make it all the more believable? They make it look like they're being victimized when actually they're the ones who are perpetrating the crime."

"And you have proof of this?"

"I had a man take some nightshots with an infrared camera. You can see the Indians cutting up cows."

"So now all you have to do is explain how they suck all the blood out of the carcass, remove internal organs surgically without cutting the body from the outside, and lastly, explain how they leave the scene of the crime without leaving tracks."

Coffin snorted. "Our forensics man said it was werewolves. You know, skinwalkers."

"That's Navajo, not Pueblo."

"They're all savages, aren't they?"

***

When someone is stalking you, you can feel it. Suddenly I was being stalked, and I felt it. I went for my usual run with the dogs. Twice a day, the way I had learned to honor the sun. My Navajo friends taught me how to do that. There are all kinds of ways. I did sun breathing where you pinch one nostril and draw sunlight into the other one. Inhale, exhale, slowly. Facing the east, then the west, moving in a gentle circle at the meridian points of the four directions while saying the Beautyway Chant: *All is beautiful all around me.* I would do this on top of a ridge in the light of the dawn sun.

I did this twice a day, morning and dusk. The sun brings the blessing of eastern light; the sun blesses the western light of day's end. It works, I believe, this simple daily prayer of harmony.

But what about the wolf I felt stalking me. Was the wolf some evil spirit from the past . . . from my past. I had no choice but to believe that I was actually haunted by the motorcyclist, the hit-and-run kid from the Gallinas canyon, who had run me down in 1967.

That night I was lying broken in the moon. Blood moon. Broken glass moon. Bleeding my life away. He stopped after the crash, his engine still growling. I saw his face as he bent over to see if I was alive or dead. Then he roared away.

My Navajo friends Jimmy BlueEyes, Ray Tsosie and Jay DeGroat said he was a skinwalker, an aberrant tribal wolfman.

A skinwalker, (He Who Walks In Skins) has nothing to do with the creature known as Wolf.

The stalker came back whenever I was in some kind of trouble. Then he would show up in my doorway. He had the mystic lupus fragrance of death all over him. Did he have fangs, claws, fur? He did not. But over his shoulders I saw the skin of a real wolf and upon his head the mantle of nose, eyeholes, the bent ears of a wolf on the prowl.

When I saw the skinwalker in the doorway, I knew who it was. I smelled the scent of swiftly moving water. The wind from Johnson Mesa. The moan of the wind coming down canyon. The cold mineral smell of lichen rock. The Penitente moon on piñon pine.

The stalker waited. Watched. Bluejay and his friends would whisper the Blessingway. And slowly, bit by bone, and bone by bit, they would sing me together again, with the help of the Ant People. I was reconstructed by poetry, song, belief the same way the Hero Twin of the Navajo after he was struck by Lightning was grafted together, one part and then another.

I used to sleep at night with a loaded pistol under my pillow. I listened to a Jesus Saves station out of Salt Lake City. The talker talked on through the night while I awaited the stalker who never came when I was waiting for him. I'd reach under my pillow, slide my hand along the wooden handle of the gun.

Sometimes I'd cock the hammer and slowly release it.

One morning I arose and wrote a single line in my journal:

We humans fear the beast within the wolf because we do not understand the beast within ourselves.

Chapter Eleven

I parked the car in a public parking lot in downtown Albuquerque and headed for the library where a calm sea of cowboy hats seemed to float upon a small group of informally clothed men and women leaning up against the walls and windows of the building.

The lines were distinctly drawn: cowboys and cattlemen mostly—large straws, small Stetsons. Some hatless politicians, Spanish and Anglo, uniformed officer here and there, and a nervous lot of newspeople, swapping notes and exchanging cards.

There was an atmosphere of a party, but no one knew exactly what was going to be served. Laughter was restrained, eyes moved from face to face, as if that was the best way to get acquainted.

In this atmosphere of indecision I found myself suddenly shy. Then a face surfaced in the crowd, a beaming smile upon it, and a straight-backed, mustached fellow came up to me. "Peter Argyle, he said, "Professor of Applied Cultural Anthropology, University of Vancouver."

I told him who I was, but I didn't tell him what I did for a living.

"You're a writer, aren't you?" he said, chuckling. "I can tell by the way you're holding your briefcase, like you've only got one chapter left to go."

"Fact is I'm just sorting through everything."

"I agree. No need to draw conclusions when there aren't any. Who knows where any of this will go anyway?"

Hats and heads began turning toward the glass doors of the library and the two or three hundred people that had gathered began to eddy into the cool auditorium downstairs.

A stage had been set by a TV crew, now swarming over hotlights and rotary cameras and myriads of wires and hook-ups.

A long cafeteria-type table was prepared at the left-hand corner of the stage and a stenographer's chair and desk were just to the right of it. Senator Harrison Salisbury, New Mexico Senator and former astronaut, entered from the wings with Brinton Shaw, the District Attorney who took a seat at the long table. The senator walked up to the podium for an opening line of welcome, but just as he got there a cameraman's hot lamp fell from a great height and smashed on the floor in front of the stage.

Salisbury seized the incident and exploited it to his best opening advantage: "These days you have to keep a lookout for UFOs even inside public buildings", he said.

The audience laughed and the tension in the room seemed to ease and I even saw a few Indians crack a smile.

"We have, as you know," the senator began, "brought about this conference, because of mounting public concern, over the 2.5 million dollars of property damage that has occurred in the past year as a result of cattle mutilations in our state. Now the hard fact for me to accept is that, up until now, no federal crime was committed. It wasn't until last week, that my colleague, Wallace Smith, our newly assigned Agent at the Department of Justice, who is with us today, discovered the two clauses of jurisdiction that will allow us to launch a major investigation.

"It is terribly hard for me to accept that we actually had to search for a federal law that was being broken before we could get moving on this thing. What Wallace Smith has done for us is find the legal loopholes, if you will, whereby we can finally act, and hopefully, prosecute the perpetrators of these bizarre mutilations.

"In brief, the laws that have been broken are these: first and foremost, the illegal operating of unmarked and unregistered aircraft, and secondly, the deliberate assault of properties belonging to American Indians; both of these fall under federal jurisdiction. So we hope today to re-affirm our goodwill with the Pueblo leaders of northern New Mexico, as well as other tribal leaders, so that they may assist us in our efforts to bring cattle mutilations to a stop in our state. Before closing my statement and going on with our proceedings, I would like to say that what makes our predicament so untenable is the unprecedented discipline employed by these offenders. To my knowledge, there has not been a crime perpetrated in twenty-three states thus far in our history that leaves us with so few actual clues. This fact alone deserves our closest scrutiny and our best scientific approach. Thank you for coming here today and offering your collective support to our cause."

The first speaker of the day was Oliver Parsons, Director of the Social Science program at Yale. He was a spare athletic-looking man.

"I belong to a nationwide network of researchers, Parsons said, "Who are trying to determine the exact nature of the mutilations. Let us say, for simplicity's sake, that we're doing our best to find out whether the facts on hand point toward a mass hallucination of a psychic order, like Orson Welles' *War of the Worlds* phenomena, where thousands responded to fear only because of a commanding voice on the radio, and thought they saw what, in fact, they only heard. What we're faced with here, in my opinion, is a frontal assault on our notion of reality, and the only thing that makes sense is that none of the mutilations make any sense. We are faced with a challenge that could very well relate to man's survival on this planet, and our methodologies, which we pat ourselves on the back and exclaim are so unfailing and precise, have failed, every single one of them.

"What we are left with is a huge riddle, a Humpty-Dumpty of the twentieth century. I want to leave you with this thought: if the mutilations happened to snakes and not cows, how many of us would be here today? And if, instead of snakes, they happened to humans, how long would the federal government have waited to spot a loophole in the laws as Senator Salisbury so eloquently put it?"

There followed a volley of applause and some members of the audience actually got up from their seats to make their support of the final part of this speech known. During this time, the senator shifted uneasily in his seat on the stage: this was more applause than his speech had gotten.

The third speaker was a Hispanic cattleman.

"I am Arturo Ortiz from Dulce, New Mexico. I have been a cattle rancher for thirty years. I have no answers; I have only questions. My first question is why do these cattle rapes and killings—for that is what they really are—happen only in certain places at certain times? And I have to ask, was this cow that I saw alive and walking around with the rest of my herd made out of some material we don't know about? Did it have a door in its stomach that opened up so that its organs popped out and flew away into the sky? Unless I am a crazy man and need to see a doctor, those are things I saw with my own two eyes. And that is all I have to say to you, except that I am hoping that someone out there knows the answers to these questions. Thank you."

The next speaker was a laboratory specialist from Los Alamos Scientific Laboratories. He was wearing a white shirt and a bola tie with a great chunk of turquoise. He forgot to introduce himself and he moved about awkwardly behind the podium. It appeared that he had been brought to trial. Twice, as he began a preamble no one in the audience could hear, he had to be told by the stenographer and the honorable senator to raise the microphone nearer to his face. "Well, the rest you know about," he said. There was a shriek of feedback from the mic after which he got going with his talk.

"I have been investigating cases in Kansas and Nebraska, as well as New Mexico, and we have gathered nine years of evidence in three categories: Predator mutilations, that would be coyotes usually after a cattle death from another source, maybe just natural death, often that's what it is, a natural death, old age or something like that. . .and then the second area would be a death and mutilation caused by unexplained knives or sharp instruments— very few of those in our findings. And the third area is summed up by the case of these young men who were caught at the site of their alleged crime in South Dakota. Just a couple of deranged kids who were cutting up cattle for the hell of it. In short, this is what we've been looking at. I have more to add but it will have to wait until my final report is out."

Professor Argyle, seated to my left, leaned over and whispered: "Some scientific method. We're going to hear a lot of cover-ups from men who know better."

The next speaker was a sort of haunted man who started off: "I am Tommy Blaine from Brown's Station, Texas and I have spent twenty-two years studying UFOs. Twelve of those years I have spent exploring the phenomena we call cattle mutilations. First, let me acquaint you with a few necessary facts. Some of you feel that while something bizarre is happening, it can probably be logically explained—if not today, then at some future date when the FBI gets it together and does the job they're supposed to do. I can tell you this much, and it isn't very comforting. Cattle mutilations have been going on since the early 1800s in Ireland and in England. At the British Museum, you can find data that shows that even the great Arthur Conan Doyle attempted to solve a mysterious animal mutilation—with no success by the way. But always under the same circumstances. That is to say, jugular veins neatly, almost artistically, punctured, blood drained from the body just like the cases we're seeing today. And we can't restrict the events of recent years to the western United States because they're happening in Russia, Australia, New South Wales, Puerto Rico, India. Pigs, cows, sheep, rabbits, goats, and horses.

"One of the most puzzling facts is that mutilated animals frequently vanish after they've been reported to the proper authorities. There was a mutilated calf in southeastern New Mexico that had been discovered by a rancher. When a team of investigators showed up only hours later, the calf had been dragged to a fence line where it just disappeared. No tracks, nothing.

"In Ohio there was a UFO sighting and a mutilated German Shepherd was found nearby; the tall grass all around the carcass was flattened for twenty feet in diameter. The most dramatic event of this kind that I have on record is a steer that had its head rotated 360 degrees. We know of several cases where shrubs were burned in circular patterns and huge boulders were dislodged and small trees pulled out by the roots. In more than one case of this kind, NORAD confirmed that 'mysterious helicopters' were picked up on radar screens and then subsequently lost.

"So, what is really happening out there? That's what all of us want to know. Frankly, I don't know. But if it's not coyotes or cultists, crazy kids or the government, it must be something none of us wants to think about. What that is, I don't know. But it has to be something like what the Mexican Indian I talked to said: "They're visiting us again." He pointed to the ceiling, and beyond that, to the galaxy.

The next speaker was a black man who sounded like a southern Baptist preacher. He had the audience though.

Dr. Argyle said to me, "Don't let his delivery throw you, this man's got some pretty interesting things to say, especially considering he is a physicist."

"I am Dr. Bob Montclaire from Sandia Scientific Laboratory. Let me just lay it on you the way I see it, and you can make of it what you will. One thing I won't do is this—excuse certain members of our distinguished audience because they imagine themselves to be a persecuted minority. You know what I'm saying? I am referring to the native population with whom I have been lately quarreling. I maintain that it is our responsibility, each and every one of us, to get to the bottom of this thing. And this is where I split paths with my American Indian brothers. Some of these people are covering up the mutilations as fast as we're finding them. I mean this literally. Yeah, the Pueblo people in the state of New Mexico are burying evidence, putting it underground, hiding it from us. They say Star People aren't going to like all this poking around and lab testing. I say we might as well bury ourselves if we're going to worry over Outer-Space People and what they might think of us. Slide, please."

The lights dimmed, the stenographer's fingers continued to dance and Dr. Montclaire spoke with more portent than before. The absence of light seemed to add a dimension to the depth and resonance of his voice. On the screen was the head of a cow, fur and flesh pulled away from its face in a grotesquery of weirdness that by now was beginning to be the poster image of the mute scene.

"This picture was taken at San Ildefonso Pueblo and we have on record the only Indian evidence that there was something very unusual about this particular mutilation. An old man told us: 'This animal had the circle of evil influence. This means no dog will go near it. When the circle of evil influence is present, nothing living, except a two-legged will go near it—not birds, not even little flies.'

"So, to complete the picture for you, folks, mostly it's people like me who get up close and personal with these mutilations. And, you know, I have to say, I believe there are secrets the Indians won't tell us and if we knew what they know right now, we'd be doing a different kind of investigation. Doesn't sound very scientific, does it? But that's the way it is. They know something. We don't."

The lights came back on and with them a brief spatter of restrained, diffident applause. I noticed two American Indian elders who looked hard at Montclaire. One of them now got up and walked to the stage.

"I speak for the Jicarilla Apache tribe," he said, without introducing himself. "We are sick and tired of having to answer questions that have nothing to do with Indian people's real problems. We're going to ask investigation authorities to clear themselves through our offices up at Dulce, and not at the Bureau of Indian Affairs. There are certain threats that cause harm on our reservation. We want these threats to stop. We are not talking anymore until the threats stop."

He turned from the podium and took his seat before Senator Salisbury came forward and asked him to disclose the nature of the threats and where they were coming from.

"We are not talking until the threats stop," the Apache elder said from his seat.

After the conference I drove home to Tesuque remembering Henry David Thoreau's comment: "A man needs only to be turned around once with his eyes shut . . . to be lost." Thoreau was right and from my point of view we were a lost nation looking for a place to rest our souls. The only words that made any sense to me seemed to come from natives who simply asked for the threats to stop. But how long had they been threatened? Centuries, I figured. Since the first twinkle of eternity. They knew something. Too bad they weren't talking.

Back home I went for a long run in the arroyo. It was, as usual, late in the day and getting near the time of deception when a horseback rider came cantering down the arroyo. I recognized the rider. It was Veryl Goodnight, our neighbor. She was an unusual neighbor, to say the least. A nationally known sculptress, she was also the granddaughter of the cattleman who founded the Goodnight Trail that ran from Texas to Montana during the great, short era of the cowboy cattle drives. Veryl was a tough, attractive, physical woman. She drew her quarter horse up next to me and said, "Don't run alone up here right now, Jack."

"What's wrong?"

"Mad coyote," she said. "It just attacked my horse."

"Rabies?"

"Just plain meanness and madness. Turn back, I gotta go."

She took off at a gallop.

I shrugged and ran up the arroyo.

I hadn't gone too far when all of a sudden, there was the coyote. It was white. The same size as the dog at the dump. No, to be accurate, it *was* the dog at the dump, and it came at me snarling, moving very slow and a little to the left of me.

Not knowing what else to do, I held my ground.

Then it came at me, directly.

I have a decent vertical jump, even though my right leg is loaded with metal and pins, and I shot upwards.

My martial arts teacher had taught me the old Mongol art of Sokol which means falcon in Czech. It is very nearly a dance, similar in some ways to tai chi.

The coyote stopped its attack to re-think. It was a few feet away from me. It looked at me warily, mouth open, growling softly.

I moved in a very tight circle, lifting my legs in slow motion. My hands weaving over and under as I turned in the circular pattern I knew so well.

The coyote growled, took a step backwards, and sat down to watch me more closely.

I did the hawk pose, one leg tucked into my groin, as in yoga, arms out straight at my sides. Then I raised my right knee to my chest and did one very straight-out flick of the right foot. Then the left, up, out and down. Then a single tumble roll forward and I lay flat on the sand.

The coyote hopped like a hare, backwards, one remove from me.

Gold eyes with the amber pine-sap streaks at the corners studied me. I could see the coyote thinking and I could hear it saying, "This thing, this so-called man, is not altogether well. I should leave it alone to work out its own destiny." Then the coyote raised its head, let out a series of wine-drunk wails, whirled around and fled to the north.

I got home before dark and told no one about this.

If I'd told Laura she would have just shaken her head, and said, "Have you *lost* your mind?"

Thoreau was right, so was Gertrude Stein when she told Hemingway, "You are all a lost generation." Sometimes you can find yourself though by facing the unexpected and doing a brave, silly little dance all your own.

Chapter Twelve

On Monday I went to the office. Marsha was setting type, her fingers clicking out a 120 words a minute at her "stand alone composer" typesetting machine. I always thought—if I could type that fast I wouldn't be writing any more. The juncture would be gone from mind/finger/word and there would be only flow, only a plumed serpent of word magic.

Marcia was cute. Freckled cute. She owned the universe with her Oklahoma brown-eyed good looks and her flying fingers.

Thomas, the adman, was another story. He was at his desk, diamond ring on his little finger glittering like a star.

Durwood, master of nothing in particular and everything in general, was correcting proof.

A title came to me the moment I sat at my IBM Selectric typewriter, *The Mute-Makers*. It was either that or *The Indisputable Mutable . . .*

I laughed. My love of rhyme often got the better of me. I canceled title number two after typing it. Then I toyed with a few others before settling on *The Star Surgeons*.

I began to write some things I'd picked up from my field research then weaving this into the conference. I tried typing fast like Marsha, no looking back, just letting the words zing . . .

A cow lying in the sun for weeks with no maggots or flies in or near the flesh is another example. These are occurrences from the Negative Plane where Evil presents itself regularly like clockwork. We need only offer our attention to this Plane and it will suck us into it. Then there are mutilations on the Positive Plane, those that cannot be explained in any other way. The clean surgical method employed by these masters of deception shows no trace of banished grace, but something spiritual has occurred when you see the muted body with missing eyes, ears, nose, or mouth. A message is being offered to us if we could only understand its meaning.

I was staring at this curious and maybe foolish opener when my phone rang.

A husky male voice said, "There is going to be a mutilation at San Reymo Pueblo."

"When?" I asked.

"Soon."

"Who is this?"

"Doesn't matter."

"Tell Andrews."

"I am Jack Andrews."

"No time to lose make it fast."

"How do you know?"

The man hung up.

***

San Reymo Pueblo was scattered out more than the Pueblos to the south and unlike some of the others, it was made up of one story adobe buildings lining a dusty road, bordered by deep green meadows—this was high country with ponderosas on the hills and higher mountains to the north towards Taos. The main cluster of adobes was on a hillside, an ancient earth-colored subdivision that sloped down toward a deep blue lake.

The air was thick with dust and pueblo dogs, but I saw no Indians, and even more strange, there were no children anywhere. Except for the dogs, the pueblo looked like it had been deserted a long time ago.

Not far from the lake's edge, some people were standing beside the carcass of a brown and white bull. There was only one Indian present, the other people were Spanish and Anglo. The grass had gone velvet in the light, the air had a hint of frost in it, but there was a reedy smell from the lake and over all of it the scent of piñon smoke.

As I walked towards the lake, one of the men, Angel Gomez, came up to me and asked what I was doing there. Standing a little ways away was Len Kreuger, the former FBI man assigned to the Santa Fe area.

"Do you remember me from a month ago?" I asked. "I'm from *The Review*. You showed me that head in the trunk of your car."

Gomez shrugged. He didn't remember me.

Kreuger came up. "By what authority are you here?" he inquired.

"My own."

"Don't give me that shit. This mutilation just happened. Who told you to come here?"

"Look, Gomez said, facing me, "This is a private investigation. I don't remember you from a couple weeks ago. This thing here is not for the press, not until we've checked it out. So you've got no business being here."

"I'm not through with him yet, Angel," Kreuger said.

I sensed they *did* recognize me and I was sure that was why Gomez was chasing me off. But then the whole thing had a surreal twist because, basically, I didn't know *why* I was there myself, or more to the point, who had summoned me on the phone. I'd been given a tip—why? I was in another of those quixotic dilemmas where nothing fit together. Did someone see a political strategy in my writing of speculative articles?

While Kreuger looked me up and down a tall Pueblo native walked up to us. He had the bearing of someone important, a *cacique* perhaps. These northern Pueblos, San Reymo and Taos, have some handsome men. This one had braids that hung down low on his chest. Oddly though he was accompanied by two white men wearing matching blue berets. One of them was tall and thin and the other was short and thin. They were pale ghosts in the fading light.

The *cacique*, if in fact he was, had his arms crossed and he stood there with a white blanket wrapped around him. I heard him say to Kreuger, "Let this one stay." He nodded towards me.

"This isn't someone we want to have around here," Kreuger said. He had a sharp-featured face, olive skin, and heavy dark eyebrows.

"He can stay," the tall man said. "By my order."

Kreuger scowled, spat, shook his head, and walked back toward the lake where the others were kneeling around the carcass.

Gomez had a good face that you could not help but like and I believed he didn't care if I was there as long as Kreuger had no say in it.

"We gotta be careful now," he said, by way of apology. "Our ass is in the sling. Len's going to have new orders any day now. As for me, I've been officially moved up—promoted. Got to watch our step real careful now."

"What's your official title, if I may ask?"

"Northern New Mexico Task Force Field Director." He lowered his voice when he said this, which meant he was very proud of his assignment. "Before you put anything down on paper," he warned, "better clear it with the tribe first and me second. But we'll have to wait on the lab results. That could be quite early in the morning. Then you call me for an official press release. I'm at the State Police Office up in Dulce."

A moment later Gomez shuffled off towards the lake. His legs were somewhat bowlegged, his boots gleaming in the damp meadow grass.

"Who sent you here?" the tall Pueblo elder asked.

"I got a call about an hour and a half ago from someone who wouldn't be identified. He told me to come. Said something was going to happen. I only half- believed him."

"You believe it now?"

I nodded.

The two Europeans came a little closer. The smaller and thinner of the men offered me his hand.

"I am Etienne Saronier," he said softly.

I knew the voice.

"It was you who called. Why?"

"We want reportage minus the hysteria," he said. "The things I've read of yours are decent and fair. They are not, contrary to what Mr. Kreuger told me, a bunch of lies. You are maybe one of the only writers talking about spiritual truths. You know, the things that underlie the events."

He was French, or sounded like it, no doubt about the accent.

"I hope you tell the truth," the Pueblo man said.

"He does," the slight Frenchman said.

Then the cacique turned away and walked toward a small queue of Indians who had gathered nearby.

"He's a good man," the friend of Etienne said.

"I would think, after today's hearing in Albuquerque, that the Indians would be a lot more cautious about letting us on their land," I said. "There's a broil of contention going on."

"You were there, too? What did you think of it?"

"I'm still sorting it out."

The tall man laughed and offered me his hand.

"I'm Harjac," he said.

I knew him from the clipping service at the paper. James Harjac was an international figure in the world of extraterrestrial phenomena. He'd had a distinguished career in physics before abandoning university life and branching off on his own to lecture and write. He was the author of many scholarly books on life probabilities in other galaxies. His latest treatise was about Jesus Christ and The Galactic Federation, a theory which cast Christ as an ancient astronaut. Harjac, only a month earlier, had talked about being taken aboard a space craft. He was returned to earth with a divine mission, but he wasn't talking about that yet.

The questions I wanted to ask Harjac would have to wait because Etienne now motioned us to follow him over to the mutilation site. The three of us came up quietly to the small circle of six or more men who were discussing things in barely audible tones. Kreuger was in there with them and he gave me a sharp look but that was it.

"Mr. Burton, what's your take?" Gomez asked.

A big man with buff-surgical gloves and a medium sized grey-blue Stetson was bending over the carcass of the bull. From where I stood I could see the clean, meticulously-cut hole in the animal's stomach, just above the genital area. The genitalia were gone and all that remained was a sooty blur of missing fur. The hole, though, was what fascinated me. In the magenta light of early evening, the deep reddish purple of the bull's missing intestinal organs showed clear to the vertebrae—the hole was like a mystic portal suggesting that it had always been there. Instead of repulsion, I was mesmerized.

Drawn in by the dusk lit scene and its shadowy participants. I overheard Burton say, one decibel above a whisper, that the bull's organs except for the genitals, had been sucked out as if by, or through, a tube.

"Some kind of blood evacuation system pumped the animal's heart dry as it stood there, not knowing what was happening to it," he said.

"You mean," Gomez said, stooping down on one knee, "that this bull was alive when it was being drained of blood?"

"Yes, and conscious, too. My opinion. Tests may prove otherwise."

"Well, how in the hell. . ."

"I don't know. But there's not a speck of blood anywhere around here, and the way the animal fell over. Well, it kind of toppled over—as if gravity brought it down, its own 2400 pounds just felled it like a tree.

"Meanwhile the animal's heart was pumping blood to keep it alive as something else, some device, was emptying its system of life-blood and then its internal organs too.

"Far as I can see the genital removal came after the animal expired. The whole operation lasted, I would guess, a matter of moments, and I don't think the bull felt a thing while it was going on. That's another opinion. But I've been looking into the faces of bulls since I was nine years old. Under such circumstances an animal's eyes register shock and fear, but not in this case."

"I have a grim feeling about this place," Harjac whispered to Etienne. "The vibrations tell me this is a bad place."

Gomez stood up and looked at Harjac.

"What's so bad about it?" he said. He put a stick of gum in his mouth.

"The owls, for one thing. The woods around the lake is surrounded with owls, spirits of death. It's no accident there's been a mutilation here and the Indians know it."

"I bet I know more about owls than you do," Gomez said. "My grand-mother told us kids, my brother and me, when you see an owl with a red face, you get home fast because that is the Devil."

He let out a small sinister laugh, and went on. "Well, the Apaches up in Dulce say a man can travel in the form of an owl, but that's medicine-man talk.

"So when it comes to mumbo-jumbo owl talk, I don't listen much anymore. I was raised Catholic, I believe in God, the Holy Ghost, the Trinity, Angels and even the Devil . . . yeah, I believe in that old bastard too."

"As do I," Harjac said quietly. "But I also believe that Christ, the Lord, came here from a world that was light years away. He came to save us, but we wouldn't let him. Now, before our eyes, is proof of another power—and we must take notice of it. We shouldn't assume that it is intrinsically evil. It has emanations of power."

"Well, you got me, Professor," Gomez said, rolling his eyes to indicate to Burton and the others that Harjac was a bit woo-woo. "I can't disagree with what you say. Fact is, I don't understand what the fuck you just said. I'm just a dumb cop and you're a smart-ass doctor of something or other. Well, put it into your report, that's what you're here for."

Gomez walked over to Burton and Kreuger and the two men moved off from the rest of us and talked. I faced Harjac by moving into the place vacated by Gomez. I looked into his eyes and saw that he was both touched and wise— maybe there was too much air and not enough earth in his astrological sign. But no matter, Harjac was a story all by himself. He was a man of knowledge. A lightning rod. A mystic man.

"I find what you say very interesting," I told him. "I'd like to hear more about what you think happened here."

"They don't understand me some of these guys. They pay me to make my reports because I have a recognizable name."

"Who's they?" I asked.

"I work for NASA. I am also the Executive Director of the Academy for Cosmic Research in California. These mutilation studies of mine are probably too ethereal for these flatfoots to comprehend, but at least there is enough current interest in the subject to keep my research on course. I really don't care what they think, as long as they let me continue to reach the media—if they tried to cut me off or shut me up, I'd be up in arms."

"I don't quite follow."

Harjac had a discrete honest face and it was impossible to imagine while listening to him that he was anything but a wisdom keeper. His blue beret was pitched to one side of his head and he removed it for a moment revealing a narrow scar that intruded into his hairline like a meandering part.

"Ironic," he laughed, "I work for NASA, yet I have been commissioned by the Galactic Federation to carry on my work here on earth. Do you see this scar? It was put there by beneficent beings who put me through a series of tests. The scar was done by a man's fingers. It is my awakening mark. One day we will all have them."

"You were saying before about your work on earth—what do you mean by that?"

"Why, my purpose, of course, was awakened to help awaken others. NASA helps me to do this by paying for my research even though I think they think I'm crazy. For the time being, and that may only be for a short while, they let me carry on my work because I am a spiritual scientist and it looks good for someone of my faith to appear with them. The hypocrites like to appear open-minded—without me they would all look like desperate little bigots."

"Let me ask you this, how do mutilations tie in with your work? I don't see the connection."

"To you and the others here," Harjac said, "these mutilations must seem horrid. That is because you do not understand what is behind them. You fear they are the work of cryptic alien intelligence bent on doing harm when in reality they are only intimations of the power of peace."

"If they're mystic messages—what you're suggesting—then, why aren't we understanding them?"

"We will in time. But there are many types of mutilations. Some are the work of visitors from the Negative Plane, from the plane of the anti-Christ, and those mutilations are frightening. I have seen them: A cow that has been lying dead in the hot sun for weeks with no maggots, no flies. Such mutilations are to be shunned for there is nothing we can learn from them. But the others, like this one here today, contain a spiritual message of some kind. We think everything bizarre comes from the sky, from the stars, but these mutilations on Indian land, always near stretches of water, prove to me that our visitors are often from within."

I was struck by the phrases he used because they were the same ones I'd written in my office, but there wasn't time for any reflection, I wanted to keep him talking.

"From within you say? What do you mean by that?"

"They originate within the earth and appear above the earth at a later time. The San Reymo people have known about inner space for hundreds of years. Their reason for withholding this information is because we are not adequately prepared to understand. What would you say if I told you we could travel in inner space by finding the secret passage in this very lake?"

"Getting back to what you said before—I still don't see what a mutilated animal has to do with spirituality. I've studied all kinds of religions and have never come across that idea. Sacrifice, yes, but not mutilation."

"You're mistaken. But that is natural. At first it's hard to accept. I could show you Tibetan Buddhist tankas that clearly indicate the flaying of flesh by deities for a greater purpose. All passages to worlds of the spirit involve the shedding of flesh and its earthly ties. The ancient Hindus said that nothing exists or is destroyed, things merely change shape or form. So what is so surprising about a mutilated horse or cow—humans have done it in religious ceremonies for thousands of years—it is just as Christ was prepared for his cycle of eternal return."

"Mutilated cattle are not my idea of anything divine."

"We pass through many incarnations. The first Tibetans were monkeys with tails and their ancestors are the Yetis, or what we have been calling on this continent, Bigfoot.

"In Asia, long ago, there was a hidden kingdom, and it was a place of broad lakes that have since turned to sand. Here in northern New Mexico there is also sand, but the lakes remain, and so do their caretakers the Indians, who facially, culturally, esoterically, and in every other way, harkens back to the ancient Monkey Kings of Tibet."

There was no light left in the sky, only the silver of the lake in the moon rounding toward full, and the white moonlike fact of the fallen bull lying on its side.

"You will have to leave now," Kreuger said. "This investigation is over."

I walked to the car with Harjac and Etienne. They said nothing. As we neared the place where the cars were parked, Etienne shook hands with me again.

"If you are studying these things, we will see more of each other."

Harjac walked away into the night without saying goodbye.

"I wouldn't want to be him," I said. "He seems to carry a very heavy burden."

"He does, indeed."

"Are you part of his research group?"

"No. He took me along as a favor. Now I see that he only knows so much. Maybe it is great. But it's a little to one side, if you understand my meaning."

In the dark, this small glow-face Frenchman seemed more a person from another world than wise old Harjac who had answers in the palm of his hand.

"What do you do for a living?" I asked him.

"I have a Center for Psychic Phenomena in Santa Fe. I have friends who come and speak there all the time. One of the speakers, a very close friend, grew up on the Hopi Reservation and she has a view similar to Harjac's. She knew him personally and introduced us. You must come and hear her speak on The Hopi Prophecy. You know, that is the belief the Hopis have. They say they came from the stars, originally. As do the Navajos—they say the same thing. Many tribal people believe they came from under ground but were helped by Star People to emerge into this, the Fifth World."

"So you believe the prophecy?"

"I do. And I think humans have but one hope for the future."

"What is that?"

"To get off this planet as soon as we can."

Chapter Thirteen

Until you have seen a mutilation, you can't really write about it. The face of a leering, lipless cow with a purple cave for a lower midsection isn't something you can forget that easily.

Durwood said, with his broad-toothed grin, "You are going to the mountain and meeting the varmint."

"Only I don't know who the varmint is."

He laughed. "The varmint is you, is us, don't you see? It's what Mary Baker Eddy called "mortal mind." What we see and hear is ephemeral. Unreal, illogical, prejudicial, worthless and no-count, as we say in the South. Stay clear of this stuff and it won't possess you. It's all passing before your eyes. When it's no longer believed it will blow away like a dust of mites."

I said, "It's hard to shake."

"Of course. Yet shake it you must."

I typed up my notes and went home.

That night I dreamed about the night I was bone-crushed by the motorcycle. I was lying in the road in the dream. Then I was out of my body and I saw there was an animal licking my blood. Lapping it. My tibia was a white bone in the dry moonlight and the lapping noise was the river running . . . or was it the man bending over me?

I looked for Laura and she wasn't there. She had gone to Ray Drew's for a blanket to put over me. Was I dead? I'd bled out. But was I dead?

I waited in the darkness, an incorporeal entity, a vacancy with a dreaming mind. A series of small vortexes came out of my open mouth. Little spinning orbs of light. They were the same as the stardust, firefly-like things that had come out of the cow that Sarah and I had seen at the dump.

I woke soaked with sweat. Got out of bed and looked at the alarm clock. It was 4:30. I put on my gym shorts and running shoes and left the house. The dogs came out of their dog houses. The big collie, Mosh and the Newfy, Black Dog. The Dachshund cross, Puppa had come out with me.

We three took the arroyo north, running quiet except for our breathing. There was frost in the air. The stunted oaks were golden-leaved in the pre-dawn light. The moon was going over the hill, the stars were fading out. Soon the sun would be up.

As I ran I heard again the voice of my Navajo friend Joogii, Bluejay, telling me about the circle of evil influence. "Once you step into the circle, it will follow you."

"How do you get out of it?" I had asked.

"Ask yourself three questions: Who am I? Where am I going? Who am I with?"

"And that will break the circle?"

"It is the start. It reminds that you are not alone."

I ran with the dogs to the top of the hill beyond the fifth ponderosa. From there I could see Los Caminitos twinkling in the gray dawn just before sunup.

Jay, as I called him, always said this was the best time to say the prayer of "All is Well" from the *Night Chant*.

"When you say this prayer you will know who is with you. Good or evil." I sat down on the sand cross-legged and whispered to myself:

> For long years I have kept
> this beauty within me
> it is my life
> it is given to me as the gift of dew is given
> to the cornflower that gives pollen
> I make offerings of pollen and dew.

I said this and sun rose and the fog of Los Caminitos lifted into the sky and a little wind came up and carried the greyness away. A moment after I was covered in sun's blood, bright as if newly born, and the fog went overhead and passed on to Chupadero.

Now I was a dawn treader following the flow of light as I ran.

I am free, I thought.

The chrome killer is gone. I have nothing to fear.

He is gone and I am alive and I know who is with me. I am supported by little wind and big wind, the Sun Father, Changing Woman, the brilliance of the dawn like a blanket all around me.

I ran on with the dogs at my heel.

Where the light stopped I came into the circle of my own home.

I crossed the arroyo, breathless, and ready.

A band of light lay before me.

Where it stopped, I saw something. I bent down to see what it was, tucked into the cleft of the arroyo's lip. A small woodrat had made a home there, I could see its straws, and when I reached inside I felt around, cool stone.

I withdrew and held it in the red soft light and saw that it was Changing Woman, blanketed, head-covered, her face deep within the folds of dark volcanic rock, protected from the forces of evil. I was safe from the skinwalkers of the night.

***

Hunting with Harjac: On The Trail of the Mutes. The galleys were on my desk. Marsha could typeset faster than any of us could write or read. I still had the unsettled feeling about my visit to San Reymo and seeing the mutilated bull there. But I had the small sculpture of Changing Woman. She was in the upstairs nicho where I kept sacred things.

Laura asked me when I put it there: "How did it come to be?"

"You mean who, or what, created it?"

She held it in her hand turning it from one side to another. It was a woman made of stone. Carved? Who could know? It seemed to be formed by the deity herself. Mother Nature. Changing Woman, as the Navajos called her; the sister of White Shell Woman who lives in the western Pacific sun and sea.

"I heard a story once," Laura said. "It was about a man in Chimayo who found a fetish like this. He said it was the Mother of Jesus. When people asked him why she was robed in black, he didn't say she was made of volcanic black rock. He said she was a Goddess of the South. 'She came from Brazil,' he said."

"I know that legend," I said. "She gave birth to Jesus, not the man from Nazareth but a North American son of Jehovah. Some called him Jesus on Horseback. Some called him 'the man who rides a flaming star'. One thing everyone in Chimayo agreed on: He was black. As was Jesus."

I wondered how this went along with mutilated cows, werewolves and other things.

An antidote. Heart medicine. A shield.

I settled in with the latest clippings from the clipping bureau we subscribed to and sipped a cup of strong black coffee while waiting for the rest of the office to show up for work.

There were some funny clippings, as well as the usual, and there were a few additional lead-ins to the San Reymo mutilation. A young native Indian claimed to have seen a "bright light in the East that looked like a flaming star that streamed across the night sky just before a mutilation happened at Santa Clara Pueblo."

A Pueblo family from Taos, mother, daughter, father, uncle and 112-year-old grandmother confessed to the County Sheriff's Department that for several days prior to a mutilation down by the river they had witnessed blue lights.

When asked why they had not discussed the lights with anyone, the family lapsed into characteristic silence. They would not comment on whether they thought the lights were earthly or extraterrestrial. It was thought, and later stated, by a tribal policeman named Naranjo, that the family had been "Afraid to speak of the lights and were afraid about them coming back."

In the *Rio Grande Sun* there was an interview with Angel Gomez, in which he said the latest lab reports confirmed his suspicion that mutilated animals were being bled to death with twelve to fourteen gauge needles which were inserted into their jugular veins.

The beating of the animals' hearts forced blood into a kind of syringe-like container that was hooked up to the needles. Prior to the bleeding, Gomez said, the animals were anesthetized by a depressant, chlorpromazine, and he quoted from a recent lab report which said: "In the anesthetized or wholly sedated animal, the heart will continue to function and act as a pump until the last drops of blood have been drained. The method of death is nothing out of the realm of human capacity."

The reason many cases were getting overnight lab analyses, Gomez said, was because the carcasses they were finding were only hours old when discovered, and they offered an ideal opportunity for the inspection of chemical residue.

Other results of recent testing proved that an anti-coagulant which Gomez said "any chemist could fix" was used to rush the blood through the jugular veins. Bones around shoulders appeared to have been shattered, suggesting the animals were dropped from the air before they were found.

I decided while reading this stuff that I ought to give Gomez a call myself, inasmuch as he had offered to let me hear the lab report when it came in from Sandia. I picked up the phone and dialed the number of the State Police Headquarters on the Jicarilla Apache Reservation up in Dulce, New Mexico, where Gomez had his obscure office.

A man answered and said that Gomez would be right with me. I waited for what seemed an hour while someone poured coffee, and then I heard Gomez talking.

The amazing thing about this man from what I had observed the few times I had seen him was that he was really an assemblage of characters rolled into one. By turns he could be as tough, as innocent, as smart, or even as ignorant as the next man. But with him these different guises worked. There was something genuine about his northern New Mexico bravado. I was going to have to do some required reading on the background of Angel Gomez.

"Whaddya want?" he bellowed into the phone.

I explained who I was and that I was interested in the lab report on the bull at San Reymo.

"Not in yet," he said.

"Can you tell me what *is* in?"

"Who the hell are you again?"

"The reporter from *The Review* who was at San Reymo last night."

"Why didn't you say so?"

"Sorry."

"You were the guy talking with that Frenchy what's his name. Well, okay, I'll give you what I got. It ain't much, not yet, anyway. They tell me down at Sandia that the tongue on this one showed signs of burning, scalding-like, you know what I mean? Said it appeared to be fried in hot fat. They found clampmarks on the animal's hind legs, and some muscle extension, like the bull was lifted into the air by some device. Then it was maybe put down on all fours. For a while maybe it was standing like that. Still alive while getting pumped out. You know, bled out."

"Could the mutilation have been done airborne?"

"Weightless? Yeah. Possibly. We're pretty sure the mutilation takes place after what they call 'anaesthetization, exsanguination.' Sound asleep, drained of blood."

"'Any blood evidence anywhere?"

"Not this one."

"But on some others?"

"I've seen dark purple or sometimes black blood spore. Once I saw an electric kind of pink. Neon color almost."

"What does that suggest?

"Hey, you ask too many questions."

"That's my job."

"Well, my job is to catch criminals whether they're high-flying or low crawling."

"Thanks for helping me out. I appreciate it."

"Here's something . . ." Gomez offered. "Tell your readers these guys, or whatever they are, have some pretty sophisticated scissors."

He clicked off.

I sat at my desk, thinking.

Following these mutes was like reading an extraterrestrial detective novel. The more you knew, the less you knew. I returned to the myriad clippings from New Mexico newspapers. There were a variety of stories on subjects tangential to mutilation, but nonetheless interesting. *The New Mexican* headlined—"Solar Balloons Cause Santa Fe UFO Scare." The story was about two giant pieces of black and white inflatable plastic with a snowflake design that were seen close to San Ildefonso Pueblo lumbering at low altitudes toward the Rio Grande. Cars lined the highways from Camel Rock to Nambe to witness the long bubbles that caught the light and reflected it back as they turned, roly-poly, in the noonday sun. The mystery was attributed to an Australian batik artist, Geoff Jarvis, who was working with the Northern Pueblo Agency's Arts Experience Program. "The big plastics, close to thirty feet long were being shown off to Pueblo children as solar balloons, but were not expected to take so readily to the air."

The Torrance County Citizen reported the story of a weird light flashing in a hill which blinked at one-minute intervals. This was later discovered to be the lit end of a pivot irrigation system.

And there was a missing son story in *The Roswell Daily Record*. An Air Force 2nd Lieutenant was in a telephone booth when the line went dead and, according to observers, the young man vanished. "Harley was very strong in his religious convictions," his father commented to the press. "He had just bought a house in Albuquerque and was going to hold bible studies there. We can only pray that he is not being harmed."

A letter in the *Albuquerque Journal* also caught my fancy. It related the following information under the headline CATTLE MUTILATION NO MYSTERY:

"My father owned land east of Roy, three miles north of Solano, where I was born. I remember that in 1910, east of Roy, there was nothing but prairies, and often one could see a sheepherder's tent up on the hills, as it was mostly sheep grazing land. At that time, I recall a cattle rancher, Vidal Martinez, who owned several hundred head of cattle and they would pasture east of Roy.

"In those days I saw many cows mutilated near water lakes. The reason was that in those lakes there was plenty of vegetation inside the water which would bring all kinds of bugs and water spiders; cows have the habit of getting in the lake to drink water and would swallow these spiders, so they would swell up and if there was no one around to help them, they would die. First the vultures would pick out their eyes and tongue, then coyotes and other animals would get their genitals and rectum, where the hide is soft and thin. When biting off the flesh they use their molars, making a clean cut, and since the cow is already dead, there is no blood pressure. I also know this cow mutilation happens only at certain times in the summer . . ."

***

I was buried in clippings when Marsha came up behind me and said, "Boo!" causing me to jump.

"Sorry, Honey," she said in her husky Oklahoma accent. "You have to deal with that person in the lobby."

"What person?"

"You know. That guy who's always trying to sell you the story of Jesus on Horseback—he's back again, and he smells dreadful."

"Show him in." Marsha's eyes were round dark surprises telling me what I should have recalled: that the old Bataan March veteran in the lobby, who seemed to make a living by haunting newspaper offices with his dusty tales, actually smelled worse than his stories.

"Darling, let me dump him out the door and you can see him later," she said.

"No, show him in. For once I can use him."

Marsha left the room in a rush of loose skirts. "He's back there," I heard her say down the hallway and in another moment, the *viejo* came into my office, dragging one foot, apologizing for the intrusion, crushing a sweat-begrimed Stetson in one hand, while holding a gnarled, hand-carved cane in the other. His dark oval face was ravaged from years in wind and sun. His voice wheezed as he fought for air.

His eyes were going in different directions. He looked at you as if you were in two places.

"There's something you can do for me," I told him, "and I will pay you for it. The story about Jesus on Horseback, I want to hear all of it."

"On my grandmother's soul, that story's true," he said, his eyes roving.

"Can you describe the man for me, the one in white?"

"Oh, no. I did not see him. My grandmother, saw him when he rode into Santa Fe on his white horse, a big white horse—like this—he measured nineteen hands high."

"And how large was the man?"

"Big. Like the horse. Very large. My grandmother told me that all around this man was a ring of light, such as you see in Santa Fe after a big rain and the sun comes from behind the clouds."

"What did the man do when he came to town?"

"He cared for people. He was a *curandero*, a healer. This man was no ordinary human being."

"Do you believe he was Jesus Christ?"

"I could not say that for sure."

"Well, then, what did your grandmother say about him? Did she say he was Jesus Christ?"

"She did say that. He coughed into a closed fist, and continued to rove the room with his eyes. "My grandmother, she told me when I was very sick one time that he would come and cure me. And she said he would only come to our house if I prayed to Jesus. So I always think to myself that this man was Jesus, only I think he did not have the same face that Our Lord had when he walked on earth. My grandmother said this man was very tall and he had white hair and a yellow beard."

"Did he appear when you prayed for him to come?"

"No, but I had a dream about him. He rode down out of the sky on a flaming star, and he blessed all the earth and all earthly creatures and he said that he lived up in the Heaven and could not come back to us anymore. Then I woke up and my fever was broken."

"Was that the only time you dreamed about him?"

"No, there was one other time when I was older. It was when I had been touched by the Devil by witchery. I dreamed the man on horseback came and blessed me and I was alright again. But before that, I used to ride up into the mountains to check my grandfather's cattle. I would pass a big old house inhabited by three women who were witches.

"When I rode by, one of these women would always come out and ask me to come inside for coffee. Being a little scared, I ignored her and kept on riding. One day when I passed that house, that woman came out and beckoned and, as usual, I passed on by her, but when I was out of sight, I heard her calling my name. I turned to look behind me and I saw a coyote following me. Now there was no one in sight but the coyote, so I just kept on riding, and the sound of that woman calling stayed in my mind. Again I turned and saw that it was the coyote, so I took my gun out and I shot the coyote, wounded it, and left it there dying. The following day I was doing some errands in town, and I heard that one of the witches had been shot and wounded the day before. When I told my grandmother this story, she gave me a little brown bag with a root inside it. This root had lots of threads coming off of it, and these were roots, too. She told me to carry this *cachana* root to ward off *brujos* and *brujas*. She also gave me an *osha* root to put into my boot whenever I was clearing brush."

"What was that for?"

"Osha keeps away rattlesnakes. And it is good against witches."

"Is there another name for the *cachana* root?" I asked.

The old man smiled crookedly. "They call it Flaming Star."

Chapter Fourteen

For lunch that day I had chile rellenos at The Little Chief Café. The sopaipillas, dolloped with honey, hot black coffee. I felt pretty good, Durwood liked my Harjac story. Gomez had phoned me some extra insight. I layered it carefully into what I had already written.

After lunch I walked around the Plaza, gazed at the pigeons as they fluttered park to bench, eave to eave, corbel to corbel. I breathed the new-minted autumn air, catching that first cold-leaved hint of coming winter Soon snow would come into the Tesuque valley. It had already put a white saddle blanket on the Sangres.

Okay, but, for now, the autumn sun warmed the soul as well as the sky and I felt some release from the mute madness that had seeped into me and didn't seem to want to go away.

After the cleansing walk I hung around the office for the rest of the day not doing much of anything except keeping out of Durwood's sight as he did his bookkeeping in those tall blue ledgers with the nubby covers that he carefully maintained like some old Bartleby-bent scribe. Best to leave him alone when he was doing "end of month."

From time to time I thought about the old storyteller man and what he'd said to me, and how his words tied in with some of the things that Harjac and Etienne had said. It didn't make a lot of sense, but I had a glimmer of an idea. A connection between the sacred and the profane. I was toying with the notion that the mutilations might be an intermarriage, a blood-wedding of good and evil.

I decided to stay with the extraterrestrial theory. Perhaps another visit to the State Library, the labyrinth of Southwest archives. I headed over there, across town, met the gnome of a librarian who disappeared into the dusty stacks to emerge with the tome of my choice: the Bureau of Ethnology Report for the year 1933. Without looking too deeply I came upon the Cherokee legend of the star people.

The hunters were camping in the mountains one night when they saw two lights moving along a distant ridge. They watched and wondered. They saw them the next night and the next. On the third morning they crossed to the ridge and found two creatures round and large with fine gray fur and little heads like those of terrapins. When the breeze played upon the fur, showers of sparks flew out.

The hunters kept them several days. At night they would grow bright and shine; by day they were balls of gray fur, except when the wind stirred and the sparks flew out. They were quiet and no one thought of their trying to escape, but on the seventh night they rose from the ground like balls of fire above the tree tops climbing higher and higher until they were only bright points. The hunters then knew they were stars . . .

My mind returned to Etienne's remark about the Hopi Prophecy. I thought about the Navajo emergence myth as well.

What are myths but the deep dreams of the ancients?

No doubt, we modern folks have our myths too. Superman, Frankenstein, Count Dracula, and that got me thinking once again about mutilations and how blood, as symbol, could be good or evil.

There was a native saint who appeared in a stream of starlight. He seized whomever he chose and cut them with a sharp flint. He then drew out the person's entrails, performed some of kind of psychic surgery on them, and restored them from whence they came. He left no mark on the person's body. This saint could break and set limbs in seconds. The moment he placed his hand on a wound it was blessed and healed.

The saint appeared often as a man but also as a woman. He was known to enter an adobe house and make it soar up into the sky where it appeared to be a streaming star in the heavens.

Bluejay once described a star car that came out of night sky. His father, a medicine man, rode in the car.

Within was a driver who had the face of an innocent child. The driver laughed a lot. Bluejay's father laughed too. The story played in my mind like a cartoon.

The myth of Cabeza de Vaca, the Spanish conquistador and healer, also seemed to fit into this context. Naked and barefoot, Cabeza de Vaca healed thousands of Indians with the touch of his hand. He came not with the intent of stealing precious metal from the Indians but to rid them of disease. "The wound I make," he said, "appears like a seam in the palm of the hand."

Yet moments before it was a gash in the chest of a dying Indian. According to the old texts Cabeza de Vaca recognized that the power within him came directly from God. And while other conquistadores cut off the hands of miscreants, he returned the sick to a state of well-being.

I had a feeling I was in an area that would yield more good things. Another article was coming, I could feel it.

That evening after leaving the library I phoned Etienne and arranged to visit him at his Center for Psychic Research. It was a little ways off Cerrillos in a small strip mall. I drove there, parked and knocked on number 110, the door of the suite on his business card.

Etienne answered the door. As he stood under the street light looking at me, and I at him, I saw how pale his skin was and how elfin he appeared, almost otherworldly. "Come in," he said casually, "I have been expecting you."

The room was furnished with an oriental carpet, a small devotional stand with a candle and incense holder, and a number of plump pillows for seating. "Please remove your shoes," he said, which I did, and then we sat facing each other on separate pillows.

I asked Etienne if he had ever witnessed a faith-healing or perhaps a psychic healing.

"Yes, but I do not know much more than this. Recently my tonsils were so enflamed that I could not eat or sleep or speak because of the pain. First I tried acupuncture but that did not work. The pain got worse. Soon I had no strength at all. Then I heard of a Filipino healer, a man who has brought about many cures all over the globe. I called him and he said, 'Come right away.'

"My wife, Mina, drove me to Albuquerque. I was to be treated at someone's home because the AMA wouldn't allow this man to do his work openly. When I first saw him in that very moment I knew he had powers. He seemed to be in a light trance. 'I don't guarantee anything,' he said. 'I am nothing by myself. I am not the healer. I carry the light of Christ and His Father. Now, tell me, Mr. Saronier, what is your trouble.'

"I pointed to my throat and he came very near and asked me to open my mouth. I did so and he studied my throat. Then, as a joke, he said, perhaps to take my mind off my suffering: 'I know what color underwear you are wearing.'

"He then told me that the color of my undershorts was blue. I laughed at this even though it hurt. He had intuited correctly. He next told me to lie on a table he had prepared and pray to God. I did this thing. Then, with no other preparation, he cut open my throat with his thumb. I felt warm blood on my neck. And I saw some on his hands as well. Then he placed one hand on my forehead and the other hand on the center of my chest. This, he explained, was to make the energy flow between my forehead and abdomen. I felt a natural current moving between and he then told me, 'The rest is up to you.'

"The whole operation lasted two and a half minutes. A day later I was completely healed. There was almost no scar tissue. Look for yourself. Do you see anything there?"

I looked closely at Etienne's neck. I saw a faint pinkish line.

I asked, "Did you see him again?"

"Yes. When I visited him again, he looked at my throat as you just did, and said it was good. What else was bothering me. I told him that my stomach was troubling me. He did another operation quite like the one before but when he finished he blew gently all over my body. When he did this I suddenly felt renewed, full of strong positive energy. My stomach stopped hurting. After that visit, by the way, I quit smoking and drinking. I couldn't touch either one of those ever again."

Etienne fell silent, remembering.

I asked, "Was that everything? I mean all that happened to you?"

Etienne thought for a moment. "Let me see . . . oh, yes. After the stomach operation I remember feeling so good that I began to cry. I burst into tears and they poured out of me like rain. I felt completely cleansed."

Once again, Etienne lapsed into silence, so I asked him, "Was that everything?"

"There is a little more," he said. "The healer told me that he had just returned from Atlantis."

"Atlantis?"

"Yes. He explained to me that Atlantis was where he had learned to heal people with his hands . . . ."

Chapter Fifteen

My next article, *Mystery Healing: Holy or Unholy?* drew forth a raft of readers who were eager for more information on the mutilations.

Durwood was enjoying the notoriety. "You got something going here, pal, keep up the good work."

I waited. Usually, with Durwood, something else was coming at you after he complimented you.

"So you like the tact I'm taking?"

"Except for one thing," he said.

I waited.

"You've missed the point a little bit."

"Which point?"

"The one about all of us being mutilators."

I chuckled. "What have you mutilated lately?"

Durwood smiled. His perfect white teeth, a little larger than life, glistened. He caressed the knot of his dark red tie to make sure it corresponded with his collar: yes, dead center. Still, he fingered it to make sure. Or maybe he just liked the bulge of a tight Windsor knot. He was one fastidious dude.

"I can think of several mutilations I've done in the past twenty-four hours. This morning I mutilated a pig, last night a lamb. There's nothing mystic about meat eating."

"No?"

"No."

"Durwood, do me a favor. Don't wreck my morning with this, OK?"

He bristled. "I have news for you. You've gained an audience with this who-done-it stuff. It's good. I just want you to follow through on the human angle. In other words, try to stay in both worlds, the real and the unreal. Otherwise we're just teasing the public."

"My tease seems to be working."

"What I'm pressing you for is a human interest story about the nature of meat. What are cows anyway? They're to be eaten. Right?"

"Vegetarians don't see it that way."

"Yes, I know. Vegetables don't scream when you drop them into boiling water."

"Neither do hamburgers."

This sort of foolish fencing could go on for hours, Durwood actually enjoyed it, and it gave him something to do beyond his bookkeeping. His Bartleby ledgers, I called them. However, usually at this point he'd give up, walk away, having annoyed me just enough to suit himself. But this day, he dug deeper.

"Make it real," he said. Then, under his breath: "Atlantis, my Mississippi ass!"

Durwood was a wunderkind boss. A boss of bosses. He feinted and tucked and played with all of us who worked there, all in the name of numbers. When the numbers were high he gave us grief anyway. You never knew where he was coming from. Sometimes it was tough being in the same room with him and his Binaca breath spray with which he punctuated his sentences. Then, again, he might just touch you gently and the feel of that touch was like Cabeza de Vaca—it was truly the most delicate and compassionate of human energies. It elicited complete calm and compliance.

Frankly though, I liked the Atlantis angle and I was proud of the way I covered Etienne and his Filipino healer. But I also knew that Durwood was heavy into Christian Science. Psychic healing was part of the Mary Baker Eddy program but not so loosely defined, in other words not as out there as Etienne's healing ceremony. The Christian Scientists might've called Etienne's psychic healing *animal magnetism*. Animal magnetism was bad; prayer was good. Any time you became fixated on something other than the Christian Science view of healing, you were into animal magnetism.

Therefore all American Indian rites were primitive and opposed to Christian Science prayer. What intrigued me and what I wanted to write about next was more healing rites. For instance, the Penitentes. The Spanish sect that practiced crucifixion. On my first date with Laura back in 1966 we had gone into the Gallinas Canyon, the same place where I would be run over two years later, and listened to the Penitentes singing Moorish-sounding chants that echoed off the canyon walls. There were times when I wondered if our being in a place where few white people and even Hispanics feared to tread, a place where men were if not nailed to a cross were tied so tightly to one that injury and occasionally death occurred. Plus the practitioners were men of such manic and crazed belief that they beat themselves with cactus whips.

I wondered now, sitting in my cozy office at *The Review* if I might've triggered a death wish up there in the canyon, sitting on a flume sixty feet above the canyon. The flume was a four-foot wide water chute that once brought water down into the village of Montezuma. Was it a death wish I had? Or was that the wish of someone who knew we were there and wanted to get rid of us? I had a friend at that time, a photographer, who tried to get closer to the *morada*, the adobe Penitente church in the pines. He was fired at and the bullet passed harmlessly through his shirt and struck his camera bag.

Holy Thursday. The night of nights. I often thought: hole-y Thursday. The brothers of light, they were called. These men with not less but more faith than their predecessors in Spain; men wedded to their beliefs in the crucifixion of Christ. In the canyon, I imagined that phantoms watched them. We'd seen the claw-marks of wolves and big cats on the wine-colored bark of the juniper trees.

I remembered the *cholla* house of thorns and how it tempted the flesh of the penitent who was one with Christ when he used the whips. The wail of the wind, the drum of the Pueblo. The Indians of ancient days mixed some of their own self-sacrifice into the Penitente rituals. Spanish and Indian faith seemed to have melded like blood in the river of sand.

The night we heard the Penitentes sing, I thought the wind-borne voices were not human. I thought it was spirits carried on the wind, which of course it was. But, to me, it seemed to be the spirits of the lost, other sacrifices from time immemorial. The ritual spoke to me in a profound way. This was the way it was in the beginning. The wind carried the souls of the dead, and in so doing, these souls were resurrected.

Historically, in the early part of the 1500s, the crucifixion re-enactment was completed with the penitent's death. In the minds of the old believers from Spain, transplanted to New Mexican soil, a righteous transfiguration took place on Holy Thursday.

The landscape warranted such devotion, they believed. The old religion, as practiced in Spain, wore away in the wind. The Penitentes were brothers of suffering and they asked no praise or reward for their love of God and for their triumph over the body. Their reward for religious ecstasy was excommunication from the Catholic Church. Thus the Penitentes were outlawed right at the start.

However, they didn't care. They were already cut off from Catholic approval when they entered the world of the mystic. They were in their own world now, one of their own making.

***

The following day I went to the State Library and dug into some books that dealt with witches and werewolves, Penitentes and other prisoners of the flesh that offered a glimpse into the world of half-light where madness verged on revelation. Again and again, I found that cause and cure, reason and unreason, were two sides of the same ancient coin.

Reading about witches, I learned that sometimes they appeared as fireballs. Neither meteor nor comet, these bright orange discs often appeared grey, blue, yellow or pale white. They passed silently through the sky. Sometimes they came with thunder and took giant strides upon the earth. Other times they clustered like small birds in a winter-branched cottonwood, so said Joseph Baca, a contemporary witness in Las Vegas, New Mexico:

"Looking ahead I could see nothing but darkness down this narrow alley in my home town. But then quite suddenly three big round fireballs, the size of medicine balls, appeared to my left. There they sat in a straight line hovering about an inch off the ground amidst the tumbleweeds that did not catch fire. There was bright pulsating light coming off the fireballs in front of me. The following day I told my mother what I had seen and she in turn told my father. He said, 'It was the Devil after you because you haven't been going to church.' But I thought: Neither had my father. So how come the Devil in the form of fireballs hadn't appeared to him?"

An older version of the fireballs story was printed in the *Taos News*:

"A family was bombarded by fireballs in full view of the neighbors and police. Stones accompanied the lights and came out of the night sky and hailed down upon the roof of a house. In keeping with the traditional belief in sorcery, the neighbors of the family in the house, formed a circle around it. Holding up lanterns and torches they waited to see the witch who had cast this spell. Their intent was to capture and confine her in a closed circle where, by calling her out, she would be made human again. Throughout the night the fireballs and stones rained down. Only at first light did the stones stop pelting as the fireballs faded. Only in the light of day did the witch appear, and only then was she identified and turned back into her former self."

Another account that I found in a privately printed book at the College of Santa Fe went like this . . .

Once two girls spent the night with an old woman who lived in their village. Late at night they heard a peculiar noise and got up to investigate. The old woman had left her bed and was seen applying a strange ointment to her naked chest, face and arms. Muttering some incantation, the old woman exploded into a fireball that went up the chimney.

Reading on, I learned that when witches danced the circle dance they became fireballs. To trap them, villagers used the traditional circle of flame. It was a kind of science. I learned that the Devil appeared at the juncture where four roads met. But unlike the witches he was not vulnerable in the same way. To trap an evil spirit, a witch, you had to have a holy circle or hoop, as the Indians called it. When the circle closed it was possible to disembowel the witch or possibly transform her. A circular body of water, a spring or lake known for its purity, was the right place to reveal the identity of a sorcerer, as in this account:

In the center there was a limpid pool. Juan bade the be-witched girl to look into the pool. Soon a face appeared in the water. The mad girl recognized the face and at that instant her mind was restored. Then Juan dropped his knife into the pool. The water bubbled and then grew calm. Down in the clear depths he could see the face of the one who had bewitched her.

So I learned that there were many kinds of witches. They could be harmonic, like curanderas or healers. In the case of the Pascagoula Indians who were aided by a deity who was a mermaid, they protected her and she protected them. That is until a Catholic priest decided the mermaid was evil. He sought to kill her but the entire tribe sacrificed themselves by drowning. People in Biloxi, Mississippi still say that the mermaid returns on Christmas Eve, but only when you drop a silver crucifix into the center of Biloxi Bay at exactly midnight.

In 1896 there was an epidemic that ravaged the pueblos of the Rio Grande. At Cochiti the sickness was attributed to witchcraft, according to the Catholic priests. They noticed two dogs, one white, one black, that walked around the outskirts of the Pueblo. Then one night a man appeared and his body was painted white. He had black hands and black rags tied around his shoulders. The priests sought to catch him and when they finally pinned him to the ground he exploded into a fountain of blood. The epidemic ended after his death.

I was learning that good wasn't good and bad wasn't bad. In many of these Spanish and Indian legends the two shared a complex dual identity. Coyote, the cosmic bungler, was both transformer and trickster. A clue to the cattle with missing parts—Coyote lost his eyes only to regain them. In one account from a medicine man Coyote proved that things that come from the stars are earthly in origin.

Was it possible, I wondered, that Navajo skinwalkers also had a good as well as a bad side?

Were they, too, a trick of fur in a trick of skin?

***

Ray Brown was an old believer, a Navajo stuck in the old ways. We knew each other for more than twenty years. The first time he came to our house in Tesuque, he walked in with his wife, Ethel and his son Gerard. Ethel wasted no time. She got busy in the kitchen making fry bread. Now . . . there is fry bread. And then there is Ethel's fry bread. When I first tasted Ethel's fry bread, I said, "Navajo heaven."

"There's such a thing, you know," Gerard said.

Brown snorted. "No, there ain't."

Gerard said, "Yes, there is, Dad. When Grandpa died that time he said his spirit went up into a cloud. His body was dead in the desert sand, but he was up inside that cloud. He told me."

"Grandpa didn't die?" I asked.

"Not that time," Ethel said, patting fry bread dough.

"But another time?" I asked, sipping coffee.

"Not this time, but some time," Ethel said.

"Hey, Ethel," Brown said, "our damn kid knows more about Grandpa than we do."

"He ought to, he's with him all the time," Ethel said.

"What happened to Grandpa up in that cloud?" I asked Gerard.

Gerard said, "Well, he stayed up in that cloud four days. He told me it was lucky a witch didn't pull him down while he was up there because they do that, you know."

I poured myself a cup of black coffee, and offered one to Brown. He pushed back his heavy forelock and took a sip.

"What would the witch have done with Grandpa's spirit?" I asked.

"Put it in a coyote," Gerard said.

Brown snorted, laughed. "Always a coyote," he said with a chuckle. "What a cliche."

"No, Dad, not always. Witch could put it in a owl too. But a coyote's better."

"Who says?"

"Grandpa."

"See, Ethel? Kid's a know-it-all."

"Just on certain Navajo matters," Gerard answered sensibly.

"Listen to him," Brown said, laughing. "The old professor."

"It's true what I say," Gerard said.

Ethel came over to the table with some golden fry bread. "I should know Grandpa's teachings pretty well myself," she said, sitting down with a cup of coffee. "After all, he's my father."

Everyone at the table nodded.

"I think there's more to that story, Gerard," Ethel added.

Gerard didn't say anything for a while, but then: "Could be the witch would put Grandpa's soul in another animal. Could be a wolf, too, you know. But first that witch'd have to make a pact with the devil and the deal would be maybe fifty years of power, and then the devil'd have him for keeps. That's the way Grandpa said it."

Brown snorted. "Could be *who knows*." He looked critically at his son and laughed.

Everybody had some more coffee. The fry bread was gone.

"One time," Brown said, "I was hiking in the San Francisco Peaks. There was me and Ethel and another guy we knew who was a skinwalker."

Ethel nodded. "It's true," she said.

Brown went on. "So we were going up this steep trail. Ethel was in the lead. The Navajo wolf was second and I was third. Ethel was bending real low to get around this ledge and her pants ripped in back. Ripped wide open, too. He looked around the table, his eyes glittering with ribald humor.

We all smiled. Ethel too though she looked in another direction.

"Anyways," Brown continued. "That guy busted a gut laughing. He wasn't supposed to do that either."

"Why not?" I asked.

Gerard said, "They have this code . . ."

Ethel said, "Those guys aren't supposed to reveal themselves to us. The wolf part of them is secret. They break the code, the Devil breaks his pact."

Brown gulped some coffee, swished it around in his mouth, swallowed. "Once the Devil's pact is broke, the wolfman's finished. I knew that and I went up to him when we made camp that night and I said, "Look, man, me and Ethel both know what you are, and now you got just four days left.""

"That scared the shit out of him," Gerard said. "Didn't it, Mom."

"That was his death warrant," Ethel said, calm and sure.

"Yeah," Brown went on, tossing his head.

"Four days later that wolf was shriveled up dead," Gerard whispered to me.

"But there's more," Brown said. He peered out the kitchen window to see if someone were coming. But it was the wind brushing a cedar branch against the adobe wall.

"That guy begged for his life," Ethel said. "He offered me his truck."

"He offered me his girlfriend," Brown said.

Ethel scowled. "You wouldn't have!"

"Might've . . . you hadn't been there," Brown said.

"Well, we wouldn't touch any of it," Ethel said.

"So where's that guy now?" I asked.

"Werewolves don't get to go to heaven and they don't get to eat Ethel's fry bread," Brown said, "and that settles it."

Chapter Sixteen

Brown and family departed the following day. I had gotten used to Ray sitting in one of our kitchen chairs watching his tiny TV. He and our parrot George had a funny relationship. George yelled at Brown. Brown yelled back at George. It all started a few years earlier when Brown showed up at our Tesuque house and our family was away. He often visited at night when we were asleep and I'd find him sitting in the kitchen. Alone.

He came for a night visit that time and just walked upstairs. Usually when he did that, he'd talk to me while I lay asleep in my bed. I'd hear him in my dreams and work him into a story I was writing. But this time, as I say, he was alone and I wasn't there. George was.

George knew Brown's voice. He neither liked nor disliked him. They had a mildly adversarial relationship. They cursed softly at each other.

Brown told me that he'd come up the stairs and stood in the doorway under the clear-story window on the roof. Normally there would've been moonlight or starlight, but this New Mexico night was moonless and starless. Brown let his eyes to adjust to the dark bedroom. Then he heard a voice.

"Get out and go home," the voice said.

Brown got a little chill. "Granny, that you?" (He told me later he thought it was my mother.)

The voice said, "Hi'ya Woo."

"Sarah, is that you?" Brown said.

Silence of the dead.

Brown got a second chill. Maybe it's a skinwalker, he thought.

"Mara, is that you?" he said to the dark.

The voice said, "Get lost."

"How come?"

"Get out."

"Who do you think you are?" Brown said.

The silence of the dead, darkness, and evil.

Brown stood his ground. But he thought better of it. He did as he was told. He drove all the way back to Window Rock in his truck. A few hundred miles or more. The next time Brown visited he asked me how Granny was.

"She's in a nursing home in Las Vegas."

"Does she still stay upstairs sometimes?"

"Not anymore."

"Was she upstairs a few weeks ago?"

I shook my head. "Been in Vegas Grandes Nursing Facility for a year now."

So Brown told me what happened and I told him that he had heard George talking. George doesn't like night visitors. And as I said he doesn't much like Brown either.

But I was thinking about the time Brown visited and then left abruptly. Laura and I went to bed that night, and for some reason I awoke in the early hours of the morning. Brown's visits were always mysterious. You didn't know when he was going to show up or take off. You always knew what was on his mind though.

Anyway I was awake and it was around 3 AM and Laura was asleep and the kids were as well and the house was silent, and dark. A little wind crept around the buried back of the adobe house and the junipers rustled.

I heard the front door open. It creaked. The heavy, hand-carved door had a steel latch rather than a door knob. I heard the latch clink once as someone— Brown, I thought—entered the living room, downstairs. Whomever it was stood there. Brown was a shadowman. He usually made himself known, then unknown. Then known again. As if he could erase himself if he wanted to depending on where he was and who he was with.

Strange feet shuffled across the black brick floor. One foot dragged. I knew then it couldn't be Brown. Brown was large and soundless except for that characteristic snort.

Whoever it was didn't come upstairs. He routed around downstairs. I heard a filing cabinet open and close. A tearing sound.

George was in Mara's downstairs bedroom. No noise came from there. More file drawers opening and closing.

I got out of bed and I was about to turn on the light when I heard the soft foot and the heavy foot start up the stairs. No hurry about it. The steps were slow. On the stairs the dragfoot made a sort of clicking sound.

What was this animal? We had bears. And sometimes they sometimes got drunk on fermented apples from the farm at the end of the road.

Now a drunk bear will do most anything. Sleep in your parlor. Shit on your rug. Eat your Snicker's bars right out of the fridge. But this bear, as I believed it to be, was now in the upstairs in the bathroom taking a shit. I could hear it. The sound of poop plopping noisily into the toilet.

Drunk bears don't poop in toilets. Or do they?

The bathroom window was open.

I heard a fat bag of fur moving thickly through the window casement.

Then I heard squishing sounds. It was slogging through the mud that had welled up by the back window.

This whole time I was standing there in my underwear in the bedroom. Listening. The intrusion was over. The wind rose. Made a whistling in the chimney and a rattling in the open window.

I didn't want to wake up the house. But by then I was shivering.

I went into the bathroom. I was afraid to turn on a light. I looked in the toilet. The lid was down. I lifted it and in the half-light I saw the bowl was full, and empty.

I walked downstairs, barefoot. The filing cabinet was jerked open. The drawer where we kept turquoise jewelry was open. All the children's silver bracelets and rings were gone. The black velvet bag where we kept them hidden in a file folder was on the floor lying among a pile of torn paper. Even in the semi-darkness I could see that the papers were the scattered parts of a novel I had written but not finished. The working title was *He Who Walks In Skins*.

The moon had broken free of clouds.

A pale blue blade of light lay upon the first page of the novel:

Out of the brittle shell by starlight, wolf fur on human skin.
The scents come back so that soft hands leave hard paw

treads. He knew they would come after him for what he had done, the sheep he had killed, maybe a hundred of them. The herder he had torn to shreds. He needed to stuff his skin in a hollow tree. He knew that he was known as He Who Walks In Skins, but aside from the killings, the blood, the beauty of it, the running beauty because no one could catch him, he was only dimly aware of who he really was in human form. He would wake up naked. He knew that. There would be four-legged and two-legged blood on his flesh. He would wake cold and uncertain. And they would be hunting him.

I smelled the sheet of paper. It smelled rancid. I cleared the crush of paper and shoved it into the open drawer of the filing cabinet. Then I sat in the chair that Ray liked with my Smith and Wesson chrome-plated 38, and waited. I knew it wouldn't do me any good. To sit there. But my heart was still pounding. The only thing that would do any good was the light of day.

***

"Tell me again what happened," Laura said as she made breakfast. We were all together, it was Saturday, and we couldn't seem to draw any conclusions about what had happened last night.

I told Laura what had happened again.

She said, "We need help with this. We just lost all the old turquoise given to me by my grandmother in Farmington. It can never be replaced. But maybe it might be recovered. I think we should go to all the pawn shops."

I shook my head. "This guy doesn't want to sell that stuff. He wants to hurt us in some way. He already has. Besides, what if he isn't . . . well, human." She shook her head. "Call Bluejay. He'll know what to do."

She was right, as always. Bluejay would do a corn pollen blessing, or maybe his father could come to do The Evil-chasing Way. That is a long saga of Navajo songs that worked power over the treachery of witchcraft. Jay's father was a very well-respected stargazer, a medicine man who sees things far beyond the eye into unknown spheres of the human psyche. In my belief, the man could do anything. I called Jay.

"I'll come," he said, "soon."

Well, that could mean a day, a week, a year. Or even a number of years. Once I had waited for him for ten years and then one day he showed up with a juniper root that looked like a heron. He said, "This is the heron that saved the Navajos once. I give it to you now as a protection against evil."

I kept him on the phone this time a little longer than usual and told him about how I found the Changing Woman sculpture. "I found it in a wood rat's nest out in the arroyo," I said. "The Spanish people here call it a black madonna."

Jay said, "You know about Woodrat, don't you? One of our deities from long ago. One of the Holy People. It's a good sign that Woodrat gave it to you. A good sign." Then I told him, in detail, how our house was violated.

Jay explained that he needed to ask his father about the Antway, the coming-up ritual, the moving from darkness to light part of the Navajo emergence. The ants, he told me, might protect the house if a certain gift were given to them.

I said I would do that thing.

After breakfast, Laura and I went up in back of the house. Sarah and Mara played Little Animals, a game they'd devised wherein a whole tribe of plastic creatures that lived in a cardboard house did stuff together. It was like a soap opera the way they played it. They could play, totally absorbed, for hours. Days sometimes. It was a kind of magical oral novel played as a series of adventures one after another.

On the hilltop in back of the house in that place where there was always mud from run-off from the shed roof, we found two suspicious tracks.

One was the left foot. A slightly worn leather shoe.

The second track was the same kind of shoe, badly worn down.

This number two track was unusual. The man's foot had come through the leather toe part, and the toes had imprinted the mud. The toes had extended nails like claws.

Chapter Seventeen

I know why we felt so close to the Navajos. We weren't far from them geographically but that isn't the reason you bond with people. For me it went back to the hit-and-run night. I'd come so close to dying on that canyon road. No one but Laura, my brother and his girl Alice knew that I was scraped off the dirt road and was now flying-low, sequestered in an air-splint in an ambulance. On my way through the high desert night to St Vincent's Hospital in Santa Fe.

The operation to put my right leg back together with metal and pins took hours. There were fourteen breaks below the knee, all of them had come through the skin. I was a mess. They might have cut my leg off. They didn't. I woke up in the early hours of the morning and out of the haze of Demerol and anesthesia saw four Navajos sitting in four gray hospital chairs. Bluejay DeGroat, Ray Tsosie, Ron Brown (no relation to Ray) and Jimmie BlueEyes. I slipped back into a dream of canyons, roaring water, chrome and neon motorcycles and broken lines of poetry tinctured with gob spots of blood. My blood.

When I awoke again, Jay was there, by himself.

In my mind, heavily drugged, I saw a Tibetan priest whose nut brown face was neither smiling nor frowning. But his lips were curved a little bit like a cat's. And his haunted, slightly slanted, epicanthic eyes told me that I was, if nothing else, being prayed over, not preyed upon. I felt safe in Jay's watch.

When I woke again it was night and my nightwatch person was a nun on soft squooshy shoes. She brandished a silvery needle.

"Do you have pain?" she whispered.

I nodded and she gave me an injection of Demerol.

I closed my eyes, and dreamed.

I dreamed of the Blessing Way. The *hozhonii* way of harmony. All things woven together in beauty. Like the great blanket of life that depicts the rising out of darkness into the light of a harmonic sun.

I woke, it was morning again. Jay was there. Then he was not there. He came and went like night and day, sun and moon.

Once he spoke to me and said, "I saw the wolf, the skinwalker, who follows you. When I went after him, his face was different. It changed from wolf to owl. The owl lifted out of the wolf, claws spread. When it lighted, landing on the earth, it changed again, and it was the wolfman. Both, as you know, are clawed. Sometimes though he was an old man with a bad cough. His mouth open and he breathes with a foul breath. He speaks with the voice of a wind, a dark, bad, foul-smelling wind."

"Can he be killed?"

"If we don't believe in him. That will take a ceremony."

"Could you sing me one of the old songs of harmony?"

He shook his head, "Not here."

Then he smiled, said, "Sometimes I see the old ones coming out of dark earth up into the sun. They are singing. I hear the earth singing with them. The corn is singing. The old ones singing. The earth singing as they rise, as the old ones rise out of the earth, into the light."

This was the song I repeated in that hospital bed of mine. That white sheet bed that held my body in a blurry transcendence of consciousness that came and went, came and went like Jay.

***

All of this that I tell about now happened twenty years before. That was then, this is now. I still walk with a limp. I jog with that disability—one leg shorter than the other. Jay is still my mentor, my friend, my diviner. We have never lost touch. The day after Brown left, Jay drove up in his pick-up truck. He and I drank herbal tea and talked of old times. Jay in his unruffled, easy going way seeing things that cannot be seen. He is like his father in that way.

"I wasn't expecting you so soon," I said, standing in the sun and staring at the Navajo logo on the door of his car. The four sacred mountains. The corn plants. The circle of rope-encircled arrowheads.

"It seems like," he said, easing himself out of the truck, "that we Navajos can't be without a logo." He laughed at this. I noticed he had gained some weight since I had last seen him.

We stood in the golden afternoon. Together again. Already I felt stronger.

"I have something to show you," he said. "Can you take a little ride with me?"

"Let me tell Laura we're leaving."

***

The ride wound away to Rio Puerco, the place where the river ran with high levels of radiation, contaminating everything around it.

"This is a bad place," Jay said. He stopped the truck.

"So, why are we here?"

"You are always asking me about animals. And people who are animals, so I thought you'd like to see it with your own eyes. I have those mute articles."

Jay rubbed his chin.

Then he drove a little ways to the south and parked under the flat roof of a rundown, deserted gas station. It smelled of tar, spilled oil, and if there is such a smell, danger. I asked if this was near the same place where they had dumped the uranium deposits.

Jay nodded.

"Do you see that old man sitting there by that empty oil drum?"

"I see him."

The old man was small and almost a part of the landscape. He wore a beat-up, winter coat and a pair of bald-kneed corduroys.

"What about that old guy?" I asked.

"He lives here. Like the sand he sits on."

I did not see the point, but that was no matter.

"We'll wait until it gets dark. Another hour or so. You'll see why I brought you here."

We were on the other side of Albuquerque by a flea bait, broken down, service station and it was several hours until sundown and I was tired and bored. But nonetheless I sat patiently and, as we didn't talk, I dozed for a while in the warm sun of the pickup.

"Keep your eye on that old man," Jay said, stirring me with his hand.

I blinked and gazed and grew sleepy again as Jay tipped his black cowboy hat over his eyes and dozed off himself.

I had nothing else to do so I studied the old man whose back was up against the oil drum. He was asleep too, I imagined. Or maybe dead. He had not moved. There wasn't anything to see really and the day wore on, and I stared at the old man until my eyeballs burned. Then I fell asleep.

When I woke Jay was getting out of the truck.

"We're going to follow him," he said.

"Where?" I wasn't fully awake yet.

Jay moved off, walking slowly, almost absently, toward the oil drum.

The old man wasn't there but his tracks were in the yellow sand.

We followed them over a small ridge, tussocked with spare dead grass. The wind howled. The old man's faint tracks started to seem familiar to me. One foot made a rounded, worn-soled footprint. The right one came down harder, dragged a little, and left what appeared to be claw marks . . . or toenail marks.

A long time passed while we walked silent as shadows that were eaten up by the loss of light.

The sky lowered down dark with cloud.

Night was coming the way it does sometimes on early winter days in New Mexico. Slow at first, then, by degrees, faster. Soon, trudging on, the darkness swallowed us and we seemed to swim through it.

"Get ready," Jay whispered.

The tracks disappeared into the blue-black mystery of nightfall.

They disappeared, as we had vanished ourselves—devoured by the lack of sun, the hunger of sand, the emptiness of wind.

I was shivering. Then Jay got down on one knee, and sang the song of protection:

White man's ghost that threatens my clouds
White man's ghost which knows no resting place

White man's ghost which comes on skittery feet
pawing at my body, my junipers, my clouds

I wear now dark flints that protect
I dance as they rattle on my skin

The dark bear I borrow the flints of his dark hands
The flying eagle I borrow the flints of her feathered hands

Now I wash my body in the pollen that rests on blue ponds
A fine yellow pollen, water-pollen makes my skin shine

My heart is great so the white man's ghost can no longer
threaten my body, my junipers, my clouds

So it is done in harmony for protection
In harmony it is finished

When Jay finished the song, which he had sung in Navajo, a thin leprous wind rattled in the junipers and I saw the owl coming with open claws.

It was larger than any owl I'd ever seen in this life, not as large as a man but maybe big as a boy. It came quick and fast, and the only reason I could see it at all was that its body was darker than the surrounding sheath of night-fall.

I was surprised how fast Jay moved. He took off his hard felt cowboy hat and as the owl crashed into us, he crowned it on the head with that cowboy hat. The sound of collision was that of a dull bell. The stunned, or thwarted, owl veered to the left. It beat its soundless wings and tried to grab hold of a juniper branch. Then it rose thrashing its whispery wings toward the north.

"Let him try that again," Jay said, smiling.

He didn't mention what it was.

I knew from long ago what it was and why I couldn't get rid of it.

***

On the way back to Tesuque in the pick-up, Jay and I said very little to each other. There was not a lot to say. I understood that he had shown me how to be blessed. How to be safe when evil comes. Sometimes it is necessary to fight back. Hard. The prayer of a fist or a knife. Or a curious cowboy hat, which Jay sometimes admitted was his ego.

As we got to La Bajada hill and began our ascent towards Santa Fe, Jay broke his silence. "I let my ego speak for me this time." He laughed.

Then he continued, "You know when I went back to Rainy Butte that time?"

I said I remembered it.

"Well, you see my father warned me. He said, 'Don't be afraid of what you see up there.' I didn't know what he meant starting out but after a while I felt it more than thought it. At the top of the butte a horse came out of the sun. A golden horse with a mane of sunrays. With hooves of flint that left butterfly prints.

"My father said, 'Don't be afraid of what you see up there on the butte.' I was afraid but I stood my ground. The horse came on and I stood fast. In the horse's mouth there was a wildflower hanging down. He galloped right at me, the same way the owl came on tonight. The way it came on us with that sudden crazy power. On Rainy Butte I took a deep breath, released it, closed my eyes. Then I said the prayer to the roundness of things: the sun, the earth, the bracelet on my wrist. And the great horse kept coming and the hooves, I knew, would crush me but what my father said protected me. That sun horse ran right through me and pounded the butte and raised a ghost of smoke and then it disappeared."

I sat in silence seeing, over and over, the image of the sun horse, Jay standing there bravely before it.

Over La Bajada the diamond lights of Santa Fe twinkled in the desert darkness as we streamed through town. Then headed north to Tesuque and the dark veils of hills.

Jay said he would be back again soon. He said this after he left me off on the top of our ridge and turned around wending his way back to Crownpoint. I walked down the hill in the starlight, thinking about what a strange day it had been and an even stranger night. Not to mention, a weird week and an insane month.

Jay showed up sooner than I thought he would, and this time he had his family with him. Jay's father, the stargazer, sat in our living room. Jay's mother sat near him. The old man spoke no English, but she spoke it well and translated, as did Jay.

Jay's mother's clothes were straight out of the last century. A loose blouse with a turquoise and silver squash blossom necklace; her dress was full and long. Jay's father wore a large Stetson and familiar-looking western clothes—jeans, boots and a blue, pearl-snap shirt. Jay's wife Ethel was also there. She looked very contemporary. She had curled hair and make-up.

I made strong black coffee, but we were out of propane so I boiled the water in our fireplace and made the coffee there. I think they liked that. In the old days I would have offered them cornhusk ceremonial cigarettes, as was the custom.

Jay knew the tack I was taking on the mute articles and he also knew I would greatly appreciate his father's opinion on these matters. When everyone had a cup of coffee, Jay opened up a conversation.

"Seen any new UFOs?" he asked me.

"Not lately, only mutes."

Jay and his father spoke to each other then in Navajo.

"My father says he saw something evil. A bunch of sheep were killed the other day. He says this happened at night. My sister-in-law was supposed to be watching the sheep but she went away for a little while and that's when the sheep were killed."

"Any tracks?" I asked.

Jay asked his father and the old man sat back in his chair and thought about it. He sat in silence, thinking.

Finally he spoke again to Jay, who turned to me and said, "He thinks it was dogs. No tracks. Fifteen sheep killed. Says he saw two white dogs, twice the size of normal dogs that night."

I asked, "Were the bodies defiled?"

"What do you mean by defiled?" Jay asked.

"Were they mauled, ripped apart, bloodied?"

Jay put this question to his father. The old man shook his head. His face was set in stone. He spoke, looking at Jay as if he was the one who desired the information, not me.

"My father," Jay said, "thinks the sheep must not be moved until a certain passage of time. Then they will have to be burned. That is the only way, he says, to discourage the evil."

"What about the blood? I have seen mutilations where there's no blood at all, not even in or on the body of the slain animal."

"There was a lot of blood," Jay said. "It was a slaughter to no purpose. Nothing eaten."

"If they were wild dogs," I explained, "they would eat some of those sheep. If they were domestic or even recently feral dogs, some part of them might be eaten."

Jay smiled. "Maybe it wasn't dogs."

"Your father did say dogs, didn't he?"

Jay's mother joined the conversation then. She looked only at Jay's father but she and the old man both were acutely aware of my being there and listening. Jay listened to his parents conversing, then he said to me, "My father says this thing could have been anything at all."

"What about skinwalkers?" I asked. The conversation might have ended there. But it didn't.

The old man spoke to Jay and then Jay said to me, "My father says it could have been anything. Mountain lion maybe."

"I have a feeling it was something else," I said. Maybe I went too far, I thought, with this logic of mine. But on the other hand . . . I had learned you only get somewhere by gently pushing in a discussion like this. So far no one had given me a sharp glance when I used the word skinwalkers. The old star-gazer knew that word in English even if he knew no other. But such a word was so profane for some of the elder Navajos they wouldn't even say it, let alone converse round about it.

After a long silence during which everyone sipped their coffee and I added a little more to their cups, the conversation continued. Or rather I should say, Jay and his father spoke together. Their talk last about twenty minutes and I only caught a few words I understood.

Finally Jay turned to me. He said, "My father says maybe it wasn't dogs. Or if it was dogs, they were commanded to do what they did by something."

I decided not to use the skinwalker word and instead chose some others. "Was it an evil intelligence? I asked. I'd heard Jay use that expression before."

Jay asked his father. The old man nodded grimly, then spoke a few more words.

Jay told me, "My father says minds that can do these things are nowhere near the place where they are done. My father is blessed with the knowing of things that are in the future and he told me that this thing would happen because of something that happened before it. This what my father said:

"There was a squaw dance last summer and it was done in The Enemy Way. To protect our family from harm. In the door of our house I had found bullet. No gun had been fired at that doorway. But there was the bullet buried in that wood. A bad thing was stalking the house and we had to be aware. To exorcise the evil we did the dance in The Enemy Way. We killed sheep for the dance and the hides should have been destroyed. Instead we sold the hides in town because we needed the money. Later, four lines were drawn on the skins. Four lines for the months that were going to pass before the evil would strike. No one knows who drew those lines.

"In November, right now, this month, the bad things started to happen. I got sick and almost died in the hospital. A little bit before that I was cleaning my rifle and I accidentally fired a shot that almost killed my daughter. But the worst did not happen to us. It happened to those fifteen sheep. The Enemy Way did protect us. There are those on the Reservation who fear us because of the things we have achieved. But we have wisdom and these things cannot hurt us if we are careful."

I asked Jay, "Were the sheep killed by an agent of evil?"

Jay didn't bother asking his father. He just told me, "They don't have to lift a finger to accomplish their work."

"And they never leave any tracks, right?"

Jay asked his father about this . . . the tracks.

His mother got into it again, and spoke directly to her husband. Jay translated what both of them said.

"They say they've both seen tracks. They say the tracks are very small. About the size of. . ."

He pinched his fingers five inches.

"Like a child's footprint?"

Jay grinned. "Like this . . ."

He did the inches again, and said, "Like a monkey."

I thought about this for a moment. A Navajo woman had once told me about a baby who was born with canine teeth and hands the backs of which were covered with soft, light hair. The feet of this baby were shaped differently than a human. More like a monkey.

"My father says to tell you that he has seen the face of this thing and it's not wolflike," Jay said. "It's an ape face and it looked down at him from the smoke hole of our summer hogan out in the desert."

***

When they left it was sundown again. It seemed to me there were but three times of day: dawn, dusk and night. I walked them out to the door and the old stargazer spoke some words to Jay on leaving. Jay smiled and said to me, "Tell him the man who built this house is a good man." It was a blessing; I knew that. We, Laura and I, were blessed. And the house and its people were safe. For a time.

As they were about to leave, they invited us to their wedding in a week.

"Their wedding?" I looked at Jay. "They've been together, you said, for fifty years."

"They were married according to Navajo custom fifty years ago to the day next Saturday. My older brother who is a Christian wants them to get married now in the Christian way."

"What does your mother say about that?" I asked.

"She doesn't care," Jay said, "She was raised in a mission school."

"What does your father say?"

"He doesn't care either. He's agreeable to it."

"Another fifty years then," I said.

Jay's mother laughed.

They all got into Jay's truck and drove off.

The last thing I saw was the stargazer's hat in the rear window.

Chapter Eighteen

Every year I went to the Deer Dances at San Jacinto down the road from our house. It was one of those ceremonies that takes you out of the century you're in and puts you far back in time. This cold moon November night I needed the dances because I knew they would lift me out of my mute-mind, as I was now calling it. Just give me a few hours of peace, that's all I ask

The pueblo was hushed and still when I got there and the people stood in groups wearing heavy coats with Pendleton blankets thrown over their shoulders. Some of them wore beaded moccasins, but most had on the low-cut squaw boots with silver conchos on the side. The women, round shapes beside the slightly taller men, had blankets raised over their heads, and their round faces were lit up by the moon.

The stillness was a living presence in the plaza and even the mongrel dogs succumbed to it by lying down in the cold dust and not moving. The children were either held on their mother's hips or they stood beside them with black shocks of hair squared off in bangs at the eyebrows.

As my eyes grew accustomed to the night shapes around me, I noticed that there were luminarias fires stacked and ready to be lit all over the plaza. There must have been a hundred of them stretching as far off as the church, a great-shouldered shape that seemed out of place until I saw that a torch-lit procession was emerging from its huge wooden doors. The figures in the procession moved with a somber pace: thirty or forty Indians led by a Catholic priest and followed by a man who fired a rifle every ten or fifteen steps. The sound of the gun wracked the adobe plaza with triplicate blasts.

The procession moved snakelike around the old cottonwood in the center of the plaza, and then it turned east and a man with a torch came out of the dark and began to light the cones of piñon wood, which burst into flame. I moved out of the shadows where I'd been standing alone and joined a group that stood in a circle around one of the fires.

They greeted me with courteous nods and moved their circle outward so that it would include me. In time, as we waited for the dancers to emerge from the kiva, the Indians in our circle moved to other ones, and the circle thinned out so that after an hour's wait there remained around the dwindling fire only myself, a man and a woman.

"You from Los Alamos?" the man asked.

"I live in Tesuque."

"Not such a long ways away," the man said.

"You got a wife and children?" said the woman.

I smiled, nodded.

"Bring your whole family next time—childrens love dancing."

"Wonder when the dancers gonna come out now?" the man said.

"Soon. They come soon," said the woman. And as she spoke a puff of snowflakes came out of the sky, and in a moment the whole plaza was a maze of white. Then there were strong voices from the clusters around the fires, laughing and excited talk, and I peered into the snow and saw that the dancers had come out of the kiva at last.

First came the rows of buffalo-headed men with black chests that heaved up and down when they stepped with a rush of bells and gourd rattles. A deer-skin drum thumped steadily as more and more dancers appeared out of the clouds of new snow. Then the deer-dancers were moving toward us with their hands gripping sticks that prodded the earth just like deer, and as they did their stiff-legged dance, they made cries that were quick and sharp. The heavily antlered heads tossed this way and that, and you could see eagle down on the tips of the horns that looked no different from the storm of flakes, and were actually supposed to be one and the same.

It seemed there were only men dancing around the fires, but there were also women moving, straight-backed, blanketed pueblo women holding sprigs of evergreen as they stepped lightly from side to side.

There were the children dancing too, dressed as antelopes, they kicked up their heels and sported about with white bobs of tail and two-pronged heads.

When the animal dancers began to file back into the kiva, the snowfall lessened and the Indians who had gathered around the piñon fires started to leave in small numbers that spread out toward the parking lot. The engines of pick-up trucks coughed on in the cold air and headlights dispelled the lingering magic of the dance.

Reluctantly, I headed toward my car, where someone waited for me in the dim shadows, a small intent figure. Right away I recognized the round face and deep eyes of Joe Juan Cello, the governor.

"Something has happened you could want to look at," he said.

I followed him to a San Jacinto police car and got into the back seat. Quietly, the car rolled out of the parking lot and headed in the direction of the fields that lay below the plaza. The moon was out and the meadow grass shone with snow. The driver cut his headlights and the car traveled evenly and quietly through the open fields.

The car stopped in front of the huge carcass of a steer tilted on its side. Its head was arched upward as if the neck had been snapped. We got out of the car. There were just the three of us.

"Just like the last one," Joe Juan Cello said. "Look here."

He bent down and the uniformed Indian driver did the same, both of them squatting by the cow's head. "No blood anywhere."

I leaned forward to look into the steer's open mouth: the absence of a tongue made the mouth look almost abstract. The moonlit teeth seemed to be laughing at us. The flesh around the mouth was missing, surgically removed. This gave the steer's face a cynical expression. The tribal officer with the governor moved to the back of the steer.

"No balls," he said. "Been cut off."

Another incision so clean it appeared like a pencil mark. The officer got down on his knees and sniffed the steer's fur.

"There's that smell again Joe" he said, "that burned-hide smell."

"I smell it too." Singed hair.

"Same old story," Joe Juan Cello sighed, "no blood, no tracks, no tongue, no balls. No nothing."

"What about that smell?" I asked.

"They smell like that," the officer said. "Every one of 'em."

"Sandia Labs doesn't know what to make of it." The governor added, "There's a radiation check they do, but so far nothing's come of it."

"May I borrow your flashlight?" I asked the officer.

He handed me a flashlight with a foot and a half handle, and it occurred to me that neither of them had bothered to use the light up close. I beamed into the cow's mouth where a thin wisp of steam was coming out. Then I shone it around various places on the body and handed the light back to the officer who quickly snapped it off.

"We don't want the Pueblo to know about this one," Joe Juan Cello said. "It would spoil the dances." He looked at me for a good while without saying anything.

"You pick up any clues?"

"Not a single one."

"Some mutilations are uglier than this one. They're getting it down all right. Getting it to the point where one night we'll be down in this meadow and there'll be a man lying here instead of a cow. And what'll the State Cops say then? What would they say if it were one of their boys lying here without any balls?"

"They'd take it personally," I told him.

"Well, right now they're just . . . curious."

Then I saw what I hadn't seen before: the cow's head was much larger than the rest of its body and seemed disconnected at the neck. The mid-section had fallen in on the ribs, as if the cow had been starved to death. Its broken-neck and laughing face . . . I knew I'd see it in my sleep for some time to come.

And yet I could still hear the ankle bells of the deer dancers. The night was heavy with the acrid smell of burned cow's hair, but the bells sang on and the snow tumbled down in windy gusts.

In the police car going back to the village, I noticed that the rest of the San Jacinto herd had gathered under a cottonwood, shoulder to shoulder. They looked impassively at us as the car passed by them, an unbroken wall of staring eyes that followed us as we left them alone in the darkness. I thought . . . if they could only say what they saw!

***

On the way home I turned off State Road 22 down the incline that made so many of our friends wary of visiting us, the now famous dirt road that made your forehead bump up against the dashboard of your car, if you were not careful. The road wound like a spool of kitten-strung yarn, dipped into the arroyo lined with sage and chamisa, came up on the other side; two more winds and turns and I was heading up the last slope to the house, which was lit in the moon like a magnificent white mushroom. A dust of snow lay frayed and wan in the blanket moonlight all around.

Laura was awake when I came up to the side of the bed and undressed. I slid under the covers. The sudden embrace startled me.

"I'm scared," she whispered.

"About what?"

I felt warm tears on my cheek.

"Are the kids alright?" I asked.

"I just checked. They're OK."

"Then . . . what?"

The house was silent.

Laura held on to me and I could feel her shiver a little.

"Do you hear it," she asked.

I listened. I didn't hear anything.

"It's an animal," she said.

"What kind of animal?"

"I don't know."

"How long has this animal been out there?"

"I'm not hearing things," she said.

"I didn't say you were. I just don't hear anything."

Then I heard it. A high-pitched scream. I got out of bed, went to the window and looked out. The night was as still as the desert, the desert of dream, for it looked unreal, all dressed-out in cactus, pine and snow.

"You've been hearing that strange wail since I left?"

"Yes. Ever since the kids went to bed. Thank God it hasn't gotten them up."

"Sounds like the sort of whimper a screech owl makes."

She shook her head. "It doesn't always make that noise. It does other ones, too. Twitterings, moans, cries that sound female."

"Okay, I said. "I know what it is. Barred Owls make every kind of sound in the book—hiss, wail, shriek, moan, cough. They can sound like a dog in heat or a couple of horses fucking."

"One owl can do all of that?"

"One little owl," I said. "Well, they're not so little."

"I've been listening to that for hours, but I still don't think it's an owl."

"Be still for a second. I just heard it again."

"Now maybe you'll believe me . . ."

There was a rustling sound at the window.

A dark face with a mantle of fur. A flash of sharp canine teeth.

"I saw it," Laura said, "but it's gone."

"I saw it too." I was trying to stay calm.

"Was it a man?"

"I think it's the same man I saw with Jay at Rio Puerco."

We were both standing still under the moonlit clear story window on the roof. The moonlight was very bright.

The window to the right of our bed was where the face was and now all I could see was the sloping hill, tussocks of moon white grass, some pine cones under a dwarf piñon tree.

"Do you think it was the same person who came into the house the other night?"

"It could be."

"Well, he's gone."

We went downstairs and had a shot of Jim Beam. One, and then another. Then we went back upstairs and lay awake for hours listening to the night. I put the black madonna in the deep window well and the little crosses on the floor around our bed.

Maybe we dozed off a few times. The wind came up once but it was a whispering, not a stalking wind.

***

In the morning the kitchen was full of ants. There were rivers of them. Funny little black ants that didn't bite but were everywhere—the whole downstairs was a syrupy stream of fast moving ants.

In the Navajo way you don't kill them, you gently sweep them out. But the more we swept—and this was a family affair, with Sarah and Mara helping with all sizes of brooms, all of us sweeping the dark ant river out the door, the more they came.

Ants.

In the bathroom.

In the kitchen.

In the living room.

They boiled out of cracks in the brick floor. They filled sugar bowls and breadboxes and poured up and down the chimney and in and around the fireplace. It was like the great flood.

Chapter Nineteen

Jay told me this story and I believe it is true.

In the beginning there was Water Woman, and the world, her world, was calm and still.

And Water Woman made Earth and Sky, who were twins. In time, the twins made Black-Belted Mountain, Turquoise Mountain, Colored-Cloud Mountain and Big Sheep Mountain.

After the mountains were made, there was still no life, such as we know it, so Earth created Black God, who is the god of fire. Then she made Horned Toad, Locust, Blue Lizard, First Man and First Woman, and Ant.

There was Red Ant, Yellow Ant, Black Ant and Many-colored Ant, and all of the Ant People had light coming out of them.

Still, there was no life.

Then Earth breathed life into Wind and, in turn, Wind breathed life into all things, and the things of life came alive and lived.

***

So the house was still full of ants. They were everywhere—on the walls, bookshelves, in the cracks between the bricks on the floor. They formed vast ant lines on the sheets of all of the beds. We brushed them out, they came back in. We gained only a moment between the time that it took them to turn around and reform their steady march.

In the end, much as we hated to use chemical warfare, we got out the Raid. We sprayed. Surprisingly, it slowed them. But didn't stop them.

Jay came that afternoon.

He surveyed the coming ant lines but said nothing about them.

After we had our usual cup of herbal tea, he took off his black cowboy hat, which was just like his father's, and placed it upside down on a chair. Then he sighed, looked me in the face.

"What's going on, Old Man Coyote?"

He didn't seem alarmed by the ants.

I told him the tale of the night before.

He listened, then, "Anything a man does has consequences. Even when he does nothing about something, he makes himself heard. Because nothing is something."

"I have to admit. I killed a bunch. Had to."

"That would only bring on more ants," he said.

"There were just so many," Laura explained as she came into the room. "You couldn't walk without stepping on them."

Jay picked up his hat and ran his index finger around the brim.

"Whenever you kill something," he said, "you have to cleanse yourself. You remember the story my father told about the sheep and the Enemy Way ceremony?"

"I remember."

"You need to burn some cedar in the house."

I nodded. "Okay."

Jay put his hat on. "Come outside," he said.

We went out, all three of us.

Jay breathed the air in front of the house, eyes closed. When he opened his eyes he knew where the ants were and walked directly to a tall conical ant hill. We stood over the ant hill, Laura and I, but Jay stood back a ways.

"Don't let your shadow get ahead of you," Jay said, amused.

His shadow was well behind the ant hill.

After a little while, Jay knelt down. I thought he was going to do a chant.

But he didn't. He talked to us in a whisper, "Tell the ant people you didn't mean to hurt them. Tell them you apologize for your mistake. Tell them you're sorry and then say you won't do that again."

"All right. Is that all?"

"Tomorrow go out and find Horned Toad. Place him at the top of the ant hill."

"Is that it?" I asked.

"Well enough. For now."

***

That night I burned the juniper bough in the house filling it with cedar sweetness. I went from room to room with the fragrant, flaming stick and then I put it outside and walked to the ant hill and said I was sorry. In the morning, I found a large sun-dappled horned toad and placed it by the hill and left it there and went about my business, which is writing. I drove to the office and wrote an automatic story that I titled, "Wolfmen and Ant People."

It was my good luck that Durwood wasn't there. I left the clean unedited copy on his green desk blotter. Then I drove home in the old Chevy feeling especially light-hearted but I took care not to get a lead foot.

Laura met me at the door. "You won't believe it. No ants in the sugar bowl."

"The beds?"

She shook her head.

"Walls?"

"See for yourself."

I went all over the various rooms. Antless.

I asked Laura in the kitchen, "No ants anywhere?"

"Nope."

"Jay's a mystic man."

"He's the son of a medicine man."

"Either way."

She made some good French Roast and we walked outside into the New Mexican sun, sat on a juniper log, watched some black and white magpies do a kind of hop-skip-dance in midair over a piñon tree.

We finished the coffee, set down the cups. Then we walked over to the big ant hill. The horned toad was still there. We watched it arch its back, lift itself up. Then it made a calculated stab at an ant emerging from the hole. The toad was faster than an eye-blink. The ant was there, then it wasn't.

I wondered if the ants, these particular ones, knew who Horned Toad was. Did they know the ancient myth? Did they know the Book of Rules? We watched one ant after another get eaten up.

"How much different is that from our way of killing them?" Laura asked.

"In Jay's mind, all the difference in the world."

Then, as we gazed upon them, the antique fable unfolded.

I could hear the dialogue in my head . . . .

Lone Ant Rider, larger than all the others, came from the lip of the mound that was the Ant People's home.

He said, "Where are the four Ant People who were just here a moment ago?"

Horned Toad said, "I ate them."

"What did you do that for?" Lone Ant Rider said.

"I cannot help it," Horned Toad answered.

"Why can you not help eating them?" Lone Ant Rider asked.

"Because it is just that way."

"It wasn't always that way."

"Maybe you never noticed," Horned Toad said.

"It is not good for our people," Lone Ant Rider said.

"Don't worry," Horned Toad said, "I will leave enough of you. Some of you

will always be here, for that is the way it is."

I told Laura the story I'd spun.

"Sounds like Jay wrote it," she said.

"I believe he did."

***

And that night, as if arranged by the Hero Twins, Jay drove up in his tribal truck with the Navajo symbol on the door. Jay had created the logo for the tribal flag when we were just out of college thirty years earlier.

Jay eased himself out of the cab and came into the house and asked for some Sleepytime tea. We made some and then sat around sipping it.

"Ant people still around?" he asked.

"We did what you told us to do," Laura said.

Jay didn't say anything.

He put a spoon into our honey jar and ladled some into his tea cup. Jay smiled at the cup, then looked at Laura and said, "Some time ago, Earth got tired of the ways of the Ant People and she told Black God to set fire to the corners of the earth. That got all the created beings to move to the center where they were pushed to the top of the sacred mountains and then into the next world where everything was much brighter. Some say there are four worlds, you know. Some say five."

"Which one are we in now?" Laura asked as she put a plate of chocolate chip cookies on the long wooden kitchen table.

Jay took one and nibbled at it. I thought how unlike Brown he was. If it were Brown's cookie, it would be gone. Wiping the crumbs from his lip, Jay said, "Fourth or fifth, depending on how you see it."

We continued to eat cookies and sip tea, and then the kids came in. They had been playing "Little Animals" down by the arroyo.

"Cookies!" Mara said, "Any milk?"

Laura got two glasses and a carton of milk.

Both girls were respectful of Jay, looking at him with quick sidelong glances.

He smiled at them though, and they smiled back.

"The ants are gone," Laura mentioned to Jay.

"Not gone," he said. "Lessened."

"Each world gets brighter?" I asked him. "Is that the story?"

"So they say."

"Are we like the Ant People?"

"You mean is there a big toad eating us?"

Everyone laughed, especially Mara and Sarah.

"Something's eating a hole in the sky," Jay said. "Maybe it's Martians or Neptunians."

***

Later that night, after everyone was in bed, I put some ganja seeds by the top of the ant hill.

In the morning the little seeds were gone.

In their place there was a tiny piece of turquoise.

Who put it there?

Ant?

Horned Toad?

Skinwalker?

Was *hozhonii* returned to the Andrews home?

Chapter Twenty

Above Abiquiu on the road to Chama and Pagosa Springs the land of sculptured rock changes dramatically to sagebrush and pine bordered by snow peaks. The road winds past towns of wood and mud with red tin roofs. The muddy Chama River slams down from the ice mountains, spills over its banks into rivulets lined with young red and green willows. Occasionally you see the skin of a coyote hanging on a barbed wire fence to ward off other predators. It's a beautiful, lonely, sometimes forbidding and yet alluring country.

The time had finally come to meet Angel Gomez on his own turf. I was traveling with Etienne to Dulce, the Jicarilla Apache Reservation where Gomez had his remote headquarters. This was high mountain country, rolling hills of blue sage, mud ponies, and empty-engine hulks of rusted 1952 Chevrolets. We came into Dulce late in the day. BIA housing and cinderblock, dull, brick buildings stood out everywhere.

"Is this the State Police headquarters?" I asked an Apache man who was hosing down a tribal police car.

"Supposed to be."

Etienne and I parked and went inside the drab government building. Once inside, we stood in a small hallway that had a dented snack machine and a couple of metal chairs. There was a dispatcher behind a glass window in the next room. The man was wearing a big brimmed cowboy hat with an eagle feather in it, and he was speaking Apache into a C.B. radio.

"We're looking for Angel Gomez," I said through the hole in the window.

"He's on his way . . . you from KOB news?"

"No, but we made an appointment with him."

"He'll be here in a couple minutes."

That could mean anything. So we sat on the tailgate of our Datsun camper and ate chicken salad sandwiches. I went over in my mind the questions I knew I'd forget when I saw Angel Gomez. Earlier that week the *Enquirer* had run a photo Gomez had taken of a UFO. The accompanying story carried his remarks and theories. Since then, he'd been interviewed so many times that media attention had made him an investigative hero.

In 1977 Gomez was named Policeman of the Year for capturing a convicted murderer who had escaped from the penitentiary just outside Santa Fe in Cerrillos. For over a year the escapee had evaded capture. He left messages in Spanish to taunt Gomez. The officer went from mountain village to mountain village sleeping on spare cots and corn cribs or the back seat of his car.

One day in February of '77 Gomez finally caught up with his quarry and they had one of those Mexican stand-offs you see on TV. Both men had cocked 38s and crazy grins. Neither one laid down his gun and they were that way when reinforcements showed up and talked the prisoner into surrender. By then the man's smile was gone. Not Gomez's. He strutted around smiling from ear to ear.

I wasn't surprised when Gomez got the drop on us as we were eating. He came up quietly in his tight, dark blue uniform. I introduced myself and Etienne. Gomez seemed to remember me. He motioned for us to get into his car.

"How about some coffee?"

He then drove us to The Little Beaver Coffee Shop. Once there Gomez asked, "You hear about the latest cut-up cow?"

"There's a new one?"

"Story isn't out yet. We're waiting on the lab check to see if the blood's been coagulated."

Inside the café we saw the usual, wrinkle-eyed cowboys hunkered around Formica tables drinking coffee. The place was run by large Apache women with narrow watchful eyes and small smiles.

Gomez said, "Coffee!"

The coffee came moments later.

"There's a lot of air turbulence talk," Gomez said. "Sticks and stuff blown all around. But we can't prove nothing up here in Dulce."

"Why's that?" I asked.

"Well," Gomez answered, "you can do turbulence tests where there's lots of sand. Here's it's all sage. So we have no way of telling what kind of aircraft's being used."

Etienne questioned Gomez about UFOs. "Do you still maintain that they exist?"

Gomez ran his fingers through his hair. "If you can call it proof . . . I don't know what to call it anymore . . . seems I saw one thing one time, another thing another time. I change my mind a lot. What's proof anyway? What they say in the *National Enquirer* ?"

Almost on cue our waitress appeared with a copy of the newspaper.

Gomez said, "OK, here's a picture of something I never saw. The infrared caught these balloons, puffs of smoke, flying saucers, airborne mushrooms, or what in hell they're supposed to be."

"Apache smoke signals," said one of the cowboys sitting near us. A couple people laughed.

Etienne and I looked at the newsprint photograph. We saw two round shapes that looked like thumb prints against the corner of a chromium sky.

Gomez commented, "They're what you want them to be, I guess."

"It says here," Etienne said, "that you saw a UFO one week ago."

"What I saw a week ago was an aircraft moving low in the sky with a big white floodlight. It could've been a UFO, or maybe something else. It was shaped like a round bubble and made no noise. No lights, except that one floodlight. When they—whatever was in it—turned off the flood, you couldn't see anything. It was pitch black. If I'd had my AR 16, I would have blown the son-of-a-bitch right out of the sky."

"You would kill them for flying over your head?" Etienne said in surprise.

"Not for flying over my head. Just to *prove* that they flew over my head."

"Everyone wants proof, too bad there isn't any," I said.

"You know Dr. Sigmund?" Gomez asked.

Etienne said, "He has some believable pictures of UFOs."

"I've seen his photographs close up and I think they're real," Gomez added. "Makes me think that an advanced civilization could be taking bone marrow from the pelvis, the lymphatic node, the . . . *chingado,* the tongue, facial tissue and blood for a specific reason. What for? Because those areas of an animal or a human being are what the medical people call *repositories*. They take the eye . . . why the eye? Because whatever that animal eats shows up in its eye.

"You've heard what some old Navajo said about a hole in the sky and things coming out of it? Well, things are going back into it too. Who knows how many human beings have disappeared on this planet? Who knows how many have been operated on by technicians from another planet."

"This gets us into the old conversation about germ warfare," I said.

Gomez nodded, said, "Have you ever thought that the whole UFO business could just be another government cover-up for something much worse than little green men in flying saucers. The little green men, who knows, they might be friendly but maybe their little green germs aren't friendly. Who knows? One thing for sure governments, at least on this planet, are far from friendly."

Gomez signaled for his sixth cup of coffee. He treated them like water chasers.

"But you would kill the little green men even though you say they might not be aggressive?" Etienne asked.

Gomez grinned. "They love space ships in France, don't they? Is this some kind of a religion with you?"

Etienne smiled. "In fact, it is. And I believe what you say about the hole in the sky and visitors from beyond our galaxy and the possibility of germ warfare. All of it is possible. But my religion is love."

Gomez said, "Good for you. He looked at both of us and nodded his head a few times. "Not a bad way to go, or to be. But you know they killed hippies up here for that. Remember the communes in Taos? What an ungodly mess."

I changed the subject. "Maybe the star people and the government people are seeking the same thing. As you say, who knows."

Gomez offered me a wry smile. "Not love, that's for sure. I'm waiting right now for a lab report from London. They just had a cattle mutilation over there. Blood removed through the jugular vein with a blowing and sucking machine. Indications of the same anti-coagulant we've been picking up over here."

"How does that show up in the mutilation?" I asked.

"Bright pink blood. Sometimes little spots on the ground. Maybe in the animal itself. We have our suspicions. But none of our national security people gave a damn about my lab reports two years ago when I found anthrax showing up in mutilated cattle. I don't want either of you to write about this, it's still classified. Last thing we want in New Mexico is an anthrax scare on top of this cow scare."

"So why do you think there are so many mutilations up here in Dulce?" I asked Gomez.

"Do you remember back in 1967? That thing they called Operation Gasbuggy? The government exploded 29-T-megaton bomb, buried underground, twelve miles from here. They say the Atomic Energy Commission wanted to open a natural gas shelf and they spent 33 million bucks . . . to get what? I'll tell you. High radiation in all the wells around the Rez."

Gomez swiveled around in his chair and waved at his dispatcher, who was sitting nearby. "Hey, Gray Eagle, how come you guys are the ones always get fucked?"

"Because we give white people the benefit of the doubt, that's why. And why shouldn't we, they're crazy."

Chapter Twenty-One

Our plan was to rest up after the long drive from Santa Fe to Dulce. I wanted to interview Gomez again in the morning.

Etienne and I rented a small cabin for the night. It was just out of town and close to the Chama river. The snow-water coming down from the high country was so loud we had to almost shout over it. I made some coffee on a hot plate and we ate some more of Mina's sandwiches. It was the best chicken sandwich ever, made with some secret spices.

"Your wife can make sandwiches better than anyone in the Western world," I said to Etienne.

"That's because she's from the Eastern world," he said.

I looked at Etienne while he was eating. He was a sort of raggle-taggle person made up of many parts. His teeth did not match, nor did any other part of him. Sometimes I thought he was an elf.

"Where is Mina from?" I asked him.

"Detroit. She's Japanese of course, but more American than you. Her parents were in the internment camps during the war. But this had only a small effect on her except for her passion for food and eating. She can, I admit, make a hotdog into a banquet."

"How long have you been married?"

"About three years. Our Akido master married us in Santa Fe. I was named Kimito by him, but I have since dropped that name. I'm more comfortable with my given name. Her given name was Frances but she changed it to Mina."

I finished my sandwich and went to the window with my coffee cup. I opened the calico curtain and looked out. Sundown was creeping into the red willows by the river. Tendrils of ice, the sheathing off the willows, had melted during the day but they hung about like silver swords in the late day sun. Etienne joined me for a moment and stared at the river light.

"This country around here reminds me of the place where my father had a chalet in Switzerland. I used to go there often when I was a boy."

I looked from the willows to Etienne. I had now known him for a couple of weeks. I'd been to his house, met his wife, played with his little girl, Tiemi, and now had come 300 miles into a desolate place to interview a man who was considered to be a madman by some, especially certain members of the press. In truth I trusted Gomez about as much as Etienne.

Etienne was a puzzle; Gomez was an open book.

There was nothing secret about Etienne except himself. There was a part of him that was cut off from the world. He was secretive in a strange way, as if there was something dark in his nature that couldn't come out. He wasn't earning money like I was by doing interviews. He seemed to have his own money. He paid for the gas and had brought enough sandwiches to last another day. He was generous.

Laura had thought that traveling a long distance with a stranger wasn't a particularly good idea. But my thought was that Etienne was becoming a part of my interviews. If I could get to know him better, I could learn some of the things that he already knew about UFOs and other mystical things.

As the day ended, we lit two kerosene lanterns and repaired to our beds to read. He was reading Meyer Baba. I studied him again for a moment. His overall appearance was studied neglect, as if he'd read all the manuals on human dress and had been unable to incorporate them into his own being.

Etienne's skin seemed a bit transparent. I decided that he had a certain amount of immateriality about him. Like he might rise up at any moment, float out a crack in the cabin and drift away into the night.

Etienne was pretty good at mind reading and he also had a great sense of humor. While I was looking at him, he was thinking about me.

Suddenly he looked over at me and said, "You wanted to ask me a question?"

I laughed and he did too.

"I wanted to ask you what you're getting out of this. For me, I get paid. What do you get? Are you gathering information for your future work at the Center?"

"Good question. You know, the last few years Mina and I traveled around and conducted interviews just like the one we did today."

"But why?"

"I haven't any choice. I must have answers, so I can continue to live as my life must be lived. For eight years I studied Aikido. Then I reached a point where it didn't matter if I could deflect a blow coming at my head. It mattered only to know why such a blow had to fall in my direction. So I prepared myself for a different kind of study. Less action, more thought. I am not disappointed in the path I have chosen. I am beginning to understand the why of all whys."

"The nature of good and evil?"

"Yes. But more than that. You see, for me all these things are one. To know how to protect yourself is useless. I'll tell you why . . . ."

Momentarily, I visualized Etienne as an Aikido master. It was impossible to see him that way.

Etienne went on. "Self-defense is after the fact. One is taught to defend only after an attack has been launched in your direction. It has taken me some time to figure out how not to be attacked. That is the true art of defense—diffusion. Finding out how to diffuse the emotions that instigate violent actions."

"That's been your secret study then?"

"No. It's what I have been thinking about since I stopped studying Akido in the formal way. This is why all of these interviews are so important. They point to the way that one can disengage, while being fully engaged in the present moment."

"My own answer to that is to trust your inner nature. I grew up in a place where people came at you suddenly for reasons unknown. You had to be ready to fight at the drop of a hat. When the adrenalin starts flowing, I get as crazy as old Gomez."

"Gomez," Etienne said mildly, "is one type of man who should be regarded as dangerous. You have to keep an eye on him."

I laughed. "Gomez is like a character in a movie. Part clown, part heavy. I try not to take him seriously—except for what he says. He knows a lot about these mutes, some of which he's still not saying."

"You really should see him the way I do. But it's OK if you don't."

I got out of bed and made some more coffee from the same grounds.

Walking outside I submerged the coffee pot into the river which was ice cold. The mountains had a ring of fire but the night swallowed everything else. I came back inside with the coffee pot and set it on the hot plate. Then I cracked an egg from our cooler and dropped the shells into the pot and swallowed the raw egg. The shells would revitalize the old grounds, a trick I'd learned from an Idaho sheepherder who used the same coffee grounds, he said, for weeks.

When the coffee was just about to boil, I filled our tin cups and gave one to Etienne and sat down on my sagging bed again. It creaked. The coffee steamed.

"Etienne, I have to tell you something. You're much more programmatic than I am, right? I see this interview as a means to an end, but unfortunately, I am in a muddle about it. In the beginning, the mutes scared me, unnerved and sometimes made me sick to my stomach. I began to see how unnatural all of it was. The weirder it is the less I'm convinced there is any theory to cover what we call a mutilation. No suspect—neither witches, nor aliens—fits the bill.

"I'm not even sure what I'm seeing any more. It's like a bad dream, someone else's dream, not mine. But I'm having to live through it."

Etienne said, "I agree with that point of view. But is there anything that does make sense to you?"

"I spoke with a veterinarian a month ago. This man claimed to have seen a helicopter that landed in back of his house in Cerrillos. Afterwards, in daylight, he found a mutilated steer. He saw the copter's runner marks in the sand and he swore the steer had been mutilated in the same way described by Gomez. A blood collection device, a pump perhaps, was used to siphon the blood out of the animal. There was a precise removal of tissue around the mouth and anus. His opinion? He told me that a cult of wealthy, bored, but scientifically minded men in Texas were performing many of these operations. I asked him if the CIA could possibly be involved and he seemed to think so."

"Absurd."

"You don't believe it?"

Etienne chuckled. "That vet was misled by what he *wanted* to believe."

"Well," I said, sipping my coffee, "I'm just saying this reputable veterinarian had one of the more acceptable answers I've heard."

Etienne set his coffee cup on the pine plank floor. But he didn't say anything.

I continued. "I think there may be more answers along the road of discovery, but at least I have one that makes some sense."

"You should be very careful," Etienne said. "I thought you were rough on my friend Harjac. You sort of betrayed his confidence."

I finished my coffee and got up and poured one more.

"Sorry about that but I had to do it. But I don't think I did him an injustice. Just showed what some of his views were like, and by the way, they're pretty far out, don't you think?"

"You need to exhibit more care in your writing. You don't want to hurt someone's feelings, if you don't have to."

I sighed. "Most of what I write is bound to offend somebody. But what I saw of Harjac was a well-armored man who wasn't about to be offended by anyone. Least of all me. I did get some hate mail though from a few people who are really wound up in this mute thing."

Etienne creaked up out of his sagging metal bed and opened the valise he carried everywhere with him. He selected a magazine called *True Space Odysseys.* "Okay if I read a little of this to you?"

"Sure, go ahead."

"On April 19, 1897 at 10:30 PM, a Kansas farmer named Hamilton who was a former member of the House of Representatives woke to the sound of cattle bawling. Out of his window he saw an airship descending upon his cow lot about 40 rods from the house. A great turbine wheel about 30 feet in diameter, which was slowly revolving below the craft, began to buzz and the vessel rose lightly as a bird. Then the craft hovered directly over a two-year-old bawling and kicking heifer, which was caught in the glare of an unearthly light beam and looped about the neck with a cable that swung it up into the air. As the brilliantly lit cigar-shaped airship vanished into the northwest sky Hamilton began to doubt what he had seen. His bafflement was no less however when his neighbor found the butchered hide, head, and legs of Hamilton's heifer in this field."

"Etienne, that's pure fantasy . . . science fiction. Either way I can't take it seriously."

"You take the myths of the American Indians seriously."

"I accept them as myths, as beliefs of the collective unconscious. Beliefs alter behavior. A person's belief system may not be able to create a mutilation but it can profoundly affect the way that person sees one."

Etienne dug into his valise and produced a folder. "These are mutilation reports I got in Marfa, Texas. They are from UFO activists who have come to the Center."

In Great Sand Dunes, Colorado, September, 1967 a full grown Appaloosa mare was reportedly stripped of skin in a "surgically precise" lifting. Pod marks, scorch marks and strange odors were found all around the area; the horse's owner, Nellie Lewis testified that her horse had been mutilated by a UFO.

In Cheyenne Mountain, Colorado, exact date unknown a buffalo caged in a zoo was mutilated within the confines of its cage. This mutilation took place within close range of a US government nuclear facility.

In Leadville, Colorado, August, 1971, an army-colored or camouflaged helicopter killed forty sheep with a spray of an unknown kind. UPI later reported that an army investigation revealed that the deaths were the result of a chemical blistering.

In Crowley and Pueblo Counties, Colorado, September, 1975, a policeman fired his 30-30 at an unidentifiable helicopter like craft which made a whistling sound as opposed to a rotary propeller sound.

In October, 1975 in Cassica County, Idaho, despite the heat of the day meat on the carcass of a mutilated cow appeared normal and untainted after more than a week of decomposition time.

In the spring of 1976, on a farm near Wildwood, Alberta, Canada, the owner of two healthy horses found both dead in a snowbank; each animal was missing its uterus and its left eye. Unidentifiable tracks were photographed near the scene.

In December, 1976, in Logan County, Colorado a mutilated cow was found and the sheriffs reported that the animal was badly decomposed and decomposing in spite of sub-zero temperatures.

Sometime during the first half of 1977, in Taos County, New Mexico an insurance claim was paid to a rancher for the mutilation of a cow whose carcass had gone from reddish-brown to grayish-white in a 24 hour period.

***

"So . . . what do you say, my friend? Is it not convincing?" Etienne asked.

"It's all believable. The unconvincing part comes in when you try to pry fact from fiction. These mute cases are happening. No question."

"Where is the question?"

"The question is who."

Etienne stretched out on his bed.

I was already stretched out on mine.

The soft globe of the kerosene lantern on the coffee table between us was a small corona of light. The darkness was deep all around it. Outside the river roared through the willows that clattered in the wind. Every now and then we heard a horse whinny on one of the nearby hills.

"What don't you believe?" Etienne asked. He plumped up his pillow and put it behind his head.

I stared into the knotholes in the rafters.

"I can accept the government having a dark and clandestine hand in all of this. What I can't fathom, or don't want to, is cultists, number one. And, number two, visitors from other galaxies."

"So you don't think they come to earth to see what's going on here?"

"No, I think they do. I just don't believe they're evil."

"You would need to talk to actual abductees," Etienne said.

"I have read plenty of books."

"Not books. People. Harjac was an abductee. He's not crazy as you imagine. He's just seen things we haven't. Maybe he was molested in some way."

"You mean experimented upon?" I asked.

"I don't know if you could call it that. But maybe so. I do know that something happened to him that he won't talk about. I myself believe in the negative plane as well as the positive. Things come from negativity. There is the circle of evil influence that the Indians keep talking about. There is the theory, you know, of the inner earth. One of our greatest writers, Jules Verne, mentioned it in several of his books."

"Etienne those are novels. Science fiction stories."

"Yes, and you know . . . science fiction writers are visionaries. They see what we cannot and tell us what we cannot imagine."

"You know how Gomez sort of flips from one thing to another. I don't want to be like that. I'd like to know from some part of myself that there's an answer somewhere, not just a heap of varietal answers for all occasions depending on what you might believe at a given time."

I could hear Etienne shifting in his bed-sprung world while I twisted and turned in mine. I was thinking it could be a long night.

"Do you know the story of Travis Walton?" he asked.

"The lumberjack in Heber, Arizona?"

"Yes, that's him. There was a UFO up in the mountains. Walton was trapped in beam of light that came off the craft. He was missing for six days. He turned up in a telephone booth in Heber, all distracted and confused. Later he said that he'd been examined by creatures with hairless heads. They looked like fetuses, he said. They had almost translucent skin and very large eyes."

I chuckled. "That's standard fare in the abductee biz. They always look like that. They have pupate fingers like tree frogs and eyes like lemurs and . . ."

" . . .You don't believe it?"

"Sure I do, man. It's all possible. My friend Jay, told me that his medicine man father rode in a starcar."

Etienne drew a deep breath. "Yes?"

"So his father said he was out walking in cactus country one night and this shooting star landed very nearby and he went up to it and there was a crater and the soft sand was still warm and a breath of smoke was coming from it. He went down into the crater and there was a little car giving off rotary pulsations of light."

"You mean like a cop car from outer space?" Etienne laughed.

"All right. But he, Jay's father, was convinced that it was real. There were like these little people inside the car-like object—he said it was pill shaped."

"Like one of our French Peugeots, eh?"

"OK. And he saw these little monkey-like men inside with heads that looked like earth children only no hair and huge eyes . . . and so he gets inside that starcar and they take him for a ride."

I was quiet for a moment listening to the wind moan and the saber rattle of the river willows.

"Go on," Etienne said, "please."

"Not much more to say," I said sleepily. "He rode in a starcar. End of story."

Etienne turned on one elbow and propped up his head with his hand.

"There must be more to that."

"Well, Jay told me his father said they never talked, the little men, or whatever they were. They just made a high pitched little whistling noise, like you do sometimes when you laugh."

"That's all?"

"That's it. They flew around for a while and then they took the old man back to the crater and they went off, swish, and that was it."

Etienne murmured, "You believe this, Jack?"

"Yeah. I do."

"Why?"

"Why not?"

"Well, it seems to me you have a kind of prejudice for the Indian stories but not for the others."

"You have that right. Let's sort it out in the morning, I'm getting sleepy." I creaked out of bed and blew out the lantern. Instant night took over the cabin. It was so dark I couldn't see the bed. But I managed to walk very slowly and I got into my sleeping bag and was tight as a tick and off to sleep in a few minutes in spite of all the coffee I'd drunk.

***

I dreamed I was thirteen again and I was up on the top of Slide Mountain in the Catskills. I was counting star formations and trying to identify them with my Outward Bound companions when we saw the light. It was a very cohesive point of light that moved in the pattern of a parallelogram. Never in exactly the same pattern though. It veered sometimes. Glided smoothly then slowed, then stopped, then went forward again.

As we watched there was auditory accompaniment too. A bobcat was screaming somewhere near our camp and a ground-level mist crept into the campsite. The fire coals were down to faint embers. But the unidentified light in the sky did not change course. It followed the pattern of the parallelogram. Unchanging except in velocity.

I woke up and remembered one of the boys was so disturbed by this event plus the bobcat screeching that he woke our counselor who built up the campfire and reasoned with us about UFOs. This was the first time I had ever heard the word. It was 1958. The next morning when we got back to base camp the counselor phoned some kind of *Project Blue Book* hotline and spoke to someone there who said they were receiving hundreds of calls in that part of northern New York.

I was back there in the dream being scared by a bobcat-UFO. That dream kept reeling me in. I'd sort of crawl out of it into consciousness, lie there and listen to the willows lashing and then I was asleep on top of Slide Mountain twenty years ago and a bobcat was screaming in my adolescent ear and a star streaming parallelogram was bewitching a bunch of batty boys who were scared shitless.

Chapter Twenty-Two

Angel Gomez was at his gray government desk when we came in to see him in the morning. He took one look at us, rolled his office chair over to a rusted filing cabinet and pulled the top drawer wide open.

"Help yourself. I got nothing to hide."

"Do we need clearance for this?" I asked.

"I'm getting you cleared right now." He was talking to someone on the phone.

Then, "You're clear. After you get through we can go up to Stone Lake and see that miserable little bull . . ." He continued to talk to someone: "I need clearance from the Tribal Council for the same two newspaper guys, they're going to come up to the lake and see last night's mutilation . . . yeah, I'll hold."

He turned his swivel chair in my direction. "Don't look so worried," he said with a laugh. He still had the phone up to his ear and I heard him say, "Yup, I'm still here. It's all right? No, they're good boys. No, they wouldn't do anything like that. They're just writers, y'know, they like to look around. Yup, I'll be watching them."

Gomez swiveled back to me. "Don't ask a lot of questions, OK?"

"I always have the feeling some tribal people think we not only write about the mutilations, we also help to perpetrate them."

Gomez narrowed his eyes and rubbed his chin. "It's the nature of the business, but the Jicarilla Apache people are a lot less conservative than your northern pueblos. And a lot more cooperative too. Do you remember the big honcho from the Colorado FBI you saw at San Reymo? He's got jurisdiction over southern Colorado but he imagines Dulce and points south belong to him as well. After last night he's going to be on the defensive."

"So what was it that happened last night?" Etienne asked.

"Are you guys through looking at the funny papers in those files?"

I shrugged. "We barely started."

"Can I save you some trouble?" Gomez coughed into his fist, cleared his throat and said, "Paperwork such as you see in those files is worthless. I do it for the BIA, for government access in general and for my own department. But what happened last night throws a new light on what's happened in the past. Come on, let's get outta here and I'll tell you about it. You can come back and look at that junk anytime you want."

We went out to his green Scout and he removed a few boxes of paperwork which he called, "more junk." We climbed in and Gomez left his little gravelly precinct and headed upward into the hills.

"Here's the story," Gomez said over his shoulder while the Scout seemed to be driving itself. He had his right knee cocked up against the wheel and was hardly using his hands at all. He was a man who did most of his talking with his hands. Then, every once in a while, he'd make a mad grab for the wheel as we hit a bump or a dip. Then he'd pay attention to the road for another half second. He was so engrossed in his own story that I imagined he could have been a pretty good B-list writer.

"This old lady sees a UFO down in Taos. Less than ten minutes later, we see the thing up here. Sailed over us at two thousand feet. Dropped a beam on a herd of cows. I was four miles away from where it was hovering and drawing toward it as fast as I could when one of my men calls in and says he's right there where it came down."

Gomez returned to his predicament with the wheel and the rough road.

"What did it look like?" Etienne said, animated.

"Damn thing made no sound at all. Wasn't hardly visible until the flood light beamed down. Then it came real low, moving about ten miles an hour . . . a round thing with a great light beam popping out of its bottom. By the time I hit the cattle guard on the east end of the reservation the thing was about to take off. When I came around the side road by the gravel plant I saw red, white and green lights. The same as an airplane has, only more of them. It lay there between earth and sky, but kind of low, like a big trout trying to figure whether it wanted to swim up or down. Right then, as I came up near, the lights shut off, it went straight up and headed north-northwest, smooth and slow. Didn't move like   anything I've ever laid eyes on. No sound, no lights, no nothing. Just a darker spot in a dark sky."

"How come you didn't shoot at it?" Etienne asked.

"Didn't have time," Gomez said, "or I would have gotten off a few good sound shots."

"To what purpose?" Etienne asked.

Gomez ignored him. "Next thing I did was radio Farmington and Farmington relays my message to the FAA's air traffic control center in Longmont, Colorado. Same time I lost track of the thing, they pick it up on their radar screen traveling at three hundred miles per hour, twenty miles north of Albuquerque. Then it just vanishes."

***

We were nearing the open country around Stone Lake. The road came up over a ridge and veered to the right around the north end of the lake. Tribal pickups were parked at eighty degree angles to the shore. Some families were smoking fish and drinking coffee around small campfires. The lake was muddy close to shore, but farther out it was turquoise.

The road veered to the right again and we headed east to a bunch of cars parked under a dark stand of pines. Cop cars and government vehicles were there along with more tribal pickups.

The moment Gomez's Scout came to a stop several people came up. One of them, was a reporter from the *Espanola Sun*. Behind her, wearing a gray raincoat was a FBI man I recognized from San Reymo. Behind these two, a couple tribal policeman and a cameraman from KOB TV. Gomez slid out of the Scout, removed his hat, slicked back his hair with his palms and then grabbed his clipboard. I turned away from Gomez who was already into his spiel and noticed the small brown bull lying on its side. Its hind legs were spread out and its front ones were pulled forward. The animal looked like it had been running when the mutilation took place. Its face looked perfectly normal, tranquil, unmolested.

Yellow string tied to red stakes marked an area twenty feet in diameter. The men who stood within the lengths of tight laboratory string were comparing notes. I heard one say, ". . . eleven month old Charlais-Hereford bull with all the classic mutilation signs . . . incision at the rectum, looks like it was drawn with a compass and cut out with a scalpel, but the incision is so clean and self-annealed . . . take a look you'll see what I mean."

I was standing about as close as I thought they would let me with Etienne right at my side, both of us feeling privileged but yet wary of when we were going to get kicked out of the inner sanctum.

The bull's mouth was partly open, eyes glazed. The liftings were so neatly done it looked like the bull was born earless and tongueless. There was a v-shaped incision showing where the tongue had been. I was thinking that this was a case for the Humane Society, the SPCA, not these clever technicians with their open notebooks and plastic gloves.

I felt a tap on my shoulder. "Come over here and meet Mrs. Trujillo, Gomez said. Her story sure tops mine."

I wondered why he was being so nice to us. But, in truth, I knew. His kindness would be returned by my kindness when I wrote about him. That's what he was betting on. He was right, I had a soft spot for the guy. He was an actor, but that's what the camera likes. So does newsprint.

Gomez sort of pulled me by the elbow over to this old lady. "Mrs. Trujillo, I want you to meet a couple guys from the *New Mexico Review* in Santa Fe. OK if they ask a few more questions?"

Mrs. Trujillo looked worried. She had an old fashioned woolen coat buttoned up and collar high. "What is it you want? I've said everything I know and now I wish to go home."

"Mrs. Trujillo," Gomez said in a soothing voice, "We want to hear one more time what you saw last night. Once more, then you can go."

As he drew me closer to Mrs. Trujillo, he took his place on the other side of her and nodded to the KOB cameraman to get just the right focus. "Please continue, Mrs. Trujillo." Gomez smiled at the blank lens.

Mrs. Trujillo looked around apprehensively. Then she turned to me and said, "I had just gone to bed, as I told Officer Gomez, when my small room lit up bright orange. I thought maybe it was the neighbors throwing firecrackers like they do sometimes, but I hadn't heard any sound so it had to be something else. So I went to the window and opened it and now I could hear some crackling. The light out there was so bright I could see for some distance. At first I thought the neighbor's house was on fire so I went to the other window and then I saw this roundish thing about as big a two cars maybe bigger. By then I didn't see the orange any more the sky was dark gray. Altogether it stayed for about two minutes. When I saw it rising I rushed into the other bedroom and pulled the curtains and saw the thing go to the north. It disappeared in two seconds and all you could see was a reddish light where it had been. It was sort of like the light was streaming, the way a falling star looks and it happened so fast and I got real scared."

"Was there another sighting of the same craft?" the cameraman asked.

"Yes," Gomez confirmed. "The same craft we spotted here on the Rez was also seen hovering over a service station by a five-hundred gallon tank truck and pickup in Taos. There was some dust—we don't know yet what it is—sprinkled on top of the pickup's cab."

A man in a brown suit and string tie came up to Gomez with a microphone. Gomez, keeping his usual confident look came close to the mic. The TV reporter said, "You have just heard the eyewitness account of an actual UFO sighting in Taos. Now let's continue our probe by speaking again to Officer Gomez who has been following these bizarre mutilations longer than anyone else in the state of New Mexico. Officer Gomez, do you feel the Taos sighting is related to what happened here last night?"

Gomez gave a quick smile, then grew serious, "Right now the lab people believe the dust on the pickup has significant levels of potassium and magnesium. The same elements found on the hide of this mutilated bull. I think it's possible to find these elements in the soil, but they don't occur naturally in the air."

"Officer Gomez, do you think that perhaps this dust was sprinkled here for some unknown or possibly unnatural reason?"

Gomez grinned at the preposterous question. "Well, let's just say we think the cattle in this particular area, as well as that truck in Taos, may have been marked for some reason. Those elements don't show up except under ultraviolet light. Further, the potassium content on the hides of several of the cattle in this vicinity is seventy times above normal. How it got there, I don't know. And it's not my job to find out. That's up to Schoenfeld Laboratories at the moment."

"Officer Gomez, you've seen plenty of strange things up here in Apache country. What do you think of Mrs. Trujillo's story?"

"I have no comment, but I am curious about the yellow-colored, petroleum-based substance we found by this mutilated bull."

"What are the findings on that, Officer Gomez?"

"The results of that test aren't in yet, but I'd say *that* petroleum is like nothing we know at the present time."

"Then how do we know it's petroleum?"

"We don't. This game has plenty of questions and few if any answers . . . like the liver of this little bull. When we found it lying by the carcass, it was all white and mushy. Now the lab men say there's calcium, magnesium and phosphorus in it. There are also some unidentified burns on the animal's hind legs where the rectum was removed."

"Are these laser burns?"

Gomez sighed. "I have no idea. They have acid in them, but the fur wasn't singed or burned by anything heated. All I can say for sure is whoever's responsible for this mutilation has more money than our government's got."

"I know of no sophisticated muffling equipment that could hush the rotors of a helicopter." Burton was talking to a reporter from the *Rio Grande Sun*.

"Do you think the "helicopter", or whatever is, a classified government aircraft?"

"I don't know where you guys get this stuff. No helicopter I know of can fly hundreds of miles an hour. Nothing at the Kirtland Air Force Base fits the description. What's more, the thing soared over twelve-to-thirteen-thousand-foot peaks. Who knows how fast it was going at that time?"

"Can you explain," a man in jeans and a cowboy hat said, "why there was no log report at the FAA, even though you state your message was called in last night."

"I have no comment on that except that it is not common to log all the flights that come in."

"Are you presently using psychics to interpret certain data?" a woman asked.

"No comment."

"Our paper would like to know what your agency thinks of this picture." A man in a well-tailored suit held up a four by five inch print of the mutilated body of a cow. In the print a pillar of white mist was coming out of the incisions in the animal's stomach. The man holding the photograph had a *New York Times* identification tag.

"I am told," Burton said cautiously, "that these rather bizarre images turn up only in the developing tray. They are picked up by infrared film, not seen by the human eye. I have no idea what they represent, but to us they're unscientific."

"We want to know what they are!" someone shouted.

"So do I," said Burton.

A woman in her early thirties wearing a ski vest pushed her way to the center of the group. "Senator Salisbury is pressing for a major FBI investigation. We'd like to know exactly what efforts your agency has made, Mr. Burton, to track down mutilations in our state of Colorado."

Burton shook his head. "You really have it in for us, don't you? Doesn't matter if we're doing our job to the best of our ability as long as you've got a scapegoat."

"Can you tell the difference between pork and beef?" a familiar voice called out. When I turned to see who had spoken, Officer Gomez was staring at his highly polished trooper's boots.

"The majority of our efforts have produced no definitive results," Burton said, but we've maintained daily checks on flight schedules at Fort Carson, we've kept in close touch with the Department of the Interior, we've worked with Fish and Game people, wildlife research groups and undercover investigative teams. All in the hope of pulling something tangible out of nothing. Our findings in over twenty-three recent mutilation cases demonstrate that only nineteen postmortems were good enough to yield a reasonable patholog-ical exam. Roughly ten of those nineteen died a natural death: five were killed by predators and five died of unknown causes. Only four were considered willfully mutilated by a sharp instrument, which some say is predator-related. In other words, claws or teeth. So, we don't know, do we? We just don't know."

"When will you know?" someone asked.

Burton leveled his cold gray eyes at the man. He was not going to tell the press anything he didn't want them to know. Unlike the last time I'd seen him at San Reymo, he was no longer an investigator, he was a spokesman. Word had come down.

"As an investigator of mutilations in Colorado," he explained stiffly, "I've been unable to determine for a fact if a person was involved in the more than two hundred cases which were examined. Does that answer your ques-tion, sir? The bottom line is to go about your work in a sensible manner. If you want quicker results than I've been able to get, all I can say is good luck."

I watched him as he pushed his way to his car, dropped heavily into the driver's side, and chunked the door shut.

Gomez said to me, "There's the kind of man that made this country what it is today—a friggin mess. You know what he told me, that sonofabitch? He said that colt they found in Arapaho County was mutilated by juveniles. He told me that out of twenty mutilations in Wyoming, nineteen were classified as *probable death from natural cause*. He even went so far as to say that pred-ators were responsible for all of the recent mutilations in Oregon, Idaho and Nebraska. If that thing I saw last night was a predator then there ought to be one hell of a bounty on it." Gomez spat on the ground and strutted back to his Scout.

Etienne gave me a bemused look.

"So what did you find out?" I asked him.

He shrugged. "Everything." Then he smiled faintly, said, "All of it adding up to—nothing."

Chapter Twenty-Three

Etienne arranged for us to interview Dr Daniel Frey, one of the most interesting abductees in America. However, while for some reason his story was well known in Europe and Asia, it wasn't as well known in America. It felt good to be on the road. I was missing my family and my solitary runs in the Tesuque back country, but I hoped to be home in a few days.

I was growing tired of the mute thing.

But there was a part of me that believed that the mute affair was not going away any time soon. It was starting to feel "old" to me but then I remembered: "Out of the heart proceed evil thoughts, murders, adulteries, fornications, thefts, false witness, blasphemies . . ." So the Bible did say; and so most of humanity did believe.

***

We had just left the town of Duran, between Clines Corners and Carrizozo, New Mexico when we began seeing them, one after another, in various stages of decomposition. I was traveling with Etienne, and it was through him that we were to interview Dr. Daniel Frey who, while working as technical engineer at White Sands Proving Grounds had the singular experience of observing and then riding in a flying saucer. His comments on ufology and its relationship to mutes had not yet appeared in any major newspaper and I had no idea why except that Etienne told me he was a sworn recluse.

The first possible mutilation we saw was a deflated brown husk wizened in the sun, the projecting points of which were the lovely, curved horns. It lay on its side flat as can be. There were no unusual features on hide or head. After that one, others began cropping up: several deer with holes blown in their bellies, some crawling with maggots, some clean and untouched.

Then, farther down the road, dogs and more deer and a bunch of steers with their ribs (in Pueblo legend, they're called "windows of the fox") gleaming white clean in the noon light. Our destination for nightfall was Sierra Blanca, the mountain where the missing fighter planes had been tracked by radar before they vanished from the screen and from everywhere else.

That was just one incident which the Air Force simply called "missing aircraft". Military spokespersons stated publicly that the two planes had been on an air combat training mission out of Holloman Air Force Base near Alamogordo, New Mexico. Supposedly, the planes were modified to resemble Soviet MIG fighters. One was camouflaged and the other was silver and both had red stars on the tail.

After a thorough ground search combed the deep canyon and heavy underbrush foothills southeast of Carrizozo in an effort to recover the F-5 jets and their missing pilots, the recovery mission was suspended. At least twenty civilian aircraft flew twelve hours daily for eleven days along with Army aircraft from the National Range Operations Directorate that racked up 122 search hours.

They vanished into thin air, as the expression is, and this is especially applicable in New Mexico where the sky is limitless. Whether shimmery blue, deep cobalt or brilliant turquoise you are always looking up and feeling sort of dazed by the openness and color.

Nearing Carrizozo at dusk, dark clouds came up and capped the heavens for miles, but as we drove the copper light of the sun glinted on the horizon creating the illusion of a world illumined by an underground sun.

Tricks of light are common in the desert. Now, as the sun set fire to the cloud base, it made a circular tent of bright pink above. Objects on the ground isolated themselves so that each green *cholla* and each clump of sagebrush was solitary and the red earth shone all around.

"You know," I said to Etienne, "It's hard to believe that anything could get lost in this place but then there's so much of it to get lost in."

"Time is lost as well as missing persons," he replied. In one time-frame the fighter planes, those fake MIGs, have just taken off. In another time frame, they have not yet left the ground. To say they have disappeared is irrelevant and it doesn't explain anything. It's a mere convenience from my point of view."

"That sounds like Einstein," I said, chuckling.

"Well, yes, it does. He said, in effect, that things come and go in the time-space-continuum. Why? Because it's limitless. Even in the cattle mutilations, we see this thing happening. An animal disappears in one place, and reappears in another. Things are hardly ever completely lost and they frequently turn up again. Take the case of Travis Walton . . . or the missing calf that appeared a month after it was reported missing. Was Walton lost? Was the calf lost? The word *lost* is just the flip side of *found*."

"You think these Air Force cover-ups are another aspect of this?"

"Of course. Did you ever hear of the Lubbock Lights?"

"Yes. Project Blue Book, if I remember right."

"They were described by observers as a flying wing one and a half times the size of a B-36. Soft bluish lights. An employee of the Atomic Energy Commission at Sandia got a good look at it. This was in 1951. Just twenty minutes after the Albuquerque sighting four professors from Texas Tech in Lubbock saw the same lights pass overhead. The incident was kept pretty quiet . . . for a while. But it wasn't hushed up as cleverly as the Socorro sighting of 1964. That was the one where a policeman saw a space craft land in the desert. He swore that he saw two humanoids, as he put it, climb out of the craft wearing sort of white coveralls."

I actually remembered this story quite well. It still shows up in the UFO magazines. The significant thing was the official report. The Air Force and FBI agents assigned to the Socorro cover-up told the policeman not to mention two of things he saw and put in his report. These were a certain pyramid symbol on the craft and also the humanoid figures themselves. All of this was part of the mythos and backstory of ufology in general. Just about everybody knew it at this point. I asked Etienne, "You remember the story about the lab analysis of some of the rocks found near that landing?"

"Everyone in France knows it. So the way it goes there was some foreign matter on those rocks. Something not from our galaxy. A zinc-iron alloy, the report went, you know I just read it again the other day. The lab said there was a combination of elements presently unavailable to us at this time."

"Etienne, in this country all this stuff was quite common in the fifties, so much hoodoo you couldn't begin to see through it. Do you recall reading about the Farmington incident?"

"Of course I do. The whole town was bombarded by UFOs. Let's see, that was in March, 1950. Massive daylight flights of silver discs. Half the population of Farmington reported seeing them. But due to media coverage it made it seem like Jack Arnold's film, *It Came From Outer Space*. Few believed it . . . that is, outside of the actual observers who were puzzled but greatly disturbed by it. So I guess it's not surprising that these cattle investigations have taken more than eleven years to become official."

"You're definitely up on your research," I said. I think you know much more about it than I do."

***

We drove up Sierra Blanca in the dark, our way partially lit by a cloud-covered moon which, when it shone more or less directly on the mountain, made a huge slab of snow above us turn a bright bluey white. We pitched a two-man pup tent off the road below the snow-face and ate a couple of sandwiches in the dark.

The air was chill and the evening clean-smelling and full of moths that dive-bombed us, pelting the tent once we were inside it. Their bodies tapped the canvas musically and furiously. Once deep in my bag, I dropped into a sleep that was unbroken until just before dawn when my eyes opened and I had the memory, the weird aftertaste of a strange, frightening dream.

Etienne was awake, rolling up his sleeping bag when I told him about some of what I had dreamed.

In the dream, I was lying in the tent when fingers began to brush the canvas. Exploratory hands or perhaps paws. I awoke from the dream. Moonlight on poplin canvas. Shadows and moths. I lay there with my arms on the outside of my sleeping bag.

Gently my hands were intercepted. I felt them being raised and then licked. Not as an animal would do it. The tongue was short and quick. It sort of flickered across my skin like a beam of light, if light had weight or could softly pressure a hand.

The licking continued.

It went moistly from hands to abdomen and from abdomen to genitalia.

In the morning I felt wet. A little sticky. The way you feel when you camp out and there is a heavy dew on the ground.

When I smelled my fingers, they smelled of the sea.

Why didn't I wake Etienne?

In truth, I thought it was Etienne. But I couldn't tell him that. Nor could I admit to myself that this was so.

But perhaps it wasn't so.

Perhaps it was all a dream.

Sometimes fear locks you up and throws away the key. I had felt myself frozen the night the skinwalker had come into our house.

This was another of those times when reality is immeasurable.

When things are not as they seem.

A shiver went through me because, wakeful, I couldn't say what I had dreamed and what had really happened.

Was I still dreaming . . . ?

***

The first thing Etienne said to me while we were eating our breakfast of granola and apples was this: "We were approached last night."

"What do you mean approached?"

"It was outside the tent. But only at first. I didn't fall asleep for quite some time. It, whatever it was, was all around us. Then I felt it looking very closely at us. Inspecting us, physically. But I had no power to stop it. His voice trailed off. He crunched his granola for a while and looking through a lapse in the trees where we could see all the way down to the white desert of Alamogordo.

"It went away at 4:00 AM."

163

"You heard footsteps?"

"I heard it breathing. I felt hot breath on my face. At first I thought it was you." He sighed, looked at the ground, shook his head. I don't think it meant to hurt us and whatever it was, it went away. It was no terrestrial animal or human."

"What then?"

"Did you feel something licking your hands?" Etienne asked.

I said, "Yes, I think I did. But I can't be sure."

We both sat in silence for a while after this.

I thought about the absurdity of it.

At ten thousand feet on Sierra Blanca two men were examined in their sleep by an extraterrestrial.

Etienne seemed to read my thoughts, for he said suddenly "Can you accept that, my friend?"

I said nothing.

"Look," he said, "I'm wet with . . . saliva."

"It smells like . . . " But I did not finish.

"Semen."

"Did you masturbate last night?" I asked.

There was an embarrassed silence between us for a long moment.

"Will you believe me if I tell that someone, I mean, some thing did that to me without my being able to stop it. It happened so fast, it was over before I knew it."

"Was there an orgasm?" I asked.

He gave me a wry smile. "I hardly felt it coming."

We both laughed at his choice of words and that seemed to dispel the tension for just a little while. Then Etienne spoke again. "What if we both agree to say that it was an animal. A bear. We were both sleeping and —"

"— I felt something, well, *indescribable*. So it happened to me, too."

"We left the tent flap open," he said, "and got rained on."

***

As we drove away from our camp in silence, I felt our separate but similar quietness was so forced you could feel the wall building between us, an effort for either of us. Bizarre things were running rampant in my brain. Some things are so dense you leave them until you can take them apart and put them back together again. But there was a way to comprehend what had happened to us unless it was a kind of dual and mutual hypnosis. Or a dream of that supernatural kind. My mind jumped back to the face at the window in Tesuque. Could a Navajo wolf do the thing that happened last night? The answer was yes, I had read and heard of many molestations by skinwalkers, who were as sexual as they were effectual in their manner of killing and disappearing.

***

After a second breakfast in the town of Ruidoso, we tried to climb back into our natural selves. The harmony of sunlight on the running backs and tails of pinto ponies on the Mescalero Reservation which borders part of the highway on the trip to White Sands was like a healing salve on our minds.

Slowly, delicately, we got easy with each other again. We laughed and made jokes about a Sierra Blanca skinwalker who gave mystical blowjobs. But the joking didn't rest easy with me. The sensation of having my hands in the soft wet mouth of a creature was as weird to me as the feeling of having been abused below the belt. But abused was the wrong word. There was probably no word for what this was. As close as I could get to it was my readings in Tantric sex where nothing happens, nothing is done, but something is felt and transcendence is given through the act of sharing one's physical and spiritual self. Is this what happened at ten thousand feet on Sierra Blanca?

Chapter Twenty-Four

Coming down out of the ponderosa meadows of Ruidoso and the lower desert, you saw immediately the long white scar, trembling in the sun: White Sands.

It sat like a scarf of snow under the blue of the Organ Mountains, a long way off. The next town down from Ruidoso was Tularosa, a patch of green with irrigation scents and secure lawns, and I remembered Billy the Kid hung out there, and how grubby the little town must have been then, not being much better off now. And finally, Alamogordo, a town made possible by Air Force personnel.

Dr. Daniel Frey was at the west end of town in a common grey tract house.

When we arrived it was past ten o'clock in the morning and the sun was already hammering on the rooftops. A rather tired, but bright-eyed man in his mid-sixties met us at the door, introduced himself as Dr. Frey, and took us into the living room, where his wife offered coffee and some comfortable chairs.

Dr. Frey had a care-worn face, a hounded look in the shadows of his eyes, and I noticed that he punctuated his speech with short breaths, as if he were in need of air even at this low altitude.

At first, he was not particularly open or receptive to our visit, he seemed somewhat wary of us.

Etienne explained that we were interviewing people who had clues to the cattle mutilations. We had chosen him, Etienne said, because of his well-pub-licized experience in a saucer. Were the two events, saucers and mutilations, related, what was his opinion?

"I will tell you something," he began irritably, "and you may or may not believe me. I have not bothered to follow the cattle mutilations in the papers or anywhere else. The reason is simply this: it's perfectly obvious that extra-terrestrials, as they're being called nowadays, have as much interest in us as we have in them."

Dr. Frey's wife, a thin white-haired woman with a disappointed face, entered the room and said, "Don't you think they have as much right to look at us as we have to look at them? Our friends in space are medical technicians as well as scientists, travelers, and what have you . . . . sugar or cream? Let me warm your cup for you . . ."

"Dr. Frey," Etienne asked, "what do you think of *etheric beings*? Since no one ever witnesses cattle mutilations, do you think there's a possibility, that some are being done by beings that we could not *see* even if we wanted to?"

Dr. Frey touched the fingertips of both hands together, giving the impression that he was preparing to do a magic trick.

"I used to answer that question by flashing a silver dollar—that was when I was on lecture circuits—and I'd say—to my audience—this looks pretty solid, but to a scientist, it isn't. And that's because only one million-millionth part of the average atom is occupied by nuclear particles, the rest is occupied by space.

"What I was getting at in my lectures was that almost any nuclear arrangement other than what we perceive as normal could seem rather improbable. And, yes, I believe in etheric beings, but I also believe in beings made of lead, to whom we earthlings must seem so etheric as to be almost invisible."

"What is the possibility," I asked, "that some mutilations are the work of beings that are, in some sense, malign? I know that sounds a trifle Hollywood, but . . ."

"Listen, good and evil are the most relative terms we have in our language. We define good as what is *good* for us. Don't you think there are those who would differ with us up there?" He gestured upward. "It could be very good for the—who's to say—to remove the heart of a cow and carry it a million miles away."

"Would you agree that we may have enemies in outer space?" Etienne questioned.

"An enemy," said Dr. Frey," "is someone, or some thing, who wants something you have. Conversely, an enemy can be someone, or some thing, who has something you want. Does that answer the question?"

"But if they are more advanced than we are, what could they possibly want that we have?" Etienne asked.

"Maybe they want nothing more than a legal landing field," Dr. Frey said.

"Did you know that it's a legal impossibility to visit earth from space? You couldn't legally answer a radio message if one was received, because if you do, you're communicating with an unlicensed vehicle. Extraterrestrials are what we really mean by illegal aliens. Without a birth certificate, a health certificate and God knows what else, they couldn't save us from our own inherent self-destruction."

"Would you mind telling us what happened to you the night of July 4, when you were abducted?" Etienne asked.

"You sound like an attorney. Why don't you read my book for that information?"

"I have read your book, but I want to know why you didn't run away when the craft approached. That's the one thing I don't understand. It would be perfectly normal to get away from there."

"If there's one thing Dr. Frey isn't, it's normal," his wife said. "It should be obvious to you fellows that Dr. Frey is one of the most brilliant intelligences we have in our society. For that reason, he was *chosen*."

"That's all right, dear," Dr. Frey said. "I can come to my own defense, if I need to. So, to answer your question, I have to ask one of my own. Why did a group of my men leave the Proving Grounds to witness a fireworks display in Las Cruces? Here were men who spent every day of their lives playing around with rocket nozzles. You'd think they would have been sick of rocketry. Well, in fact, they weren't.

"Watching a fireworks display was just as interesting as anything else they did but the men needed a break. They could watch rockets explode all night and not worry about whether anyone was going to get hurt. Now, Aerojet, the company I worked for, provided a sort of limo to take us into town, but there wasn't room in the car for me without crowding, so I offered to take the bus. The dispatcher told me that the bus left for Cruces at 7:30, so I went back to my room to read a book. At about 7:30, I showed up at the motor pool and discovered that the dispatcher had been wrong about the departure time and the bus had already left. So there I was stuck at White Sands on one of the hottest nights of the year. I went back to my room. Those wooden barracks houses were burning hot, but with the air-conditioning on it was somewhat bearable and I settled back down to read my book again. Then the air-conditioning shut down and I knew I couldn't fix it because it was up there on the roof, and there was no sense in being trapped inside in that heat, it was cooler outdoors, so I decided to take a little walk out in the desert.

"I was walking toward our test stand about a mile from the base when I spotted a dirt road I'd never been on before, so I took it. It was 9:00 or thereabouts, sun was down, sky still fairly light—when I saw a star blink out, then another to the right of it, and two more below it, and while I wondered about those dark stars, maybe twenty or so seconds passed. I saw that the area of eclipse remained constant, the original star did not come into view. Then I saw something descending at an angle of about forty-five degrees. I described it later as an *oblate spheroid*, but at the time, the only thought that registered with me was that its bearing was constant. It came within twenty feet of where I was standing, and touched the ground at zero velocity, settled itself on a clump of stout brush that crackled. The object was twenty feet in diameter and about sixteen feet in height."

"Weren't you scared?" Etienne said.

"I have been asked that question," Dr. Frey said with a sigh, "thousands of times. *Of course*, I was scared. But like a cat that has the forethought not to run before the approach of a dog, I decided to stay put. An even greater deterrent—and this puzzled me until it was explained to me later on—was the vision I kept having of all the men back at the base laughing at me." He chuckled at this and it was the first time I saw *him* sort of laugh.

"What did the surface of the object look like?" I asked.

"Silver. It hadn't the hard-bright finish of nickel or chromium but what it most resembled was platinum, impervious to corrosion. Naturally, my next impulse was to touch it with my hand, curiosity being as strong an impulse as fear. And I suppose it was curiosity that got our ancestors down out of the coconut palms where they were hanging by their tails. So there it is . . . anyway at that point my logical mind was at work. I was thinking—if the craft had approached earth from the sunlit side of the planet, its surface ought to be warm. On the other hand, if it had come from the shadow side, it would have been cool. But when I stepped up and touched it, the surface was frictionless, as if there had been ten thousand infinitesimal ball bearings between my fingers and the metal. The oil on your skin will provide drag on even the smoothest of glass, so this was unbelievable. Then I heard a sharp voice crackle out: 'Do not touch the hull. It is still hot.'"

"When I read that in your book, I was surprised. Forgive me, but it doesn't sound real," I said.

Dr. Frey smiled a little crookedly. "It was fake as a four dollar bill. Why? Well, it was explained to me later on, and I'll tell you in a little while. You know, the rest of the story has been told and re-told and it's quite boring to me now, but as you know if you read the book, I took a ride in that saucer and it went from here to New York City and back in no time at all. The inside of the craft was bare, almost ascetic in appearance, and there was no pilot. Later on, I learned that it was remote controlled and the voice I was hearing was beaming down from a mother ship somewhere off in space."

Etienne said, "The voice, then, was telepathic?"

"For lack of a better word . . . actually, the way the pilot spoke to me was through a direct modulation of the auditory nerve, without a sound current and so the effect on the brain was the same, but there was no interlude in the air, no sound waves at all."

"Was it also possible that the pilot had been tampering with your thoughts prior to the flight?" Etienne asked.

"I don't consider psychic contact of extraterrestrial beings *tampering*. How else are they to communicate with us? This is their only legal means. If you want to get technical about it: there is a pact within the Galactic Confederation which forbids outright mind control. This is a kind of Monroe Doctrine of the cosmos."

Dr. Frey shifted his position on the sofa and took a sip of his coffee, which, by his expression, had grown cold. He did not seem to care, and drank it anyway. In a certain way I felt he lived outside of his physical senses, or strictly within his own mind rather, and this was why he'd appeared insensitive to me at first. But now he continued, rattling the cold cup of coffee back into its saucer and licking his lips. He stared vacantly out the window at the sun glare.

"Let's see, where was I? Oh, I was also to learn from the pilot of that little remote controlled craft that his name was Al-lan, and that he had broken this pact in order to set me up, as it were, for the flight. He had arranged things to his advantage. For instance, when I considered running back to the base when I first saw the craft, it was Al-lan that dissuaded me. He showed me what would have happened: the derision of my staff. Oh, there had been many UFO sightings at White Sands, but none like this, none of this magnitude. So I guess he prevented me from making a fool of myself, while keeping me there so I could ride in that saucer. As I later learned, he also arranged for the dispatcher to say 7:30 instead of 7:00."

"Was the failure of the AC also pre-arranged?" I asked.

"Probably not. That happened all the time. But he did make me want to take a walk on that deserted road. I felt quite a compulsion to walk on it by myself, even though it was terribly hot out."

"And you don't consider any of this tampering with your mind?" Etienne wanted to know.

"Not when I learned what Al-lan was trying to accomplish on this planet," he said. "Al-lan explained to me on that first flight, and on subsequent contacts, that he was an emissary whose orders were to ensure the continuance of this planet. After the discovery of the atomic bomb, there was considerable doubt in the minds of many extraterrestrials whether we'd go the distance. So when people ask me if Al-lan was successful in his mission, I always refer them to the obvious truth. We're still here."

"Did you ever actually meet Al-lan," Etienne asked, "I mean, physically?"

"You mean was I ever in the sphere of his physical presence being? The answer is yes. I once flew on a TWA flight with him, we went from Medford, Oregon to Sacramento, California. After the so-called White Sands Incident, Al-lan enlisted my assistance in various ways, such as providing him with a bank account, birth certificate, immunization documentation and other necessary things. And he scolded me for not making his message clear to all Earth People but now I'm getting ahead of myself, that came much later. At first, he wanted secrecy. His purpose demanded that he pass as one of us. His greatest test, this creature with powers far beyond ours, was to settle in amongst us and look so much like us that you'd walk by him at the mall and never know it."

"How long did it take Al-lan to prepare for this naturalization process?" I said.

"About four of our earth years. And then around three weeks with me up in Oregon on his second visit. Four years had elapsed from the time I rode to New York and back in the little craft. I hadn't told a soul about it, hadn't even thought of writing my book. I was up near Medford, Oregon, where we have a small cabin on eighty acres. You drive three-miles on a deserted road to get to it, an isolated place, but that's why we like it. Anyway, I'd gone into town to get some supplies and coming back on a three-mile road, I rounded a turn and there it was, a small saucer, like the one I'd ridden on. It was dusk. And there standing by a barn was a man I'd never seen before. He was just standing there, a stranger."

We waited for him to go on. He breathed deeply, exhaled. He looked tired and I thought maybe he was unwilling to continue the interview. But he went on without pause.

"I knew it was Al-lan the moment I saw him. The rest is rather comic. I taught him how to drive, which was damned hard for him to do, because whenever he came to a stop sign or cross-traffic, I had to shout to get him to stop. His inclination was to increase acceleration and go right over any obstacle in his path. He had a hard time accepting vehicle limitations. The notion of braking seemed quite laughable to him."

"You spent three weeks teaching him to drive a car?" Etienne questioned with a small chuckle.

"Mostly I got him acquainted with things he'd already studied, tidying up his grammar, so to say. But, as I say, the driving thing was difficult and teaching him how to do a job interview was even harder."

"Where did he find work?"

"He managed to get hired as an import-export entrepreneur. And that position afforded him time to trouble-shoot for the betterment of humankind. He was based in the Middle East."

"Where exactly?" I asked.

"Egypt, Iran and Israel, primarily."

"Do you think he was successful in his mission?" Etienne queried.

Dr. Frey frowned and looked at Etienne as if he were crazy. "If he hadn't been we'd be an incandescent gas floating around the atmosphere."

"May we assume that Al-lan's powers of thought transference, though breaking cosmic laws, were used solely for our benefit?" Etienne said.

"Correct."

I could see that Dr. Frey was tiring of our inquiries, but I had to ask a few more questions. "What were his methods?"

He closed his eyes and rubbed them softly with his fingers.

"Well," he said, "Al-lan could put a picture in someone's brain. And this picture would stay there, fixed in place, until that person let go of any destructive mental energies."

Etienne pressed on. "Just a few more questions Dr. Frey "What kinds of images . . . can you tell us exactly?"

"Once he made one of our world leaders hear the wail of two billion people burning. He told me that. Needless to say, Al-lan prevented the Apocalypse."

"Is Al-lan still with us?" I said.

He shook his head. "Al-lan was greatly disappointed with his work on our planet. He did not accomplish what he set out to do. He explained to me that Earth People were completely unwilling to embrace the concept of world peace."

"That isn't to say he has gone from our lives," Mrs. Frey said. "He happens to be with us right now."

I looked at her in surprise. Etienne and I had almost forgotten she was there. She paused, then went on. "Al-lan will not leave as long as you are here, dear."

Dr. Frey shook his head. "Hot out there, isn't it? A lot hotter than it needs to be. Al-lan's working on that, too."

***

White Sands: two hundred and thirty square miles of gypsum sand. Standing in the white immensity of concave shapes, you feel like the lone survivor of a dead star.

After leaving the home of Dr. Frey, I drove on to White Sands and we wandered around for almost four hours. Then we sat on a high white crest, listening to the dry buzz of wind and the infinite number of moving crystals. Before our eyes were mile upon mile of skunk bush, yucca, rabbit brush, saltbush, and cottonwood.

I wondered, sitting there with the wind in my ears, how many Al-lans had set up camp in the womanly curves of the dunes. I saw the pink stains on the carcasses of mutilated cattle; and the Carrizozo plains gone in a pink cloud at sunset; the pink of the Sangre de Cristos, Blood of Christ Mountains; and Christ's imitators, the Penitentes, cactus-whipped and bleeding.

The shape of a dune and the shape of a saucer are similar—the little sickle dunes, called *barchans,* look exactly the same. When the wind blows, it moves the sand along the edges of the sickle dune faster than the sand in the center. This molds the sickle and drives it in lines sixty miles long. Barchans can maneuver over anything, including high plateaus.

I thought of the barchan-like crafts seen over the Tularosa Basin, as Dr. Frey had said, moving as light upon the air, as natural as the soundless, frictionless sprawl of barchans.

The endless fascination with light and dark: on one side of the Sands lives a white mouse, and where the white gypsum ends and the crystals are black, there's a black mouse. If the black one ever strays to the white sand, it is plucked by a hawk. This plucking is the natural order. In the opinion of the mouse, if such there be, the hawk is evil; but in the mind of the hawk, the mouse is merely there to be taken.

Chapter Twenty-Five

At dusk, we drove deep into the Mescalero Reservation to a place, high in the pines, that Etienne identified as just like the spot where Travis Walton was taken. A forestry crew had recently logged the area, and their leaving were everywhere, so we made a fine pine-bough bed to go under our pup tent.

The last light lay in the basin at ten o'clock, and we could still see the surface of White Sands more than sixty miles down in the desert. We rested on the hood of the car and sipped black coffee. The stars spilled all the way into the ponderosas and firs. The wind was no longer the warm savory breeze of the desert, but a high mountain wind with a cutting edge.

"I have had the feeling since I was a child," Etienne said, "that I would one day be taken."

"I wonder how Mina and your little girl would react to such a thought. Have you ever told them?"

"Tiemi, no. Mina, yes. She has accepted it. Once, when I was a boy living in France, my best friend had a disturbing dream and he looked out his window. Down in the cow pasture was a flying saucer. At one of the openings at its side, he was astonished to see me waving at him. Ever since then I have been in touch with contactees all over the world. I know as surely as I sit here with you, looking up at the stars, that one day I will be taken."

"Why do you use that word, *taken?*"

"Maybe because English is not my first language. Look there! Did you see it?"

I saw a blue star wobble across the sky. It appeared very un-star-like.

"Maybe we will be taken together," Etienne said. This was followed by his odd, little elfin laugh.

"I'm not ready to go."

"Then probably they will not take you. Let me tell you something: I have this ability to see something in the sky just before anyone else. I don't know why, but it is true. I can also sense danger, as you know."

I was staring into the sky in the perverse hope of spotting a moving light in advance of Etienne. Suddenly I saw something. A slow steady arc, like a falling star in slow motion.

"A satellite," he said.

We spent another hour stargazing and then we both admitted how tired we were and went into the tent we had pitched earlier. The only light was the face of my watch. I glanced at it. "I hope . . ."

But I never got to finish. As always he beat me to it.

"Let's both hope . . ."

There was no reason to think the same thing could happen twice, but there was also no reason to think it couldn't.

At any rate, exhaustion transcends fear in most cases, and the long day, the heat, the traveling on winding roads into dark forest ended with yawns, and finally, heavily-lidded sleep.

However, at precisely 3:26 AM I suddenly awoke and heard Etienne breathing inside the tent, but also outside the tent. Intermittent, unison, deep drawn breaths with intervals between. The sound outside did not seem like an animal, it didn't have the resonance of a bear or an elk, or even a coyote. It was Etienne—as unmistakably him as the way he talked. Convinced that I was not imagining things, I stilled my heartbeat, lay back and listened. Half the night passed as the stars wheeled overhead in their endless revolutions. Etienne never woke, never moved, and the echoing sound of his breathing, inside and out, continued. I decided that I wasn't crazy for hearing two Etiennes. It was yet another of those things you can't explain.

First light finally came, and Etienne woke up. I told him what had happened. "What you heard was natural. One night Mina moved a foldaway bed into the living room because I had been kicking her in my sleep. She awoke to see me standing off the floor, not touching the carpet. She could also hear me breathing in the bedroom. So I was in two places at the same time. She was frightened and got out of bed to embrace the me that was floating off the floor. She realized she was holding an armful of nothing. I wasn't there, but a phantom form of me *was* there. An incorporeal me."

I asked him—"What about yesterday night—was that you doing that thing?"

"No, that was somebody else."

***

Sunday night. After the three-hundred-mile drive back to Santa Fe, a thought came into my mind. I tried to run it out of my head by jogging up the arroyo but the thought would not go away.

Monday morning. Bright and early, as I shaved for work, the thought came and settled in. It did not come and go as do other thoughts that haunt, nag or nettle. Other thoughts went by it and could not distract it.

At the office. There were clippings about retired FBI man Len Kreuger and his mute investigation. He seemed to have come through with some new evidence.

"Well, dear," Marsha said, while leaning against the doorway of my office, "you'll go on to bigger and better things. Looks like Kreuger's got it all figured out." She ran to get the phone.

I had one of those tension headaches that begins around the base of the skull and works its way upward, less an incipient headache than a vague and unreasonable apprehension.

Marsha came back. She was wearing a pretty gold amulet on a pretty gold chain around her neck. She was about forty but she didn't look all of thirty.

She had a warm Oklahoma accent and the only thing about her I didn't like was that she was always right. Still, I liked to talk to her.

"Have you ever had a thought that wouldn't leave you alone? That just bore into your brain?"

"Sure, everyone's had that happen."

"How do you shut it off?"

"You don't. You learn to live with it."

She turned away and rushed to the phone again.

I heard Durwood criticizing Thomas, the VP adman, for his general lack of refinement.

177

Thomas walked by my office, glanced at me, rolled his eyes, as if to say trouble's on its way.

Enter Durwood.

"What are you staring at the ceiling for?"

Durwood was nearly fifty but like Marsha he didn't show his age. Not even a little bit. He could, in fact, be any age. He took pride in this and glowed when anyone noticed it. We liked to make a joke about how he had a painting in his attic. A literary reference to Dorian Gray, the immortal man who showed no signs of change while his portrait, hidden in the attic, revealed advancing age.

Durwood, unlike Marsha, liked to come in very close. In fact he stood so close to me that his belt actually brushed against my ear.

"You've obviously heard the news. The question is, what are you going to do about it? I hope you got some good blood and gore down south. Did you?"

"I heard some things I'd like to forget."

"That gives me chill bumps," Durwood said, sarcastically.

I shook my head. "I'm sorting through it now, Durwood."

Then he gave me a directive. "Interview Kreuger."

And Durwood disappeared into his own office, where I heard him whistling. That famous tuneless shrill whistle you sometimes hear in supermarkets when nervous and irritating people are shopping.

Thomas stuck his head in my doorway. "Any jokes today?" he whispered.

I yawned. My head ached.

"Am I keeping you up?" Thomas asked.

I liked Thomas well enough, but his grand diamond ring sparkling in my eye was as annoying as Durwood's whistle.

Thomas faded.

I got up from my desk, walked down the narrow aisle past the production room to the back end of the shipping room and out to the loading entrance. Then I kept walking, following the sun toward the Plaza.

Leaving the building was a good thing. I sat on an empty bench and looked toward the Palace of the Governors. The native people were laying out their black bowls of incised pottery and their bright silver and turquoise jewelry. The warm sun was topping the tall branches of the cottonwoods. I watched the slow moving women setting up their blankets and wares for the day. This ritual of theirs seemed to be helping my headache to go away. Little by little, it was fading.

I knew one thing that was bothering me. I had seen an Appaloosa horse in Tularosa and it reminded me of the horse named Skippy. That was the one that had been mutilated recently, its flesh surgically carved from its head and upper body. This frightful image was accompanied by the sound of flesh being ripped from that beautiful, sinewy equine creature. The sound of the hide being shorn from the body, the auditory horror of it kept creeping through my head. I'd expunge it and it would come back. The sound and the sight. I remembered what Etienne said. "Be watchful of your thoughts, for it is as Jesus said, . . .*out of the heart of man come evil thoughts*. . ."

For eighteen hours the vision of Skippy and the sound of sheared flesh tore through my mind. I'd become a helpless captive of this moonlit horror. Over and again, I saw the dappled skin ripped from the muscled sinews of the Appaloosa mare. And then I'd see the horse, still standing, dead in the starlight, and the girl crying. It had happened. It was real. It was my worst nightmare. Literally, a *night mare*.

Had I fallen into the mind trap that Dr. Frey mentioned? Had this possibly been initiated by Dr. Frey himself? I could hear his level, unchanging monotone, which was both reassuring and troubling. His uncommon thoughts emptying into the dry banal, suburban home. Each phrase punctuated by a soft inhalation.

My weary mind also dragged me back to the tent and the double breaths of Etienne. I saw the shadow of the skinwalker. I felt his wet warm tongue all over my hands and body.

I was turning into a mental mute case myself.

That night I told Laura I was going to quit *The Review*.

She didn't try to talk me out of it.

Chapter Twenty-Six

Durwood sat at his big L-shaped desk, grinning as if he'd won the lottery when I gave him the news of my leaving. Smiling, he handed me a check. "This is for leave time," he said, passing the piece of blue paper in my direction. I could see it coming from a long way away.

My hand reached for the check, but I was reluctant to take it, especially since I had prepared a sweet little going away speech, and now I knew I would not have an opportunity to use the words I had rehearsed.

"Let me tell you a story about a friend of mine," Durwood said. "Maybe you've heard me mention the name, Pamela Gibbs, well, she has a big black cat that likes to hunt, and not long ago, this cat brought home a fat horned toad and dropped it in her bathtub. Pamela had never seen one close at hand, so she studied it carefully and the cat studied her at the same time, and then something clicked in that cat's brain. The cat disappeared and when it returned, there was another horned toad in the tub. And then another and another until Pamela was up to her ears in horned toads."

"I'm afraid I don't get the connection."

"That's because it's perfectly clear."

He picked up a sheaf of papers on his desk. I recognized the double spaced wide margins with inked corrections in my own handwriting. My reports.

"What we have here is a pile of horned toads," Durwood said. "Now, what you need to do is go off somewhere like Pamela Gibbs' cat when she told it to give it up and give it a rest. She told it that if an ugly old horned toad came around, the cat should look the other way. I'll expect to see you the beginning of next week. Meanwhile we're going to run more of your series. I think we may win one of those awards over there."

He nodded in the direction of a plaque from the New Mexico Press Association for reportorial excellence.

As I walked out the door of his office, he was typing one hundred words a minute editing my words faster than I had written them.

***

A week in the woods was what I needed. And then, if I was back harvesting horned toads, it might be different.

At home, I mixed a shandy: more beer than lemonade, and threw some things in my backpack. I didn't have much of a plan. I just pulled on my well-worn Dunham boots, and sipped my shandy.

There were plenty of possibilities: Lake Catherine on the other side of the ski basin, Horse Thief Canyon in the Pecos, maybe the Hot Springs over at Jemez.

I packed absent-mindedly in the upstairs bedroom, looking out the concave adobe window at the morning light on the piñons, the wind moving the needled branches ever so slightly.

It was a warm wind, and I knew the camping would be good. Getting away would be good, not having to think.

Laura, came up the hill in the Jeep truck and I saw brown supermarket bags lined up in the bed. The truck stopped, the engine shuddered, and the wheels lurched forward in the dust, as she put it in gear and let off the clutch.

I don't know why, but I broke into a cold sweat. Laura was outside the truck with two grocery bags in her arms. She was stepping in front of the left headlight when I yelled—"Don't!" Then I ran downstairs and went outside.

"What's the matter?" she asked.

"Is the truck okay?"

"Of course it is," she said. "Why wouldn't it be?"

"I feel like I'm going crazy."

She stood there, smiling. "Can I come inside now?"

The truck engine sprang to life, roared.

The back tires churned.

The driverless truck jumped forward.

Laura turned, lost her balance, fell away from the truck. In doing so, she threw the bag of groceries and the contents went everywhere. The truck crunched into a wheelbarrow that was leaning against the kitchen window.

The wheelbarrow hooked into the front differential and brought the truck to an immediate stop.

Laura sat in the dust and started to cry. Oddly enough, she had a bunch of celery in her right hand—and a torn piece of the brown paper bag. Soup cans lay all around her. I got down on my knees and we hugged hard and long.

After a while she stopped crying. Our lanky hound dog, Sally, sidled over and licked Laura's face in her usual sloppy way.

One of our cats, Moonie, came over, delicately stepping in between the Campbell's soup cans.

Laura was laughing with her arms slung around my neck. We were still hugging when cousin Peter, who lived down the hill, drove up the driveway. He stared at the mess of animals and groceries and the Jeep that had magically merged with the wheelbarrow.

Peter got out of his old GMC truck, moving slow and easy. He lifted the hood of the Jeep and looked at the engine. He didn't say anything. Then, "What happened?" he said, chuckling. "Dust devil? What else would do this?" He furrowed his big blonde eyebrows, glanced at us. "Anybody want to tell me what happened?"

"We don't really know," Laura said. "The Jeep started up after I'd pulled the key from the ignition and walked in front of it. I barely had gotten out of the way when it crashed into the wheelbarrow—"

"More voodoo," Peter said under his breath. "I wish you guys would stop doing that stuff." He laughed.

Then he turned and poked his head under the hood again. "Looks like the starter wire got loose, touched against something hot, which caused a short in the electrical system, which caused the engine to turn over, which caused the pistons to jump, which caused the wheels to turn, and you know the rest."

"The engine started up like someone turned it on," Laura insisted, "and from the moment it started, it acted like there was a driver behind the wheel."

"Another inch," I added, "and the truck would've taken out a chunk of our house."

Peter said, "Bad truck," as if he were talking to a dog.

"Hey, Pete," I said. "I heard her pull the emergency brake. You know the sound it makes."

"Emergency failed," he said.

"You don't believe in the supernatural do you, Pete?" Laura said.

"Not if I can help it."

Chapter Twenty-Seven

My old friend Adam Pereign who had a cabin in the mountains north of Santa Fe came to my rescue. We got together at El Nido down in Tesuque village, and Adam offered to take me up there since he was planning a fishing trip anyway.

"It'll be great to have your company," he said.

I liked Adam. He knew how to be quiet. He'd grown up on San Juan Pueblo. He was an old believer who knew how to be by himself and when he was with others he was there only if you wanted him to be. Otherwise he was somewhere else. The following day we left in his van.

***

We had driven up the washboard road in the early evening, coming to a stop whenever a creek crossed the road. Then we crept over the stream bed. It was almost summer and the heavy snows of the past winter were melting and filling the creeks and dry arroyos with ice cold mountain runoff. We found Adam's one room cabin as he had left it in the fall with an added scattering of mouse droppings and the evidence of an overnight guest, probably a local hunter passing through.

"Someone always comes by here in the winter and spends a night or two," Adam said. "I like to imagine it's the same guy. A friend I've never met. Thing is, he leaves the place like he found it, and there's always the same size lump left in the bed."

I went outside while Adam unpacked our things, and took a look around. The cabin was set in a small clearing with a hill behind it. Above the hill was a stand of pines and the remains of those that had been badly burned by a fire, some years earlier.

Below the cabin was a steep incline that dropped down to the creek. Directly over the fast-moving water, someone before Adam's time had built a well-framed outhouse that was connected at either end by two pine trees so it couldn't pitch into the creek. You could sit, flanked by those big pines, and thumb through the parchment-like pages of a 1936 Sears Catalogue.

The sun had gone and that first cold pinch of high country air came down out of the mountains and brought with it the clear hoots of a small owl. Adam was making corn beef hash on the Coleman stove by the light of a kerosene lamp when I came back inside.

"How does it feel to get your feet on the ground?" Adam asked.

"Pretty good."

Adam Pereign was one of my oldest friends. We had known each other long before we formally met, and even after that we often kidded each other about being long lost brothers. He was a dark-faced, fastidious cabinetmaker who could do most anything he chose to do. But mainly he was fun to be around because he had a gift for making as much, or as little, of the moment as was necessary. When he worked with wood there were no unnecessary movements. The same was true with the way he reasoned. No excess.

"It feels good not to have anything to think about," I told him.

"Then have some Wild Turkey," he said.

"That's something I don't have to think about."

We passed the bottle between us a couple of times before we ate the steaming rust-colored hash with scrambled eggs and chili. We also had beer from the cooler, and afterwards, hot coffee.

Then more Wild Turkey and a tight packed joint from Mexico. It was good weed and the silence made it better.

In a while the field in front of the cabin turned moon white and the air coming from the creek was cool and moist with the odor of moss and dead leaves. I took a long draw on the joint and afterwards felt very warm and well fed and a bit talkative. "It's been a long time since I got away like this. Not going somewhere on assignment, but just for the hell of it . . . and friendship, I might add."

Adam smiled. "I saw a bear come out of that upper clearing," Adam said. "It stood on its hind feet, paws turned down on its chest, funny look on its face, sniffing like this . . ."

Adam did his bear imitation.

"That bear," he said, "wasn't smoking weed; he was smelling it, and he liked the smell. You could see that."

"Yeah. Like cats going crazy-eyed over cat nip. We had one ate so much catnip it got sick and threw up all over the kitchen."

Adam passed the bottle of Wild Turkey. The sharp hard taste went well with the herbal remedy.

"You want to tell me what happened?" Adam said.

I could hardly see the outline of his face in the dark. It felt safe talking to him like this; almost like talking to yourself in the dark, but better.

"Peter told me some of it," he continued. "He said you'd been drawn into some kind of witchcraft or something."

"I don't know if that describes it—do you know about skinwalkers?"

"The Navajo werewolf kind of thing."

"That's right. I think one got into our house and somehow left its mark on us. You know how the Navajos believe in 'bad stars', well this was a bad star driving a skinwalker."

"I know about that stuff from San Juan. They used to hang witches there. Burned them too."

For a while neither of us spoke. We listened to the tinkling sound of the creek and the wind in the pines.

"Strange things happen in the high country," Adam said. "I was hiking one time and I met this guy on a switchback going down toward this little snow-fed lake, and he looked kind of strange.

"Then I saw there was a kid with him. The kid was a boy, somewhere around eight or nine. And they both had all kinds of scratches and scrapes all over their arms and faces. They looked like hell, only I didn't notice it all at once, just a little at a time. Then I saw the kid—standing there with his jaw hanging loose and his eyes staring straight ahead of him.

"I thought maybe it was a bear got to them, but as it turned out, they'd been sitting way up on one of those peaks when a piece of the mountain they were sitting on just came loose and started rolling, and they got scratched up, but the rest of their party, a couple of others, were killed. I got a helicopter from Search and Rescue up where it happened, but we never could dig down into the talus deep enough to get at where those people were buried. That was their final resting place."

"That's kind of what happened to me," I said. "A mountain fell on me. Then a jeep without a driver tried to run over my wife. An owl attacked my friend, Jay. Our house was broken into by a skinwalker and overall nothing seemed to be making sense. I got myself in a little too deep with one of those ufo nuts and the whole mute probe in general screwed up my head. This didn't happen in that particular order, but I can assure you, it really happened. It's nothing I made up."

"I heard about some of that. Pretty unbelievable. But not if you live out here. That witchcraft thing is really dark and malevolent. All the old people believe in it, including my father. I want to show you something."

The cabin was dark except for a mellow shaft of light made by the kerosene lamp on the table.

Adam rummaged around in a drawer and brought a faded envelope over to me. I opened it. Inside was a small downy feather. "This is from Second Mesa," he said, touching it gently with his fingertips. "It's from Shomopovi. A good Hopi friend gave it to me. This man died having a seizure, an epileptic fit, but after he died his spirit came to our house and stayed for a week. He just walked from room to room. I think he was blessing our house. Valerie got scared because Amy was only a baby at the time. Anyway, take this feather, it will bring you good luck, it's a kind of protection against anything evil. Bad stars. Navajo wolves. Even bad luck."

He took the four inch bit of fluff with the wine-dark tip, tied a tiny piece of string to it, and returned it to the envelope which he closed and shook a few times.

"What was that for?" I asked.

"You got to get the corn pollen on it. Without pollen, it won't work."

He removed the feather and I could see specks of gold-brown, like the amber dust wood that beetles make in a plank of pine.

"Put it on that nail over your cot," Adam said.

But as I hung my feather guardian on the nail, my limbs felt like lead, and I realized even Hopi Angels, *kachinas*, *santos*, or any other deities couldn't have kept my eyes open another minute. All I wanted to do was sleep. Looking up, I studied the four by eight ceiling beams and cross-ties of rafters where the wood rats had cleverly stuffed pillows made from old army blankets, and puffy cottonwood catkins, and little sparkles of glass from a broken mirror that caught the low light of the kerosene lamp and made it twinkle on the ceiling.

These were the last things I saw before sleep overtook me and my last conscious thought was that rodents were just like people, and those mirror-bits were an animal's attempt to beautify an otherwise drab nest with a beautiful work of art.

I slept the sleep of a drowned man.

I woke when I heard a weird noise.

I heard it once, then twice, plainly in the meadow, wondering who I was and where I was: the moonlit interior gave me no clue as to the place, but looking at my hands holding the wooden spar edges of the cot reminded me that I was still pretty stoned.

But what was making that strange sound?

The old rusty high post bed next to me was empty, a crumpled sleeping bag, thrown open at the side and half-way down its length, said that someone had left in great haste. Then it clicked, Adam—the cabin, the empty moon-filled meadow, all perfectly clear, and I was finally awake.

The noise came again, this time I recognized it as the snort of a horse, but there was another sound like that of a large fan. I got up, opened the door a crack and looked out at the moon-filled creek. I walked out onto the porch.

Down in the lower meadow, on the other side of the creek, there was the shadow of a man. And at a point where the big fir trees made a black-shaggy wall, there were two horses that I had not seen before. Snorting and stamping, they tossed their manes and moved skittishly in the direction of the forest.

It was a scene from a fairy tale, yet there was an edge to it, a tension created by the high-shouldered head-toss of the horses, and the isolated stillness of the figure whose white clothes were all the more visible in the moon.

I realized, then, that the figure was Adam—and he was wearing the white Levi shirt he had on before I fell asleep. The only thing that bothered me about this assumption was the silvery pants he wore now—or was this the poetic alchemy of the moonlight and herb turning his faded jeans to sterling?

Then came a creaking, a door turning upon a rusted hinge; looking down and to the left, I saw a blue-jeaned man emerge from the shadow of pines that shrouded the out-house, and that person was unmistakably Adam. It was definitely his way of walking, arms swaying back and forth.

Simultaneously, in the lower meadow, the figure in white turned to observe Adam and I saw the silver pants give a visible jump to one side, and then drop into a low crouch. A second later, the pants made a silvery flash run toward the pines.

Adam seemed unaware of any of this when he came up to me; I pointed urgently at the north end of the meadow, where a flash of silver shot between the pines and then disappeared. At once, the horses charged in the same direction and they crashed into the forest at precisely the same exit point where the phantom person had gone. It may have all been an illusion, but it seemed so palpable and real. I looked over at Adam to see how he was taking it.

Adam said, "What the hell's going on?"

"There was a man in white down there on the other side of the creek."

"I missed him but I heard the horses. What'd he look like?"

"Very tall."

"Where did the horses come from? What direction?"

"They were just there on the other side of the creek close to the trees."

"Sometimes there's horses pasturing up here," Adam said. "There's a guy who uses that meadow for grazing in the spring and summer. He's got a whole bunch of horses, more than two. But maybe they got separated from the rest. It was probably that guy."

We decided to cross the creek. The shallow stream bit into my bare feet. We looked around in the moonlight and found the place where I'd seen the white pants man. There were tracks, several of them, all the same size. Evidently he was moving all over the place. But for what reason?

The tracks showed ripple-soled boots and it was hard to follow where they went after he made his break into the treeline.

In the upper meadow the hoofprints were deep and wet in the spring grass. We followed them to the low slung limbs of the fir trees. There were broken branches and a strong horse smell in there. The place where they'd broken into the woods was like a mine shaft into which you could see nothing but night.

"Let's get back into the moonlight," Adam said.

"Maybe we should both admit we're drunk and stoned and go back to bed."

Adam laughed. "You're the one who's supposed to be an investigative reporter."

"You're forgetting why I'm here."

We stood there for a moment and peered into the black tunnel.

Adam shook his head. "Probably was nothing anyway," he said and turned to go back down toward the creek.

I could see from the way he squared his shoulders that he was annoyed with me, and he would have stayed that way for a while if he hadn't been the first one to see the light. It appeared over our heads, a coppery orange disc that moved like a bubble in a glass.

My first thought was that I was witnessing some kind of meteor, but that idea was corrected by the upward flight of the object, which as it accelerated, diminished in size, but not in color: the coppery glow became a greenish florescence as it mounted into the heavens, then it shrank to the size of a pin-head and was no longer identifiable.

Adam and I stood beside each other, amazed. We were in a kind of reverent silence not wanting to speak.

"I believe we've seen something we'll never see again," he said finally.

"Don't count on it."

"I still don't believe I saw that thing," he whispered.

"Did you hear the sound it made?"

"Like a raven in flight, a rushing of air, not a beating sound at all."

I said, "Even if we are out of it, half drunk on Wild Turkey and definitely high on weed, that —"

I stopped mid-sentence. There was a whinny that came from the tunnel in the trees. The sky was going gray now, it was nearing dawn, you could see more clearly, maybe fifty feet in.

Adam motioned me to follow him into the tunnel and I did somewhat reassured by the graying of the sky, the lifting of the darkness, but I could hear my heart pounding and I was walking clumsily, as if my ankles were rubber.

We went in and it got darker until it was almost night again. But Adam seemed to know where he was going, bending branches out of the way for me and ducking low whenever necessary, neither one of us talking, just moving through the pines, snapping sharp sticks underfoot and going steadily uphill, to where Adam said the horse tracks dipped off to the right and started going back down in the direction of the creek.

A pine bough caught me square in the eye, knocked my glasses off my face and like a complete idiot, I stepped on them. I could barely see, but it didn't matter. All I had to do was concentrate on Adam's white shirt and duck the branches he forgot to hold back for me.

We kept moving along like this, hunched over, going too far to the left or the right, then coming back to the deep-hoofed tracks in the pitch-black ground. There was a half-inch or more of water in these new tracks now, which meant that we were very close to the creek.

Then we could hear them, the stamping of soft earth, the occasional hard clang of a horse-shoe on cobbles, they were right nearby and we could smell them and hear the slap of the creek as it went over the rocks; here the water was filled with wind and ferns and a mist of mosquitoes so thick you couldn't miss eating a few while breathing.

"We're near the source," Adam said. "We go up any further you'll see it come right out of the rocks from underground—this is all snowmelt. Be careful, you could go up to your neck in this stuff."

We were rock-hopping when we saw the first horse already down in the muck, deep in, up to its shoulders, heaving maniacally to get free, but without success. With each thrust it went down deeper.

"Get a branch, a log, anything," Adam yelled.

I ran and tripped, falling face down in that slimy backwash. By the time I struggled to my feet and found a solid log, Adam was struggling to keep the horse's head out of the muck by pulling with all his strength on its halter, and balancing himself, keeping his two feet straddled on rocks while tugging and shouting at the horse—more likely to himself—the big animal was not putting up much of a fight anymore.

The horse's head was not wild and twisting as it had been only seconds before when, its nostrils dilating with froth, it had galloped deeper into the black mire.

"Get that thing under her head," Adam said. "Now if she'll just stay quiet, we can keep her head out of it."

You could hear the horse's constricted breathing, the intakes of air stifled by the mud that was crushed against her ribs. It looked surreal, this great brown head framed in mud and unattached to a body.

I jammed the log as far as it would go under the head by the back part of the jawbone, still shaggy with winter hair.

"That oughta hold'er," Adam said.

"She's hardly breathing," I said.

"Damn her hide, damn her muddy fucking hide, she's beginning to like it in there."

"She can't breathe with all the mud on her lungs," I said.

"That's not it, it's the cold. She's suffering from hypothermia: freezing up inside. Her body's numb."

For a moment we both took stock of the situation. Adam was covered with mud, his shirt torn at the shoulder where he had a shallow cut when a pine branch lashed him. My clothes were untorn, but I'd gone in deep at least once and I was soaked to the bone.

The sound of rushing water was everywhere; above us you could see where the source of the creek found its way from a dozen underground glacier-like tributaries and sprung out of the earth in pools of ice and streamlets that laced together into a quagmire where the horse was half-breathing.

Now the breathing came harder and was more shallow, and there was a gurgling sound coming up when she exhaled.

"She must've taken water in when she went down the first time," Adam said.

She tried to whinny. A back-up gurgle of fetid air and water bubbled out of her nostrils which opened wide this final time. I let go of the log as the weight became too great. Then I fell backwards into the mud. Adam lay flat. His right hand was braced on a rock. His left was on the halter.

"Let go, for Christ's sake," I shouted.

He seemed intent on the struggle. His arm went deeper into the mud pulling his shoulder and his face against it. The horse was gone from sight in the dark ooze.

"Adam, let go, you crazy son-of-a-bitch!"

Bracing my back against a large round rock I took hold of his bicep and pulled as hard as I could. It was then I realized that his hand was trapped by the halter.

The right side of his face was now pressed against my left shoulder. I sank my fingers into his bicep and pulled again. This time his hand came free. I then took hold of his shirt collar and began hauling us backwards out of the mud.

When his body came free there was a loud pop sound. We lay panting on the river gravel like a couple of hounds. At last we got up and resting our heads on our knees we watched the oily bubbles rise and burst where the horse had sunk.

"How's your hand?" I asked.

"Not broken, but hurts like hell."

"Let's go back to the cabin."

It was about a half hour after sunrise, I guessed. Adam led the way back to the meadow. The other horse was standing at the other end. Its ears working back and forth. With measured steps we walked toward it. The horse just stood there ears flicking, flesh rippling. We came within a few feet and stopped. The horse was still.

Adam slipped his unhurt hand under the halter. The horse lowered its head under his touch. We saw the dark purple sockets where its eyes had been. Adam stroked the horse's head.

"It's in shock. But also in darkness."

"It was so dark back there in that swamp, I didn't have my glasses on and I couldn't really see the other horse that well.

"Neither one had any eyes."

We led the blind horse back to the cabin. Neither of us felt like talking. We bathed in the creek and attended to the mare. There wasn't a scratch on her except for the empty eye sockets. If she felt any pain she sure wasn't showing it. She would even let us touch around the edge of either eye socket. Not even a shiver.

"What do we do with the horse?" I asked.

Adam nibbled the bottom of his mustache nervously. He looked from horse to creek to upper end of meadow. He shook his head, "Can't get my mind free of the horse that went down in the mud," he said.

"How's your hand, now?"

He raised it so I could see it.

The tissue over the tendons behind the knuckles was badly rope-burned.

"It's not broken, and I know more about injuries than you do, my old man being a doctor. So you can stop worrying about my injury."

"There's not much we can do," I said to Adam.

He gave me a faint, slightly twisted smile.

"We can make coffee and get that wood stove going."

We started a fire and it felt better when the cabin started to get warm.

The coffee was hot and good.

"I guess we better report this. We need to head back to the Tesuque ranger station," I said.

"I'm not so much worried about the horse, if we leave it. I'll give it a long tether and when we get to the station I'll buzz old man Gonzales. They're his horses. I've no idea how I'm going to break the news to him. To be perfectly honest I'm still shaky and scared shitless myself."

"So am I."

Adam gave me a long look. "You're not going to write this thing up in *The Review*, are you?"

"I'll sleep on it."

"It could make national news, but it could also sort of ruin your life. You'd never have a moment's peace after it got out that we not only saw the mutilation but we also witnessed a UFO."

"I feel like my life's been pretty battered by this whole bloody, or I should say, bloodless business. It's true, Laura and I both want to get away from it.

Adam dropped his eyes to the ground, exhaled and said, "If you do write it, leave me out of it. Because I'll deny I saw anything."

I said nothing. There was a part of me that was already writing about it. I'd already stuck my neck out, not like Adam, who hadn't. I was already a target. I was already known in the field of journalism. This story could be the end of my mutilation coverage. But if Adam wouldn't swear to seeing what I saw, what we both witnessed, then there was no witness.

For the moment we ate some hash and eggs without any further talk about the horses or the UFO. I couldn't seem to make any private resolutions.

My life was a mess. It had all started back when Sarah and I saw the white dog. It had gotten way out of hand when I met Etienne and Gomez and even before that when the skinwalker began stalking me. That went all the way back to 1967. For a moment I thought about Etienne, Harjac, Gomez, the guy in the arroyo, Dr. Frey, Kreuger, Durwood, even the old man who told me about Jesus on horseback. I went back in my mind to the first date that Laura and I had in the Gallinas Canyon, before the hit and run. The two of us sitting on the wood-and-tin flume that ran along the canyon wall. It was there we heard the Penitentes sing in the *morada* across the river. I saw the horse with the empty eye sockets and visioned again the Appaloosa that had its hide ripped off. These things were running rampant through my mind when Adam tapped me on the shoulder.

"Don't forget this," Adam said, as he held up my little eagle feather. "It will still protect you. If you let it."

I did not feel I could tell him that I was past protection. My blood had spilled by creek and sand bed long ago and had mixed with the souls of the flayed penitents. I myself was a mute.

**

The roads below were drier. The meadows greener. There was empty road before us and the whip of willows against our tires along the last few miles of the Tesuque fire road.

We rounded the last elbow turn. Adam eased off on the gas pedal. The van came slowly to a stop.

"Will you look at that? I've been by here a thousand times and this is the first time I ever saw anything like that. That's Pueblo grazing land we're looking at."

Scattered on the hillside twenty or thirty shaggy elk. Mostly cows, dark brown, stilt legged down from their winter range. They looked rangy themselves.

"They live off the burns in the upper meadows," Adam said. "I've never seen them down this low before. And in cattle country."

The bucolic sight should have calmed my nerves, at least a little. But all I could think of was the hunter I'd interviewed who shot an elk with a 30-30 and then watched in astonishment as the elk got sucked up into the sky by some invisible vortex. The hunter later found the elk mutilated in the classic style.

"Look how the bulls keep watch," Adam said. "Keeping their heads up all the time the cows eat."

"I wonder why they're not scared of us," I said.

"They know hunters from lookers."

The van began to roll as we went off on our way. The elk held their positions. I was reminded of driving off from the Pueblo one night and being watched by a wall of blank eyes, a whole herd of cattle.

196

After some more miles of canyon country we came out in the scrub oak and pine foothills. We could see the Tesuque valley and the valleys beyond, the mesas of the distant pueblos. Then the faraway vistas turned to haze. The warm air and the highway dust blew into us. The limitless hills reminded me of a long run I'd done at seven thousand feet. My chest ached from the twelve or thirteen miles. My right leg ached from the metal and pins.

But as long as there was a trail in front of me and nothing to stop my feet there was no stopping my mind, and it was my mind that was doing the running. That is when I realized that a runner's mind is not a prisoner of circumstances. If I could just keep my runner's mind I could defeat the dystopian visions I was having.

It occurred to me that I could burn all my mute notes and writings. A kind of transcendental self-immolation. Jay's medicine man father said that if he'd only burned the sheepskins that day, he would've saved his sheep and kept his family safe. I vowed to get into my files and destroy every last page.

***

It was Sunday but I had a key for my office. I walked past Durwood's L-shaped desk and imagined him there with a lemon yellow tie grinning at his Dorian Gray image in the reflective mirror on the opposite wall.

I went into my very empty room and emptied all of my files into the waste basket. Then I took the wastebasket to the incinerator that was used by the restaurant that adjoined our building. Some people cleaning up in back of the restaurant watched me. I smiled at them and dumped everything in and put a match to it. In that same moment I broke into a cold cataclysmic sweat.

I went back into the building and left Durwood a call-back phone note. It had one word on it.

Reviewquit.

Driving home in the old '56 Chevy I thought about the meadow with all the elk. I imagined they were gone now all except their ghost hoof-prints. Night would come to the meadow. Starlight would dapple the grass and turn to sparks of frost. Space and time and their accompanying veils of light would continue forever.

***

That night Laura and I returned to Adam's cabin. The horse was standing exactly where we left it. It was so still I thought it might be dead. But when we got up to it, it shivered, nickered, tossed its head up and down a few times.

Old man Gonzales had not made it out. Laura got some hay from the shed in back of the cabin and an old coffee can full of oats. In the gathering darkness we fed the horse and led it to the creek to drink. The animal's eye sockets were dark, bloodless holes and looked no different than when I first saw them. We heard some coyotes, maniacal drunken laughter.

Then in the distance we heard the rumble of a truck and a trailer. Old man Gonzales? He came around the bend under the bare-branched cottonwoods and got out of the cab arthritic and slow. He had a halter, not rope, but leather. He was an old man with a broad mustache curled upward at the ends. His sweat-stained cowboy hat was dented in all the wrong places. He saw us and nodded and said, *Como estas,* under his breath.

"Not so *bueno,*" I said.

He gave me a look. Then said, "There's a hole in the sky—"

"—And things are coming out of it."

"You know."

"Yes, I know."

Then Laura and I helped him lead the horse into the trailer in back of his truck. The horse's preternatural calmness was amazing. But maybe its cauterized eyes kept it from being afraid and feeling pain. Sightless, it was if in a dark trance. A lightless place where no harm could come.

Chapter Twenty-Eight

After I left *The Review* I spent some time by myself sorting things out. My cousin Peter came over one day and asked what I was doing with myself and I told him, "Nothing much." It was a lie. I wasn't doing anything at all. I was in recovery, but he knew that and he suggested something I've never regretted doing.

"I'm between jobs," he said. "Maybe we could do something together."

"Like what?" I asked.

"Well, how about . . ."

He thought for a moment.

"Why don't you and I go fly a kite," he said.

"You serious?"

"Very."

I could see by his sea-blue eyes that he meant it.

"I'm game," I said.

***

And so for a month or more we flew kites over the mesa up by Vista Redondo above where we lived. You could see for miles up there—or I should say, our kites could. Because after a while we discovered you didn't need high ground to fly a kite. High ground would lose you a kite in northern New Mexico winds that run fast and hard. So we took to lower ground, the good old arroyo in back of our house.

The time spent flying kites was wind-borne, and wonderful. We never tired of it. We woke up in the morning refreshed and ready to go to work flying our kites. We did so, as I say, for a month . . . and then Peter got some house renovation work and he hired me on as assistant carpenter. That, in a way, was like kite-flying for me. It wasn't exactly career-oriented. But it was emptying-the-mind work.

There was an old man in the house we were working on and his mind was gone, but he was always, despite the Alzheimer's that had a hold of him, cheerful. He would watch me working on the *latias*, and he would stare fixedly at what I was doing. I could see the question mark in his eyes. "What is the tool in that young man's hand?"

I told him, "It's a nailset."

The old man awakened to the word.

He knew what a nailset was and was delighted with the knowledge.

After that, for days, for weeks, he would see me on the ladder as I made my rounds, and he'd say, "Nailset!"

I'd repeat the word. It made his day. But I was growing fearful it was also making *my* day. He and I had something in common and I was afraid of what it was.

***

The following autumn I was up at Eagle Nest with Laura, Mara and Sarah. It was like a small vacation in the midst of a larger one.

We were staying at the ancient hotel where Clay Allison, the famed gunfighter, shot a man for disturbing his rest. Allison was taking a nap, and the man in the adjoining room was doing the same, only he was snoring. Allison, who was a light sleeper, woke up when he heard the snoring, and put an end to it. He fired his 44 through the wall, killing the snorer instantly. Good shot, everyone always said.

So we were in that hotel, *The Cimarron*, and it was getting stuffy. Hotels, if you stay in them too long, get that way. I left Laura and the kids, and went for a jog. It was late afternoon. I ran for about fifteen minutes, came to a place where the piñon trees were thick and hedgy along the side of the road. While resting for a minute, I heard a coyote yipping.

There was a barbed wire fence that separated the road from the back country. Hopping it, I found myself walking in the direction of the yelps, which were getting louder. There was a sandstone ledge in front of me. Below it, in a little arroyo full of pastel-colored sand, I saw a black coyote lying on its side. It was obviously dying, but there was no blood anywhere around it, and no outward sign that it had been hurt. I hopped down off the ledge. At first I was cautious, afraid the coyote might suddenly be revived, and lunge at me. But it lay there, and as I approached, it growled and showed its teeth. The coyote was completely black, a shadow on the sand. I felt a strong compulsion to pat it, to comfort it. But caution held me back.

I knelt beside it, the sun warming my back. At once a magpie—the black and white clown—showed up and made its high, fluting, popping cries. High above, a couple of ravens skirted the clouds, coughing. A trickle of sweat rolled down my neck. There was no wind, the desert was very still, breathless. A tear ran down my cheek. After all, this was Death, and any death, no matter how small, as Mr. Donne put it, diminishes us. I felt sorry for the dying of God's Dog, which, when I looked at it emptying its life, I imagined myself doing the same thing.

Then a clear thought came to mind. Ray Brown was right. The proof of a long-gone argument we'd had about the two dogs that live within: one light, one dark. The cliche question was: Which one do you feed?

Everyone knows this old conundrum. But here I was with the dark dog that I imagined I had been feeding all these years. I could never seem to make up my mind which coyote to feed. They were equally hungry. And I was equally eager to feed either one. Or both.

So here I was beside a real black coyote. God's Dog, the Plains people called it. As I drew closer to it, risking a bite, the animal stopped growling. Its tail flopped in the sand. It seemed to smile at me. I felt a huge torrent of compassion. I grew even more bold and raised its head up, cradling it. In that moment, it seemed all the compressed fear and loathing in my heart-residue of months of mute work—was spent.

The coyote died in my arms.

A part of me died with it.

***

The following day, we drove south, returning home to Tesuque about mid- afternoon. Something was happening, again, over which I had no control. But a great burden was also lifted from me. I felt a little removed from myself, a little distant, but it felt all right. There was an almost pleasant sensation, as if that which I touched was not permanent. I felt, then, as if nothing were permanent, all things connected to my life ephemeral.

While Laura unpacked I walked around our adobe house in a daze, looking at books. Nothing mattered, I told myself. The dog of death was gone. I could do—or be—whatever I wanted. There was nothing out there to stop me or haunt me. I was free. The sense of release was exaggerated, as it is often is in epiphanies. After I checked the house, I went outside, presumably to go for a walk. But I wasn't sure. Yet I knew that something awaited me. Something just beyond the next hill.

***

I walked six miles into the chalky foothills of the Sangre de Cristos. Our motley dogs accompanied me. The ancient Newfoundland, the harlequin Great Dane, the red Akita, the ego-driven dachshund, and Sally, the old hound. There is a place bordering the Tesuque Reservation and the National Forest, a kind of no-man's land where the hills are eaten away and the crumpled wastes look like the Painted Desert. The land is blistered and remote and fades to hard clay like a lopsided, over-baked pot. Resting there, on the lip of the pot, I saw a white coyote emerge from a small rise and come toward us. It was not pure white, but a kind of blonde color, with russet at the shoulders. But the overall look of the animal was white, the soft, sun-color of desert snow.

I kept still as the coyote approached, coming quite close. Within, say fifteen yards of us. Then it feinted off in the direction of the next hill.

Immediately, the dog pack went after it. And a comic procession it was: the Newfy, at first, taking the lead, the Akita next. Then the dachshund got into the front of the pack. The Great Dane bounding alongside the others.

They ascended the hill in a fine cloud of yellow dust. I watched the white coyote lead them to the top, then, calm as a queen, she—I knew she had to be a she by the grace of her—trotted back down the same way she'd gone up. Of course the foolish, tongue-lolling pack, galumphed down after her. This time she fell away from them fast, accelerating into a quick, foxy sprint. She made it back to where I was sitting, and sat on her haunches.

She wasn't breathing hard, yet her pursuers were falling over themselves down in the valley and were probably not good for another rally. Which proved to be the case. They topped the hill, too tired to bark.

The white coyote seemed to smile in satisfaction. The dogs were done, and she knew it. Then, walking past them she came within a yard of me and stood there staring. The wind ruffled her fur. Finally, somehow reassured that I wasn't going to do anything she walked passed me. A musky scent of coyote and the mist of her fur wafted by as went away leisurely into the distant hills, not looking back, not running just walking and stopping and sometimes sniffing the air.

I got up and jogged six miles back home. My dog team followed, a little worse for wear. But at least they had an excuse; it's hard to chase after a blithe spirit made of air and fur rather than bone.

***

The following day I was again tramping in the far hills around my home when I found it—and through it—him. I'd come to the top of a rise, which gave a nice overlook of the small canyon when I came upon a rock fetish. It was a bear, a large stone bear, covered with greenish-yellow lichen. Stooped, as if bending into the river in search of fish, it had its round head down-pointed, toward the earth. The bear shuffled around among the prayer feathers that someone had strung in the cedars; small downy feathers of the eagle. Some were fresh, still faintly dusted with cornmeal.

Well, Bear, what have you to tell me?

The wind hummed in the cedars. High overhead a raven sawed the air. The bear moved along in a desultory fashion. It pawed at fallen logs, chewed grubs. It glanced at me over its sunlit shoulder, and moved on.

Something unsaid was said by that bear. Like the white coyote, some archaic body language: I see you, I don't care about you, I don't want to know you because I already know who you are.

The Bear had spoken. I opened my eyes into the clear stream of daylight and the scent of pine. Time to go. I had seen the bear and it had reminded me of my friend Brown. Brown would sometimes fry piñon nuts just to see them pop in the pan. Then he would hump around picking them up off the floor and eating them. This bear was like that. In his own world.

When I got to our doorstep, Laura was sitting outside in the sun. The dogs were all around her. She had a pixie look, red-gold hair and Celtic eyes. But behind the mask of the faerie princess was the calm of deep underworld.

I sat beside her, resting from my run. "What now? she asked, threading her hand in mine. "More messages? From the animal kingdom?"

I nodded.

An old Tesuque Pueblo man came up the arroyo, she said. He was carrying a huge load of piñon wood on his back. He stopped in front of the house. He smiled at me, and went on.

"Is that all?"

"Yes."

"I found a bear up on the hill, the high beige hill at the foot of the Sangres."

Laura squinted in the sun, shaded her green eyes. "Was it a stone bear?"

"Yes. Someone had carved it out of tufa."

She didn't say anything so I continued. "There were prayer feathers all around it. I had a strong feeling, connected with that time in the hospital after I was run over, that I was supposed to touch the bear. I did. When my hands were on it, I saw something. A thing from my past. My mother explaining our family history. Did I ever tell you there was a stealer of horses, a charmer of animals in the family?"

She looked thoughtful. Those green sparkle eyes and red hair. I embraced her. She hugged back, hard, as she always does, and I felt tears come to my eyes. Rivers trembling in the sun, east and west. Bringing the gift of blood, of love, of devotion and friendship. "That old man," she said softly, "with the wood piled up on his back, he looked like Ray Brown."

***

A few days later I got a call from my good friend Marie who asked if I would like to accompany her eighth grade class from Santa Fe Prep into the Grand Canyon.

"We're going to Havasu," she said with her usual wide-eyed lovely enthusiasm for all things, "just below the *Supai* village where we'll camp. Won't you come and tell stories around the campfire?"

In the past few years I had made a tangential living telling stories—Native American legends that I'd been collecting over the years. This sounded like fun. I hadn't been to Havasu. Double-fun. I said yes.

That weekend, I found myself tramping into the Canyon by full moon.

Traveling with thirty young adults for a week's camp-out may seem to some like a nightmare, but to me it was a vacation. I like kids, I like canyons, and I like back-packing.

Thirteen miles to the base-camp by the waterfalls of Havasu is a good hike. The pack settled easily onto my shoulders, I set myself a good pace, and the moony miles of eerie landscape closed me into a dreamlike time-frame, in which I meditated as I tramped. The only night-sounds were the crunching of boots on the river-cobble. Soon even these melted away as the youthful adventurers sped off, each student trying to best his partner.

We were supposed to hike as far into the Canyon that first night as possible, then to simply stop and camp. There were ten adults on the trip, most of them teachers from the school.

As I walked along, the escarpments rose up like fingers all around me, some broad like whole hands formed of stone, others bony claws scraping at the starry sky.

I knew little of the Canyon. Each step I took went deeper into the unknown. Remembering a Pueblo friend's advice, I relished the trip all the more. He, a traditional Pueblo silversmith, had forbidden his daughter to go to Havasu without being accompanied by a medicine man. I asked him why and he told me the Canyon was full of Spirits.

"Do you mean evil spirits?"

His eyes narrowed. "I mean Spirits."

Later, I'd heard that Havasupai meant *People of the Blue Water*.

Named after the lovely series of waterfalls, the turquoise freshets that spring up everywhere in the oasis-like atmosphere of Havasu. The clear mineral waters, abundant with limestone deposits, give the pools a sky-blue reflection of such shimmering clarity that to swim them is to imagine yourself in the Virgin Islands.

But the spirits intrigued me.

I'd gone about eight miles in when I found a small encampment of teenagers gathered by the riverbed. They were scattered about, with and without chaperons. We were to camp near, but not necessarily in, any group of kids we felt comfortable with.

No tent needed. Just throw down your sleepingbag, zip down, and zip up.

The Canyon at night, even in June, is cold. I zippered the down bag over my head, rolled a time or two on the sand to make a sleeping-place, closed my eyes and felt the first waves of sleep overtake me.

I woke shortly before dawn. A mouse scampered over my head, an owl hooted close by. I drew my head out of the bag in time to hear a clattering of hooves, then to see—before I could guess what it was—a ghost pony coming up the arroyo. First one, then another. Then a Supai man, walking at his leisure, humming a little tune to himself.

The moon was down. The Canyon was now dark. All around me, in their secret cocoons, the students were sprawled, buried in dreams. It was lovely, I felt exhilarated, I didn't want to sleep another minute. So got up, packed my backpack, hefted it easily onto my shoulders, headed out. As I tramped off, some kids began to stir, sit up, yawn into the moonless dark.

They'd be following in my tracks soon enough. There was no getting lost here, it was all one way: down into the bowels of the Canyon. A few hours before daylight left. Chewing a strip of beef jerky, I considered how lucky I was to be on this trip. I could I thought, be rising to shave and shower, and off to my dreary office job. Instead, I was strolling through the dawn streets of the gods.

The arroyo soon twisted into tunnels of down-flowing stone, slippery with moss. The air was catkin-sweet, new morning night-fragrant.

Another ghost pony, saddle-bagged and empty, trotted up canyon, where it would be packed-in with either dudes or food. Or both.

The clang of steel shoes, striking of sparks. The soft chomp of the wet sand. The horse like a thing of dreams, sometimes white, sometimes black, tearing the gauze air of predawn.

I was, according to my calculations, quite near the village when I saw a fissure in the canyon wall. A cleft in the pattern of time. Within, light. A flickering, firefly dancing.

Approaching it, my rational mind was already at work: incandescence, the result of little glow-worms. I'd seen it before. But once close-up, I saw something else again.

Ribbons of blue seemed to flow out of the hole in the wall, like ghostly serpents. Particles of incorporeal matter, smoke of blue, backlit by some secret moon of blue. Blue, blue.

I stuck my arm into the wall, all the way to my shoulder, and something pulled on it. Then, before I could retract my arm, a hand took hold of my own, clasped it firmly, and pulled me half into the rock. I felt myself, swimming in the stone.

Breathing. Flexing. Moving like a fish through stone. Was it possible to swim up, up where the light of day would greet me? I swam.

The hands grabbed my shirt, pulling me down, even as I swam up. I could not see. There were blue fleeting things, a sensation of swimming.

I could breathe freely, in the stone. Stone cold. Stoned. Weightless. Swimming. But not moving.

Suddenly, I was free.

Out of the rock. Whole, breathing air. Human again.

I was lying on my backpack like an overturned bug, my feet kicking the air.

A voice near me said, "Hold my hand."

The hand took me, towed me.

He was a small man wearing a faded blue-jean jacket with a very worn corduroy collar. He had a tam on his head woven out of red, gold, green and black wool. His face was round, brown like a roasted coffee bean. His eyes were onyx black.

"Looks like you got yourself stuck in that hole there," he said.

"I guess, I did. . ." Embarrassed, I smiled.

"You did, at that," he said.

There was not much to say, except the medicine man who had said, "There are evil spirits there even in the rock.".

"Been here before?" The Supai man asked, lighting a cigarette.

Taking a deep inhalation, he offered me the same.

I took it, sucking hard. The hit, in the back of the throat, did me good.

Exhaling slowly, I said: "Something pulled me in there. A hand, I think it was . . ."

He laughed, stood up, stretched. "Couple minutes, it'll be morning."

"Morning," I said, tasting the word.

I took another long inhalation, returned the cigarette. "You keep it. I don't smoke."

"I don't go into caves," he said.

"I was pulled in, I didn't go because I wanted to."

He stared at the blossom of sun spreading on the upper rim of canyon. A sudden flamingo flood of sun color washed over the lower shadows.

"Take my advice, stay out of places that are staked off." He smoked unconcernedly, and for the first time, I felt the breath of his horse, standing next to us. A scent of alfalfa steam coming from its nostrils.

"What would you've done?" I asked, borrowing back the cigarette.

He chuckled. "What I'd do, what you'd do, two different things."

"There are spirits here, aren't there?"

"There are spirits *everywhere*," he mused, picking up a rock. "In this stone, spirits. In that sun up there on the cliff, spirits. Down here, in the shadows, spirits. You and me, spirits. What else is there?"

I laughed. He was right.

"You look out now," he said getting on his horse.

I promised I would. Then I started back down the canyon and he started back up, two ways of doing the same thing.

It was awhile, walking in silence, before I realized I was still smoking his cigarette.

Down at the bottom of the Canyon under a grove of flowering leaf trees, I burned a sordid meal of macaroni and cheese, crunching the crusted black cheese, washing it down with too-sweet Kool Aid. Then some mixed nuts, heavily salted, putting back in what I'd taken out, hiking. More Kool Aid. Then a strong brew of Kenyan coffee, the camper's equalizer.

Found myself sharing this brew with Chuck and Tammy, a Methodist minister and his wife, who were unwilling, and as they put it, "too old to backpack." They had come down the same trail I did on mule-back, an experience they'd much enjoyed. They were two happy campers, two people in love with life. They seemed to be aging gracefully. We sipped coffee under the blue stars of the great canyon night. A warm, almost tropical wind came down the trail, meandering and returning, and whispering.

"How are we're going to get out of here?" Chuck said, thinking aloud.

"Helicopter," Tammy replied. "They come down once a day for old folks like us."

The night swallows dived overhead. Then they were gone and the bats took their place. You could hear their high squeaks. The canyon exhaled cooler air which was then warmed by the canyon walls. I excused myself and went to my little square of campground. It was comfortable enough to sleep on my poncho with no sleeping bag and no cover. The locust trees rustled as I drifted off to sleep.

In the morning I was up at dawn. So were my companions.

"That was some show last night," Chuck said.

"What show?" I asked.

Tammy said, "Well, Chuck woke me up to see it, some youngster, standing right by your poncho, speaking in Indian."

"I've heard that talk before," Chuck muttered, "but this was nothing like that. It sounded like ancient Celtic, didn't it, Tammy?"

"I suppose. . . maybe. But really now, it didn't sound like anything I've ever heard before."

She was shaking her hair out, and catching loose strands with her towel, and rolling them dry.

"I guess I really missed something," I said.

"He was standing right where you're brewing your coffee," Tammy went on, "a young man about your size and height . . . come to think of it, it could've *been* you!"

"Now hold on, Tam," Chuck said, "he was sleeping like a baby, we saw him plain as day."

She didn't say anything.

After breakfast, I took a hike with some of the kids, went up-canyon to a small confluence of streams. There was watercress and wild celery growing everywhere, and cottonwood catkins blowing through the air like sheep's floss.

The Canyon was weaving a spell. Moments later, I was swimming in a pool where the many rivers met. There was white sand under me and the water was clear as gin. It was starting to come back to me. The dream of the night before. I remembered trying to wake someone up. Was it me I was trying to wake up? Was I another I altogether? The sound of the rivers coming together might have been the ancient language I had spoken in my dream. Old, dim, river-rushing sounds returned to me now.

I got out of the water and watched the kids swimming around and throwing playful insults at each other.

It was almost too cold to swim but that was the fun of it for them. For me, the chill, almost a burn continued. I found myself shivering. I wrapped myself up in my towel and sat in the sun. The kids got in and out of the water like water rats. I was lifeguard for about an hour until the last one got out and wobbled up the trail.

In the afternoon, I hiked into the Supai village. Ate chili. Watched the slow way the Supai women moved about their tasks. Listened to their voices, dreamed their language, while sipping glass after glass of cold lemon ice-water. I could not get enough liquid in me. But the sounds, the lisping canyon lilt, voices of the blue water, were not the sounds I myself had said only a few hours before. These were softer, more pliant.

In the evening, I sat with Chuck and Tammy by the Coleman burner making coffee. And, again, the swallows were followed by the bats. The surrounding darkness resonated with mating, croaking toads. We turned in early. The first aches of the long hike into the canyon were beginning to be felt and lying flat-out on my poncho I fell asleep quickly.

When I woke, it was still dark.

Someone was standing by my poncho. A man doing funny things with his hands.

I sat up. "What do you want?" I asked.

He was doing odd little pirouettes, spiral motions with his fingers.

"Chuck, you get back here in this tent right now!"

I saw Tammy's white face between the tent flaps.

She shined a flashlight on her husband who was now trying to fly.

His lips moved though his eyes were shut tight. And it was as if someone or some thing was talking through him. A kind of ghostly ventriloquism.

I got out my pen and pad and scribbled the sounds I heard.

Dah diniilghaazh nihit tikan, he said. Or something like that.

Then Tammy took him by the shoulders and guided him back into their tent. He walked like he was a bit drunk, but I knew that neither one of them indulged. A Coleman light went on in the tent and I heard her protesting, then the minister's calm, sure, resonant voice. He had returned to himself. I heard the zipper on his sleeping bag and then a groan and he went to sleep, or so I supposed.

I didn't hear anything more except the humping and pumping of the toads.

***

211

Back home after a week in the Grand Canyon, I felt the difference in me. The tectonic shift of psyche and self.

"You look different, Laura said at dinner, the first home-cooked meal I'd had in a week.

"I feel different," I told her.

We were sharing a bottle of Beaujolais by firelight and she had prepared a very fine fettuccini. The crackling fire scented the room with juniper, the wine was dry and good, and things seemed to be in harmony, or *hozhonii.*

Laura's eyes had a mystery sparkle of gladness.

"To sup early and well, to go a-bed well and soon," as the Elizabethans said, this made me feel even more well, and full of anticipation. too.

We knocked off the bottle of red, and moved on to Myer's dark rum and I felt middle-aged in the bones, but unbelievably young at heart.

We went to bed early, and well.

The canyon faded. We burnished ourselves with affection that comes of sudden separation and deeply desired renewal.

We slept . . .

. . . and chanced to dream.

***

The flood filled the desert.

I stole the Sun, Coyote said.

I took the Water-monster Babies, Coyote bragged.

I made love to White Shell Woman, Coyote boasted.

I made every Woman there was, Coyote added.

And the water rose and the seven fingered dawn was gone.

There was no laughter, except Coyote's, no sun, no language to speak of only the presence of insects, locusts, red ant people, and a few of the animals we know by name.

Where are we? I asked Wolf.

In the beginning, Wolf said.

The Dark below White Dawn is very large, he said.

Where is Mountain Lion? said Red Ant.

Gone to discover whatever happens next, said Lizard.

And what will that be? asked Snake.

No one knows, Badger said.

White Hawk returned, said, There is going to be a terrible flood.

Mountain Lion returned, said, The belt of darkness is growing.

The animal people gathered up corn and seeds, filled their pouches and climbed to the top of White Mountain in the East. But it was soon swallowed up, so they went to Blue Mountain in the South. But it too was swallowed up and they went up Yellow Mountain in the West, but it too was swallowed up and that left only Black Mountain in the North but by the time they got up top, the water was rising so fast they were scooping handfuls of earth to carry along with them to plant the seeds in.

Coyote shuffled behind everyone else. He had something under his arm. Red Ant said, You've stolen Water Monster's babies and that is what is wrong. Coyote started to run off but he tripped and fell and Water-Monster babies were free of him and they dived into the water, and were met by their mother, Water-Monster.

After that the flood stopped.

And the people moved up into the light.

***

The phone rang and I got up, answered it.

Ray Brown was on the other end. His voice sounded far off.

"Where are you?" I asked.

"Home," he said. "With Ethel."

"Your son too?"

"He's back where you are."

213

"You know that wolfman that was after you?" Brown said.

"The skinwalker," I said.

"That one."

"What about him?"

"He got killed in a fight. I saw him. Dead. They burned him."

"Who burned him?"

"Some people he wanted to kill. It's over now. You don't need to think about it but I thought you'd like to know, I got to get back to Ethel, she's making fry bread."

"Everything's OK?"

"It rained like hell last night."

"In Window Rock?"

"Way North of there. Far, far North."

***

In the old stories Diné, The People, went North when they died.

That afternoon it rained for the first time in weeks and afterwards the sky lit up with a double rainbow that arced over the house, and I remembered the old song that went like this:

> *I cross the deep canyon with nowhere in its belly*
> *And nothing in its heart*
> *I throw my friend Rainbow over the gap in the great canyon mouth*
> *Now I walk on Rainbow's Bridge that spans the world*
> *All is beautiful before me behind me below me above me*
> *All is beautiful all around me*
> *This covers the mountains whose ways are beautiful*
> *The skies the waters the darkness the dawn*
> *Whose ways are beautiful all around me*

Epilogue

The Evil Chasing Way Chant of Diné is usually sung before The Great Star Chant. The Evil Chasing Way is a curing rite that heals. It is said that this narrative song is for those who have seen such terrible things as the nightmare of war, the mutilation of animals and humans, dreams of darkness and disharmony, and all kinds of creature occurrences—visitations from aberrant owls, tricky coyotes, and other animals and ghosts that can frighten and attack human beings. When a medicine man sings The Evil Chasing Way, he brings the psychically wounded person into harmony with the natural world. As a result the recipient of the healing returns to the beauty of all things and becomes well again. My Navajo friend of fifty years, Jay DeGroat, first told me about this rite in 1965. He said, "Grandfather told it to a man named Joseph Campbell who came to hear stories about the Hero Twins. The Evil Chasing Way is about them. That was a long time ago."

GH

Coming Spring 2018

Star Song *series*
Hand Trembler
Book 2
by
Gerald Hausman

Hand Trembler is the story of one man's emergence through native rituals into the world of extraterrestrial/intraterrestrial time travel.

Throughout the novel there is the basic wisdom of Navajo medicine and a visionary healer from *Evil Chasing Way* who instructs the author in the arcane art of leaving the body and traveling through the portals of astral projection. The story is both ancient and timeless, yet the events are prescient and timely. The universal message is that we are almost out of time.

An SV Original Publication

For more information
visit: www.speakingvolumes.us

Now Available

Stories of bravery and murder, stories of love, betrayal and suicide. Sometimes it seems that the gun is doing the talking—not for itself—but for all of us.

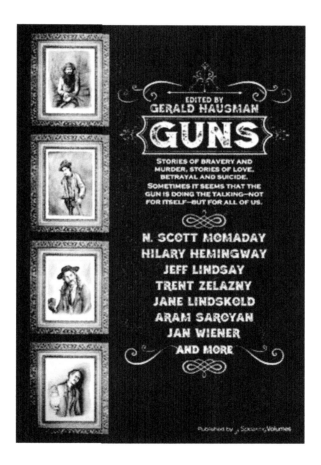

For more information
visit: www.speakingvolumes.us

Now Available

"*Tunkashila* is a book to be read slowly and with deep respect... it is like the wind one hears on the plains, Steady, running, full of music."
—N. Scott Momaday, author of *In the Presence of the Sun*

**For more information
visit:** www.speakingvolumes.us

Sign up for free and bargain books

Join the Speaking Volumes
mailing list

Text

ILOVEBOOKS

to 22828 to get started.

Message and data rates may apply.

Printed in Great Britain
by Amazon

16022218R00133